MOUNT PLEASANT

ALSO BY DON GILLMOR

FICTION

Kanata

NON-FICTION

Canada: A People's History

The Desire of Every Living Thing

I Swear by Apollo

To Lynne,
Best Regards,
Don Gillmor

DON GILLMOR

MOUNT PLEASANT

RANDOM HOUSE CANADA

PUBLISHED BY RANDOM HOUSE CANADA

 Published in 2013 by Random House Canada, a division of Random House of Canada Limited, Toronto. Distributed in Canada by Random House of Canada Limited.

www.randomhouse.ca

Library and Archives Canada Cataloguing in Publication

Gillmor, Don
Mount Pleasant / Don Gillmor.

Issued also in electronic format.

ISBN 978-0-307-36072-4

I. Title.

PS8563.I59M68 2013 C813'.54 C2012-905602-2

Text and cover design by Andrew Roberts

Cover image: Alan Thornton/Getty Images

Printed and bound in the United States of America

2 4 6 8 9 7 5 3 1

To Anne Collins

Men have been swindled by other men on many occasions. The autumn of 1929 was, perhaps, the first occasion when men succeeded on a large scale in swindling themselves.

JOHN KENNETH GALBRAITH, *The Great Crash, 1929*

ONE

SUNDAY DINNER ARRIVED WITH ITS DREAD. Harry was making a squash risotto with Moroccan lamb and asparagus. The organic lamb cost $82, bought from the swarthy criminal at the boutique butcher shop. Harry had grown up in a world where university professors such as himself were financially comfortable and well respected, and butchers were dropouts with cleavers. Now, professors were marginalized and indebted, while butchers were wealthy artisans.

Lately, Harry's debt had taken on an auditory quality, a buzzing that usually remained in the background though rarely went away. At times it was all he heard, awful moments when it had the quality of a high-speed periodontist's drill, a brilliant German instrument that was burrowing into his skull, shrieking as it got closer to his brain. He stood in the kitchen, stirring the risotto, adding wine in the dull white noise.

Tonight Ben was bringing his girlfriend, Sarah, a wiry, pugnacious psychology major who had spent their last dinner together outlining the appalling state of the world and ascribing blame to Harry's generation. He first tried appeasement, then argued unsuccessfully with her, then got drunk and blithe.

Gladys appeared behind him, dressed in a cashmere sweater and navy pants. "You're not going to fight with Sarah, are you," she said, her tone balanced between the imperative and the interrogative.

"I won't have to. She'll fight with me."

"Remember who the grown-up is."

At dinner, Sarah ignored the food. "If the money spent on the American military was used to buy food, it would end world hunger in one year," she said. Harry had heard versions of this thirty years ago when he was an undergraduate. Sarah's hair was spiky and she wore loose jeans and a second-hand curling sweater with the name "Brian" stitched over the heart. She was, as Gladys had noted on more than one occasion, extremely bright. But she used these worn liberal platitudes like a club. *Shouldn't that phase be coming to an end?* Harry wondered.

"While we're having this dinner," Ben added, "four thousand children will starve to death." He stared at his father accusingly, as if the dinner Harry had made was the actual cause of the children's deaths. Why is it never Gladys's fault? he wondered. How is it that I'm solely to blame for the world's poor showing?

"If the money spent downloading music by people under twenty-five was used to build affordable housing, there would be no homelessness," Harry countered. He felt liberated by this fabrication. He tried another one. "The aggregate annual salary of North America's athletes is greater than Pakistan's GDP." This was probably true.

"Harold," Gladys said. A warning.

"It's you people who are paying their salaries," Sarah said. "You watch them."

"I'm not much of a sports fan," Harry said.

"Dad, you are a freak for sports," Ben said. "You dragged me to those football games when they played outside at Exhibition Stadium. I'm, like, still cold from watching them."

"I lost my appetite for it," Harry said. "I was probably losing it back then." He'd thought he'd regain his interest in sports by taking Ben, that his son's enthusiasm would reignite his own. He once took Ben to an intersquad game, a father-son event sponsored by the league. Ben was nine, cold and uncomprehending. After the game, Harry took him to field level, where they collected autographs from sullen, oversized men. It was an overcast late-October day, and the icy wind from the lake distorted the players' features so they looked monstrous. Ben started to quietly cry. On the way home, Harry bought him hot chocolate, a consolation.

"I think it's pathetic that men need football as a metaphor for war," Sarah said.

"We don't need a metaphor for war," Harry said. "We have war." Who had said that? Susan Sontag? Perhaps it was Bud Grant, a glacial, crewcut football coach he remembered from the sixties. Harry examined his son's girlfriend, her fox-like face, the nose small and upturned, eyes predatory. He wondered about her sexual appetites. Was it sex as politics with them, and she a strict, non-penetrative anti-imperialist; or did they practise tantric sex, a holy ritual illuminated by scented candles and drawn out to the point of boredom; or, lucky Ben, was Sarah surprisingly wild? She caught his gaze then, returning it as if she could hear his thoughts.

"This risotto is marvellous," Gladys said. "It reminds me of that restaurant in Florence. What was it? Il . . ."

"La Fenice."

He and Gladys had gone to Florence last year, both of them careful not to bill it as a romantic vacation so it couldn't be declared a failure. They were in a marital lull and Florence became an (unstated) romantic grail. The planning, the reading of civic histories and Renaissance biographies, the immersion in all things Florentine. The hope was that when they walked its ancient streets and ate gelato in the Piazza della Signoria they would find themselves swept up in one another. They had been careful not to talk about the cost of the trip. It went without saying that it was unaffordable. But Harry had shielded Gladys from the actual state of their debt. She still had some of her own money, left over from the early retirement package she'd received from the library. She suspected, of course, that things weren't going swimmingly, but made a point of not asking, the way some people who suspect they have a health problem make a point of not going to the doctor.

When it wasn't buzzing in his head like a swarm of wasps, Harry tried to think of his debt the way governments thought of theirs, a mounting deficit that was worrisome but not lethal. Debt was a necessary burden that was passed on to others. Florence was like floating a government bond to pay for improved health care in rural areas.

He felt he wasn't extravagant but knew he hadn't entirely forsaken the sense of entitlement that he'd been born with. His generation didn't carry the deep fiduciary scars that the Depression generation did, where every nickel had measurable weight. Savers of string, collectors of rainwater, backyard gardeners, buyers of cuts of meat that had to be slow-cooked for eight hours to be edible. They mended clothes and made do. They lived the lives they could afford, measured daily in pennies. But not Harry's generation. Money was a vague ideational pool they all splashed in. Saving was futile. If Harry bought the $14 Shiraz rather than the still very modest $24 Bordeaux, what would it save him? A few hundred a month. A spit in the ocean.

In Florence he'd returned to their hotel room late in the afternoon one day to find Gladys in the absurdly large faux marble bathtub and he took two overpriced drinks out of the mini-bar and took off his clothes and joined her. They chatted pleasantly and sipped their Campari out of water glasses, but when Harry began to soap her breasts, which sat, still invitingly, partially submerged, he could see the sudden shift in her eyes.

"I'll get your back," he had said, swiftly downgrading it to an affectionate service. When they did finally make love, it was with a sense of obligation, fulfilling the (unstated) pact that Florence would bring them joy.

It was the mornings he loved most on that trip. He would get up at six and walk for an hour through the compact city, watching it come alive, people sweeping the pavement in front of their stores and cafés, deliveries of meat and fish and newspapers dropped off. He stopped at the small piazza not far from the Duomo and sat at an outdoor café and slowly sipped espresso and read the *International Herald Tribune*. As he surveyed the dinner table, Harry wished, suddenly, that he was in Florence, alone, lingering in the Uffizi, following a dark-haired Italian tourist who looked like Audrey Hepburn.

"It was a wonderful restaurant," Gladys said, bringing Harry back from his reverie. "You would have loved it, Ben. Absolutely unpretentious. Like being in someone's home. The food was extraordinary, but it wasn't fussy."

This was for Sarah's sake, Harry suspected, designed to show her how down-to-earth they were, yet how sophisticated, and how this could be the life that she and Ben would embrace in time. Did Gladys actually think that Sarah was somehow good for Ben? Perhaps she saw her combative nature as complementary to Ben's innate passivity, and that their son would need her aggression to navigate life's forest. Gladys wasn't a romantic, her judgment obscured by issues of love and sexual compatibility (though who wasn't sexually compatible at nineteen?). She was looking at survival, the maternal Darwinism that women carried in their hearts.

"Do you plan to continue with psychology?" Gladys asked Sarah.

"I don't know, Gladys. I've been thinking about environmental law. Do you know how much particulate the Sunways Paper plant put into the atmosphere in 2009? Eleven thousand tonnes. Being exposed to it for twenty-four hours can raise blood pressure, not to mention the carcinogenic nightmare." She glared at Harry as if he were the CEO of Sunways. "And we're dealing with it every day. I mean, you can almost see the stacks from here."

Harry glanced at Ben, who was examining the two women in his life, perhaps gauging that future dynamic.

"I think that's admirable, Sarah," Gladys said.

"It's a growth industry," Harry offered. He examined Sarah, her second-hand clothes and ongoing defiance. Would he have fallen for her when he was nineteen? The fashions weren't dissimilar from Harry's own years at university. The music was similar as well. Sometimes it was the same. Ben had three hours of the Grateful Dead on his iPod, which seemed like an abdication of responsibility. Shouldn't he embrace the sound of his own generation?

"Most working women leave the house each morning with 127 toxins either in them or on them," Sarah said. She began listing on her fingers, "Formaldehyde, lead, phthalates. Methyl, ethyl, propyl and butyl, which can seriously fry your hormones and cause breast tumours. Cosmetics are basically toxic waste dumps. I mean, we're killing the planet so we can look good."

"I mean, the laws are there," Ben said. "But no one has the balls to enforce them."

"Maybe it's more a question of money than balls," Harry said. "Environmental cases tend to be wars of attrition."

"Which is why the major polluters always win," Sarah said. "Someone has to stand up to them."

"One of the problems," Harry said, "is that these lawsuits tend to come down to a balance of probabilities. The company lawyer argues that the lead in the plaintiff's blood isn't from the massive chemical fire but from chewing his HB pencil in sixth grade. The irony is, as we all become more toxic just by walking around and breathing bad air and eating carcinogenic hot dogs, it becomes increasingly difficult to prove that some company was responsible for the whole neighbourhood being diagnosed with leukemia on the same day."

"So you're saying we should just give up?" Ben said.

"No, no, of course not." Even when he sought solidarity, Harry ended up drawing some line in the conversational sand.

"When I think of all the shit we put into the atmosphere," Ben said. "Those Lincolns that got, like, a kilometre a litre, everything we burned up at the cottage, those bottles we threw away. I mean, it blows me away."

"Well it was a different time, I think everyone now knows—"

"But we should have known then. I mean, it isn't that hard to figure out. The world isn't that big."

"It used to be," Harry said. He remembered that sense of space; when he was little, people still heaved litter out their car windows, confident the landscape would digest it. His son, he noticed, was more tenacious in Sarah's presence. Perhaps she was good for him.

As Ben aggressively quoted landfill statistics, Harry silently invented one of his own: If all psychologists were placed in a landfill, we would gain a better understanding of ourselves.

Harry thought about his father. Now there was a planet killer: a chain-smoking, leaf-burning, pesticide-spreading clear-cutter (slightly, at the cottage), a driver of motorboats. He never owned a car that got much better than ten miles a gallon. He shot raccoons, poisoned squirrels and once, in Florida, fished drunkenly for a marlin he later had stuffed and then abandoned (he would never have put it up in the house). He ate bloody steaks and burned trash. His only nod to conserving anything was refusing to have air conditioning installed because he thought it was vulgar.

At the moment, his father was lying in a hospital bed, his limbs and brain withering; he would have just finished commenting on the woeful, largely untouched dinner that had been presented by the smiling nurse. He was disappearing now, unable to conserve himself.

"Remember those beetles at the museum?" Harry said to Ben, trying to bring the conversation back to some environmental common ground. When Ben was young, they had taken a private after-hours tour of the museum, part of a fund-raising effort. Ben had been so obsessed with dinosaurs that Gladys feared it was a sign of a learning disability. They became members of the museum and regularly went to examine the dinosaur skeletons and listen to Ben recite their diets, habitats and idiosyncrasies with authority. In the sub-basement, there was a steel door that sealed tight. The elderly man in the grey cardigan who was giving the tour said, "Now this isn't going to smell very pleasant." He gave them a horror movie butler smile and opened the heavy door. A wave of frightening air came out, the heavy smell of decay. "Be cautious where you step," the man said.

There were bones everywhere, birds, animals, things that had been given to the museum. Hundreds of dermestid beetles crawled over everything, stripping the bones right down to the bacterial level. In this age of cleansers and technology, it was extraordinary that they used insects for something like this, and that it was done in the actual museum. When Harry examined his son for his reaction to this vision of hell, he could tell that Ben was worried that the creepy tour guide was going to shut the steel door and lock them in the sub-basement, and the next person he showed the room to would see their bones, stripped clean of all flesh. Harry knew Ben was thinking this because it was what Harry would have thought at that age. A part of him still laboured against the thought.

"That creepy room. God." Ben turned to Sarah. "Like a million beetles, they use them for cleaning bones. In this special sealed room in the basement. You wouldn't believe the smell. We smelled like death for hours after."

"In the actual museum," Gladys said. "I find it difficult to believe—

"Remember, I told you," Harry said.

"It seems so primitive."

"It is. But it was the best method."

"I'll remember that if I ever need a skeleton cleaned," Sarah said.

"Would you like more risotto?" Gladys asked her, despite Sarah's almost untouched plate.

"No, I'm good."

Harry poured some wine into his glass. He could feel antipathy building, and this made him angry, this failure in himself to put up with his son's girlfriend, to show her kindness and demonstrate wisdom. He should try to be more sympathetic. Who knew what kind of family life she'd had?

———

Gladys, who prodded Ben's friends for details about their parents, hadn't been able to get anything from either Sarah or Ben. "Why are you so obsessed with where everyone's from, Mom?" Ben had said. And Glad responded, as she always did, that she wasn't obsessed, merely interested in who her son was spending time with. To which Ben had predictably yelled, "I'm spending time with Sarah. She's who she is. Why can't you just let things be?"

"So what is it these days, nature or nurture?" Harry asked Sarah, a question that drew a sharp-eyed glance from Gladys.

"What?"

"I mean that whole debate."

Sarah reached for the wine and filled her glass almost to the top. "Is this a quiz?"

"Just curious."

Sarah stopped just short of rolling her eyes. "It's an unanswerable question."

"But a lot of energy goes into trying to answer it, doesn't it? Like the shape of the universe for physicists."

Gladys glared subtly as Sarah stared at her wine for five seconds. Then she recited in a near monotone, "The relationship between lymphocyte precursors and other blood cell lineages is basically groundbreaking. The RAG1/GFP knock-in mice experiments are . . . I mean, you can chart the entire sequence of lymphocyte differentiation events in bone marrow. Bottom line: steady-state lymphocyte formation doesn't recapitulate ontogeny."

Harry wondered how much of this was distorted and/or bullshit. "But in your own case, what would you say?"

"Is this the lame hypothesis where people go into psychology to deal with their own problems?"

"Do they?"

"Everyone has problems, Dad," Ben said, rallying to his girlfriend's defense. "It's a bit simplistic."

"Psychology is a perfect complement to law," Gladys said.

"Not everything is about getting a job, Mom," Ben said, who'd always been adept at translating Gladys's words into their actual meaning.

Sarah was twisting her perilously full wineglass, rotating it on Gladys's expensive Provençal tablecloth, a fact that Gladys registered with quiet alarm as she reached to take Sarah's almost untouched plate. The tablecloth was bunching slightly in small swirls that would unbalance the glass. Gladys stared at the glass for a second, then went into the kitchen. The background music she had meticulously chosen filled the void.

Harry stared at Ben, remembering the unconditional joy he'd felt when Ben was an infant. Those months when Harry took him for long walks in the stroller, talking to the sleeping lump curled under the fleecy with its cute, hopeful slogans. Back then, Harry had overflowed with love. He'd imagined Ben growing up and imagined new victories in his own life. Gladys had the difficult job—the nightly feedings, getting up when Ben was afflicted by some unfathomable fear, lulling him. Harry just had to push the stroller in the pleasant autumn light and change a few diapers. He occasionally imagined that he was raising Ben alone, like a valiant TV dad, just the two of them. Harry used to sit on the bench outside the organic grocery store and return the smiles of women who walked by, and then he'd stare at Ben's sweet face and think, You are the love of my life.

What was he now, Harry wondered. This young man, resentful and distant, holding his girlfriend's hand as if in solidarity against Harry. His own father had been a miserable role model, and Harry realized he hadn't done much better, despite the vows he'd made to himself as he pushed the stroller. What would he pass on to Ben? Debt, perhaps. Distrust of the world, certainly.

Ben and Sarah were talking about something, but Harry couldn't tune them in. The hum of his debt suddenly intruded, and it had taken on a new, musical quality. As Harry watched his son's mouth move, he heard what sounded like the forceful strains of Mahler's Fourth Symphony.

Gladys finally came back carrying a fruit flan she had made. Dessert arrived as a mercy, and there was a lull as she cut and distributed it.

"This looks wonderful, Gladys," Harry said.

TWO

THE NEXT DAY, HARRY ARRIVED at his father's private hospital room to find Dale in the small bathroom behind the partially closed accordion door.

"Did you manage to unhook her brassiere?" his father said.

"What?"

"Who's that? Who's there?"

"It's me. Harry. Your son."

"Teachy preachy."

Harry could see his father's thin, hairless calves, his lengthy white feet through the partly opened door. They were separated by six feet. "Dad, do you know where you are?"

There was a flatulent blast, then a high, piercing sigh. After two minutes, his father said, "She moaned and she meant it."

Harry stared upward, looking for guidance. His father's mind was increasingly erratic. Wild thoughts burst forth during these visits, followed by moments of cruel lucidity. Harry imagined a landed trout inside his father's head, flipping stupidly on the dock. After another five minutes, Dale said, "I'm finished here."

The last month had been the most time Harry had ever spent with his father. His parents divorced when Harry was sixteen, but Dale had pulled away long before that. He worked in wealth management and disappeared into money, and then into another marriage (and another divorce). After the divorce from Harry's mother, Dale was supposed to take Harry and his sister, Erin, for two weekends a month, but that arrangement petered out, and Harry rarely saw him for more than the odd afternoon.

Harry accompanied his father on the early visits to doctors, had sat as a witness while a serious woman with the pinched face chronic pain sometimes produces (a professional tic perhaps, Harry thought, a pre-emptive solidarity) explained the specifics of his father's brain cancer. Harry jotted notes as she veered into jargon ("anaplastic astrocytoma"), ascribing human qualities to the cancer ("tendency to infiltrate"). At first she lightly disguised its fatal nature ("excision may discourage but not eradicate"), then punctured any hope even for experimental treatments ("gene therapy converting adenoviruses in Russian subjects has not yielded . . ."). Dutifully searching the Internet, Harry discovered that five television series had used this cancer to kill off unwanted characters.

The curious effect of the ensuing medical sessions was that his father's cancer became more vivid to Harry than his father himself. Dale had never come into focus, a distant, silent, unsupervising figure. But his disease was visceral. Harry became acquainted with the expensive machines, the heavy artillery used in what was usually described as a battle. He examined the positron emission tomography of his father's brain, which looked like a psychedelic walnut, and wondered what it now contained. Several million memories that had been arranged by priority (the hand on the neighbour's thigh, the martinis made with mannered precision) now randomly scattered like a filing cabinet overturned by thieves.

Now Harry led him back to his bed and helped him lie down, covering him with the hospital sheet. The destruction of his father was precipitous. He didn't always recognize Harry when he visited, he spoke less, his body a venous network of atrophied limbs, the skeletal core trying to surface as his brain flailed. His face was taut, his arms laid out beside him like a child's, thin and guileless, floating through an OxyContin landscape.

Harry looked at his father and pondered what was effectively gone. He wondered if Dale pondered Harry's life as well, staring through eyes dulled by painkillers, enlarged and extruding as the rest of him retreated; what did he see in this fifty-two-year-old man? But if Dale was pondering anything in the withered prison of his head, it would be his ill luck; he would calculate the odds of his own cancer (12.8 per 100,000, thirty-two percent survival over five years) the way he had calculated bond yields. His sister, Erin, and his father's girlfriend, Dixie, hadn't been involved much at first, but they now visited regularly. Dixie was only a few years older than Harry, a handsome woman with sun-damaged skin, long-legged and purposeful, her smile honed in the hospitality industry. On those occasions when their visits overlapped, Dixie was always smartly dressed in dark clothes, and Harry wondered if she were trying out different funeral outfits. Harry was straining to recover something from his palsied relationship with his father, but he also recognized that both he and Dixie hovered over Dale with the shared expectation of a significant inheritance. Erin did not share that unfortunate bond; she and her husband were discouragingly well off.

Harry pulled out the book he had brought and started reading aloud. His father had little interest in fiction, but Harry remembered that he had enjoyed Ian Fleming's Bond books, and he found a paperback copy of *Goldfinger* in a second-hand bookstore. Sitting on the chair beside the bed, he read slowly.

When Harry had read to his son years ago, his voice became deeper, comforting both of them. Ben would fall asleep on Harry's chest, and the smell of that perfect head filled him with a contentment that was unrivalled sixteen years later. Breathing in the essence of his only child in the comfort of that bedroom, the star and moon pattern of the curtains barely visible in darkness, he often fell asleep as well. Dale hadn't read to Harry. And now, when young fathers gathered in the park with their offspring, resentfully searching for the diaper bag, wiping the non-toxic rubber nipple with the tail of their shirts, here was their triumphant conceit: we are much better than our own fathers. What would Ben say?

Harry looked at his father, who showed no sign of having understood anything about the devious Auric Goldfinger. His collapsing face was blank. Harry closed the book and wished for his father's death.

Dale died three nights later. If dying was a final leaving, then the true moment of his father's death may have been decades ago. Harry's most vivid memory of his father was the recent version, his protracted death. Yet it was Harry's duty to mourn.

Standing at the entrance to the Anglican church, he shook hands and hugged, thanking people for their presence. He smiled at aging, addled friends of his father's whom he hadn't seen in two decades and assured them (falsely) that Dale had had a peaceful passing.

Erin performed the same ritual a few feet away, clasping each outreached hand with both of hers. Gladys was beside him, offering accepting noises and sad smiles as a response to the condolences. Ben stood awkwardly with Sarah, his hands folded in front of him, gangly and useless and dreaming of escape.

As Harry finally walked toward the front pew, he surveyed the gathered—dutiful, dry-eyed, shifting uncomfortably in the warming interior of the church with unpierced hearts. The financial community had come out. A few of the old neighbours. His mother looked elegant in a midnight blue dress. Dale's second wife, Tess, hadn't shown.

He sat beside his mother and reached into his suit jacket for the reassurance of his written eulogy. *My father was a complicated man.* His mother looked at him, her face brightened by gin.

"This is no time for honesty," she said.

Harry turned to look at the crowd. Dixie was exiled resentfully in the middle rows, splendid in black, her ash blond hair effectively pinned. Near the front were Dale's colleagues from BRG, the firm where he had worked for most of his life. Harry hadn't seen them in twenty years. The heroically named August Sampson was now stooped and bald, myopic, hair bristling on his outsized ears. Beside him, Prescott Lunden sat like an aging soap opera actor, handsome and silver-haired, the reassuring figurehead. In the pew behind them was the short, pugnacious Dick Ebbetts, who had greeted Harry's mother and leaned in to whisper something into her ear for an inappropriate length of time. The financial world embraced funerals, reassurance that money was flowing downward at a sombre pace.

Harry touched his head experimentally. He wasn't sure, suddenly, if he was here. Maybe it was he, rather than his father, who was gone. Roughly the same crowd would be at Harry's service, the financial guys replaced by a smattering of academics. This thought spooked him. His composed wife, his indifferent child; would they be equally composed and indifferent if it were Harry in the casket? If it were his waxy face and black suit beneath the polished wood? He crossed his hands, clutching himself, pressing his fingernails urgently into his palms, waking himself from the dream, if it was one. "Dale Essex Salter," the minister began, then paused, as if he too was unable to recall the nobility of the deceased.

At the edge of the curving, welcome synclines of Mount Pleasant Cemetery, a few trees showed a hint of autumn. There was a soft breeze. The September sun was high and bleached the pale grass. The cemetery contained almost 170,000 dead, a city of the lost, the vicious hierarchies of money and beauty and talent and luck levelled among the Japanese katsura and red oaks. There was another funeral in the distance, the dotting of dark shapes around the unseen hole. Behind Harry, an ancient crone sat in a folding chair, the kind parents use to watch their kids play soccer. Harry didn't recognize her. *Perhaps*, he thought, *she's one of those people who spend their days attending the funerals of strangers, getting comfortable with death as it moves closer.*

The minister uttered a last few calming words over Dale's casket, then everyone drifted away. Harry lingered; he wanted to see his father lowered. It seemed impolite for everyone to turn their backs and leave while Dale still sat there exposed. When the gleaming coffin was lowered on canvas belts, winched into the earth, it made a slight mechanical clicking sound that reminded Harry of when he attached a playing card to the wheel of his bicycle with a clothespin as a boy, then cycled around the neighbourhood, listening to its motorized clack.

As Dale descended, Harry thought he heard murmuring, indistinct sounds coming from the hole. The dead welcoming a new arrival. Or the collective regret of all those lives escaping through this fresh fissure. We never bloomed.

Harry picked up a handful of earth, almost experimentally, then threw it on top of the coffin. He walked back to the parking lot to find Gladys standing beside the car. "What were you doing?"

"I threw some dirt in." Holding up his smudged right hand as proof.

They drove back slowly, Harry dreading the reception, Gladys staring out her window, Ben in the back seat texting. Sarah had gone home in her own car, perhaps to avoid this silence. At an intersection where they were stopped, Harry saw a couple on the sidewalk waiting for the light. They might have been seventeen. She was wearing a summer dress and sandals. She turned to the boy and kissed him and said something in his ear, then pulled away and looked at him expectantly. Harry remembered his prom date, Jenny Larsen, who had kissed him and mumbled, "You complete me," a phrase she'd picked up somewhere. Good for her. Complete at seventeen, and at the unintentional hand of the incomplete Harry.

The city had a Sunday hush. It drifted empty on the breeze. Harry opened his window to let in the soft air. It moved around his silent family with its false tropical breath.

Contrary to the popular dictum, Harry's father had taken his money with him. It was, at any rate, gone. The reading of the will had the giddy outrage of a practical joke. The executor, a terse stranger from one of the large, threatening law firms, revealed Dale to be essentially broke, a shock to both Harry and his sister, and a much bigger shock to Dixie.

The three of them sat in the lawyer's office as he intoned the will's clauses with appropriate solemnity, accompanied by a paper version handed out with numbers and percentages highlighted. More than half the estate went to Dixie, a fact that was quickly mitigated by the alarmingly small sums involved. Dixie received $7,200. Harry was second, with $4,200. Erin, an enraged and distant third, received $1,100.

As the lawyer, whose name Harry had already forgotten, rumbled on about various items, Harry tried to calculate how his father's estate could have shrivelled so drastically. He had assumed that Dale was worth roughly $3 million. In Harry's most shuttered thoughts, he had ascribed one million to himself, another million to Erin, with the rest split between Dixie and a few charities that Dale had supported. He had guiltily toyed with these sums. The mortgage would evaporate, then his line of credit and Visa bill. He would treat himself to a few cases of good wine (a case of a Pomerol that looked promising and a slightly guilt-inducing case of Château d'Yquem). He would fix a few things around the house, and they would rent a place in France for the summer. He would buy an expensive bicycle and join the brightly clad cyclists along the lakeshore. Gladys, he guessed, had her own math.

He avoided looking at Erin, who detested Dixie and referred to her, after two glasses of wine, as "that tinted whore," and who was now confronted by this awful arithmetic: Dixie favoured by a factor of roughly six to one.

Dixie was the first to leave, tersely gathering her papers, on the verge of tears that would flow in the hallway then let loose in earnest when she was safely home, Harry guessed. She may have thanked the lawyer as an afterthought halfway to the door, but Harry wasn't sure. His debt had resumed its roaring in his ears, an insistent martial sound that arrived in waves.

Harry was stunned by the injustice of it. I wasn't seeking riches, he thought, merely debt relief. This dream, the modest hope of a Third World nation lobbying the UN, had vanished. He was too tired to move, too afraid to glance at Erin, resentful of the lawyer, who sat mouthing something in the roar of Harry's trashed prospects.

Harry recalled the dark crowd gathered at the gravesite, their heads half-bowed. Perhaps one of them had taken Dale's money. Or it sat in his coffin with him, Harry's inheritance sent down to burn.

THREE

DEBT WAS HIS MISTRESS, the dirty siren who clawed his back. They had been together for three decades, entwined, an anniversary that had crept up. *My god, has it been that long, my love?*

Gladys lay beside him, the subtle lines of her face piled against the pillow in the grey light. It was 4:30 a.m. and an unspent erection lolled. He fell asleep an hour before dawn, his dreams descending like carrion birds, tearing expertly at his flesh, dancing away from him with strings of red sinew in their beaks.

Before waking, in that gloaming where you could manufacture your dreams and direct the action, where you were master of that bent landscape, Harry saw his father peeling off an endless succession of hundred-dollar bills, as if doling out an allowance. They formed a thick carpet on the ground, and thousands fluttered upward with every footstep.

—

Harry walked past the university gates to his bank for the appointment with Ms. Remnick. Harry and the bank were partners in his decaying house, which was being reclaimed slowly by nature. Water had seeped into the basement, spawning mildew and fungi. There were mice in the walls, and what looked like lichen on the shingles. An elm tree root had worked its way into the old clay pipes under the front yard, the pipes that carried their effluent to join the rivers of shit that bound the city. To balance this encroaching boreal world, there was lead in his soil, the residue of a toothpaste factory that had been torn down years ago. Harry wondered if that soil, with its quota of styrene, benzene, lead and mercury, was the only thing that kept nature from taking over his house entirely.

A month earlier, a terse letter had arrived telling him that his line of credit would not be extended. His line of credit had quickly become a kind of friend, someone who'd lend him money anytime for any reason and wasn't worried about when he'd repay it. When Harry's inheritance arrived, he'd planned to happily pay this friend back. Except that his inheritance didn't arrive.

The events leading up to what he only half ironically called his genteel poverty were unremarkable. Harry had worked as a journalist and political commentator for the public broadcaster, where he enjoyed a degree of success, a measure of prestige and a smaller salary than he would have had with a private broadcaster. When the government putsch arrived and funding was cut, he was surprised to find himself out of a job; he could have supplied a two-page list of deadwood colleagues who should have been axed years ago. Instead, it was him. After a discouraging interval, he found work as a sessional instructor at the university, initially teaching media studies, then catching a break and a full-time position teaching media and a course in civic politics. And now he sat, tentatively, untenured (having come late to the party), a white male at the one moment in history when this wasn't an advantage.

Harry arrived at the bank and was ushered into Ms. Remnick's small office, blinds drawn against the southern exposure, a certificate of merit framed behind her. He had opened his first account at a downtown bank, one of the pillared nineteenth-century buildings with thirty-foot ceilings. He kept his passbook in his desk in his bedroom and would regularly take it out and examine it, basking in the accumulated cash given to him by relatives on his birthday. His father had deliberately taken him to one of the downtown branches in order to instill a sense of awe. The surfaces were marble and gleaming wood, and the light was from another century, golden and hushed. Harry felt a reverence when he stepped up to the teller, as if he were about to receive communion.

Money had once sat in Harry's account and collected a dignified interest. Now it sluiced around the globe like bilge water. It was vast and abstract, unanchored by gold. A single drunken trader in London could send the global markets lurching with the push of a button.

Sitting in the diluted corporate mood of Ms. Remnick's office, Harry wondered how much of his life he had lived in the expectation of his father's money. He sat like a schoolchild waiting for the teacher to correct his test, a sick dread in his stomach. He had a combined credit card balance of $24,300, and now his line of credit, that amoral friend who had cheerfully lent him $79,000, was abandoning him. His mortgage remained a monster from a children's book, looming large in the shadows, hiding under his bed.

Ms. Remnick wore a tailored suit, and her hair was pinned up. She was an attractive woman in her forties. A few strands of hair hung down, as if they had begun an intimacy and she had started taking the pins out.

"I'm afraid . . ." she began, looking up from his file, her brown eyes filling with professional sympathy.

We all live in fear, Harry thought.

When Harry left the bank, and news of his frozen line of credit, he went south past the cheap, student-filled restaurants of Chinatown, lit like operating theatres and filled with undergraduates in front of steaming bowls. It occurred to him that most of them were in a better financial state than he was. He turned west, walking past the Victorian jumble, a line of tattoo parlours and used books and falafel spots, the street claimed by pierced and illustrated youth.

Gladys had ordered a cake, and Harry had said he would pick it up, a dark chocolate and fig production that would cost, she warned, roughly $50. The cake was for a birthday dinner Gladys and four other women were hosting for a mutual friend. Each of them was supposed to bring a dish that had significance in the life of the birthday girl. The cake had something to do with a trip to France the woman had taken when she was young.

He arrived at the bakery, which was small and cheerful and warm, and waited in line as others claimed their absurdly priced orders. The woman at the cash was French, with the girlish slimness the French managed even in middle age. She turned and plucked a smallish dark cake from the shelf, delicately placed it in a box, closed and taped the box, then put a ribbon around it and deftly tied an elegant bow. She handed Harry his cake and smiled. He handed her a $50 bill with genuine regret, and left carrying the box by the ribbon, then worried that the cake would slide around inside and get damaged, so he put one hand underneath the box and cradled it like a baby.

He walked east for half an hour, past a cloud of Asian smells, churches offering yoga classes, window displays of bondage gear. He suddenly realized how hungry he was and approached a sausage cart, the vendor with his dismal toupée and homely wife, their faces a map of Eastern European grief and a boredom that had centuries of peasant solitude behind it. The woman opened her gap-toothed mouth, an unspoken query.

"Sausage," Harry said, holding up one finger.

Some of these people, he had heard, were rich. They started with one cart, then bought another, then another, and eventually they enslaved other immigrants. Maybe this couple was rich, Harry thought. This was their cautious public life, designed to throw off the tax people, to deflect envy and discourage thieves.

The woman quickly made sharp diagonal cuts along the sausage, then flipped it onto the grill. She worried it and prodded it in fluid movements, then finally picked it up with the tongs and placed it in a bun. Harry smothered it with hot peppers and added a dab of mustard, then took his sausage and sat on a cement planter and watched the traffic go by.

He was just finishing his lunch when a man came by and asked him for change. "Can't help you, brother," Harry said in what he meant to be a tone of solidarity.

The man stalked half a dozen steps, then returned. "Buy me a hot dog, asshole," he said. He was maybe Harry's age, his swollen face the colour of a rugby ball, with a full head of longish black hair. His raincoat was greasy, and beneath it Harry glimpsed layers of discarded fashions: a green sweater, a grey shirt, a black T-shirt with gothic lettering. His dirty white loafers, the shoes of a racetrack tout, looked to be two sizes too big.

"What?"

"Buy me a fucking hot dog, you Ralph Lauren dick."

Harry stared at him.

"You don't," the man said, pointing to the cart, "I'll put my hand in that mustard and smear it all over your jacket. I'll piss on your shoes."

Adrenaline hummed. Harry reached into his pants and came out with a $2 coin. "Knock yourself out," he said, flipping it toward the man, as if for a coin toss. The man made no attempt to catch it. It landed on the concrete, rolled briefly and stopped.

"You buy it," the man said. He was leaning slightly, coiled.

"Fuck you," Harry said sharply, and stood up, fearful of a sucker punch. They both waited in that small, charged vacuum that precedes violence, then the man bent over, picked up the coin and walked over to the cart. He bought a hot dog and Harry watched as he piled an absurd amount of mustard and relish onto it.

As the man walked back toward him, he took a huge bite of the hot dog and started talking before he had swallowed it all. "You worried I'm going to give you that speech, the one where none of you assholes even see guys like me. We're invisible." Small bits of wet bun spilled out of his mouth and lingered in his beard. "That horseshit speech."

Everyone was invisible, Harry thought. He was invisible.

The man pushed the second half of the hot dog into his mouth. He made as if to shake Harry's hand, then wiped both his grimy, stained hands on the lapels of Harry's sports jacket, the Calvin Klein he'd bought on sale.

"Racquetball on Monday, Bud," the man said. "We still on?"

Parts of his hot dog came out as a meteor shower of pink and yellow and green. He laughed, a glottal sound that became a tubercular cough, then turned and walked west, his natural hunch propelling him forward, this Fagin with his greasy black hair swaying slightly.

"Christ," Harry said. He went to the sausage cart and bought a bottle of water and took a handful of napkins and very gently dabbed at his lapels. The stain was dark with sick yellow streaks. The water made it worse, smearing it into the fabric.

He walked for several blocks, waiting for the adrenaline to subside, before he realized, with a stab of nausea, that he'd left the cake back at the hot dog vendor. He turned and ran back as fast as he could, winded after the first block.

When Harry got there, the cake was gone. He asked the gap-toothed sausage woman, but she simply shrugged. Forty-nine dollars and twenty-eight cents. Harry was suddenly aware of how much he was sweating, a steady runoff that soaked his shirt and overflowed his brow. He examined passersby for clues, then looked north and saw a form curved over a subway grate as if protecting something. Harry wiped his forehead with his hand and walked closer and saw it was a woman, greyish black hair running wild, sitting in a stained orange parka held together with geometric lines of duct tape, hunched over the cake, eating with one hand, shovelling it into her dark cave-like mouth like a child.

"What do you mean, someone *stole* it, Harry? Someone stole the cake?"

"A homeless woman."

Harry had started back to the bakery but realized that the cake had been specially baked to order. There was no point in buying a replacement because it wouldn't fit the theme of Gladys's party.

"She just walked up and grabbed it?"

"Gladys, it doesn't matter how she stole it. It's gone. A mentally ill woman in an orange parka ate your cake over a sewer grate. There is no fucking cake."

They stood in angry silence, he and Gladys. There had been, he noted, an increasing number of silences like this one, charged and dangerous, precipitated by something large or small. A place where something awful could suddenly flower, like a toxic mushroom cloud in a fifties documentary.

Gladys took her coat and left, cakeless and resentful, for her party.

FOUR

THE LOGICAL PLACE to start looking for his father's money was Dale's office. Harry had toyed with the number three million for long enough that it had assumed the status of fact, a rumour repeated until it was truth. While his father may have been worth less, he could also have been worth more (as he occasionally was in Harry's head). But a $13,000 legacy was inconceivable. Perhaps there would be clues to his ruin in his personal files.

Harry intended to go to the BRG offices to collect Dale's things and talk to Prescott Lunden. But he didn't want to go in empty-handed. He wanted a little context—on the office, on his father, on his investments. So he first called Dick Ebbetts, who had worked with Dale at BRG, and Dick agreed to meet him for lunch. Dick was a stubby, coarse man—Harry's mother's description, though an accurate one. He was crude and poorly tailored, but he was considered a value savant and that was why he was tolerated at BRG, a money management firm specialized in preserving Old Money. Ebbetts had never n part of the social world at BRG and was retiring, and that reason Harry thought he might be the most discreet e to start in trying to find out what had happened to his er's money.

was inconceivable that Dale had the net worth of an .ergraduate. There had been the two divorces, of course, h of them expensive. But his tastes were surprisingly mod- although he had all his clothes made, even his shoes. And pent a fortune at Scaramouche, where he ate at least twice eek, walking there and back regardless of the weather. But was it. He didn't like to travel and had no interest in col- ing art or wine. He'd sold the family cottage years earlier. hadn't bought a new car in more than a decade and rarely ve the one he had. Harry guessed that, as he got older, his er's investments would have gotten even more conserva- . Surely he would have avoided most of the carnage of '08.

When Harry got to the restaurant, Ebbetts was already there, rked in front of an anachronistic martini. Harry shook hands ıd sat down, and they chatted listlessly about civic politics ıtil Harry got to the point.

"My father's estate, Dick," he said. "I'm wondering if you ın help fill in some gaps."

"Happy to help if I can."

"Do you have any sense of what his financial situation was .ke near the end?"

Ebbetts considered for a moment, then said, "Well, that divorce from Tess was a ball-breaker. And the divorce from your mother probably was a kick in the nuts too. It was different back then. Two kids. The courts frowned. Felicia got the house, for starters. Free and clear. But Tess was a piece of work. I mean she was laying the groundwork from day one, and she had the

Prince of Darkness for a lawyer. Dale was still using Ted Mo
with his white hair and that crinkly smile—he looked like
fucking queen by the time he quit practising. Her lawyer g
there with Ted, and it was like a pit bull with a ballerina
Dale came out of that one with a few feathers missing."

Dick took a breath and then attacked his drink. "The t
is, he talked about Tess all the time. Which for Dale . . . I th
he was really gone on her. Anyway."

"You don't think it affected his work?"

"Love," Ebbetts said, as if that was an answer. "Dale was
of those guys who was all instinct. He was conservative, but
felt those rhythms, he listened to them. He called Nortel. T
falling fucking knife."

"What kind of investments did he get his clients into?"

"Old school: banks, dividend stuff, railways, utilities. To
into junior oils for him was like stepping off a cliff. But after
was eviscerated by the whole Tess thing, he loosened up.
put money into the oil sands, figures that's the future, worl
running out, blah blah—puts it into this company, Pathos,
junior oil that lucked into a lease right on the Athabasca Riv
They don't have any capital, but they're sitting on this go
mine and they're going for, like, eighty cents a share on the
Venture Exchange, and Dale figures three things."

Dick held up his stubby left hand and counted off the fingers with the right. "One: West Texas Intermediate is going to
hit $150. Two: the Chinese need a stable energy supply for a
billion people who suddenly want Lincoln Navigators after
ten centuries of raising pigs in their living rooms. And three:
Pathos is going to get listed on one of the major exchanges and
the institutional money is going to get on it like teenage sex.
He starts buying this thing, and it starts to move, and I'll tell
you the feeling, you don't get it often—some guys never. But

back something and you're watching it like it's your kid ning how to walk and it picks up speed, lurching a bit, and ı it takes off, and when that happens, it's like you just fig- l out the key to the universe and you'd be accepting the ›el Prize but you're too busy fucking a supermodel. Pathos north of twenty bucks. West Texas hits $147. Dale's got I 't know how much in this. But he's shitting gold. And he vinds the position a bit, starts thinking like an investor ead of a lottery winner. The Chinese are crawling around oil patch, looking for a deal. It's like the Red fucking ıy—hundreds of them, I'm not kidding. And the smart ıey figures Pathos and maybe Husky are the takeout tar- , which will drive up the price, though you have to figure most of this is already built in. Then one night the entire l Army checks out of their hotel and heads back to Beijing. ıean they all leave. Not a fucking word. A week later they a $100 billion stake in a Saudi play. You know the rest."

Harry nods, but Ebbetts continues. "Oil drifts down to thirty- e bucks. There isn't any credit out there to build a $23 billion grader. The environmentalists are all over the oil sands. Pathos es to twenty-four cents and gets delisted, and Dale can't ıload this shit—there's no one out there buying—and by the me they've bagged all the bodies, he doesn't have much left."

But surely he was taking money off the table before that, Harry thought. It was in his DNA—preserve. He would have taken half, at the very least. Where was that money? He didn't want to grill Dick on this point, though, because he didn't entirely trust him.

A waiter hovered and Harry glanced at the menu, its essay-ish descriptions, the nod to provenance and odd couplings—vodka and dark chocolate with lingonberry accents. Harry ordered quickly and randomly. Ebbetts took his time.

His mother didn't like any of the men Dale had worked with, but held a special contempt for Ebbetts. Felicia had a witchy intuition about people. Harry wondered if she was right about Ebbetts.

"What's your take on Press?" Harry asked bluntly. Prescott Lunden was president of the company, and Harry had always assumed that he and Dale were close. They were certainly cut from the same cloth.

Ebbetts downed the dregs of his martini and set the empty glass carefully beside his water glass. "Press likes to come across as the kind of guy who can hold his own, a tough guy, someone who knows someone at the track, et cetera. If he loses that look, the look of a guy who knows gold is being jerked around by three South Africans he knows on a first-name basis, the guy who's got an ear on the ground in Saudi—he loses that look, he's gone. People think Press knows someone who's in a mud hut talking to Nigerian warlords about whether they're going to blow the pipeline and oil's going to spike. And they like the excitement, they like the information. People have something on the inside, it gives them a hard-on. They walk around all day like they have a little piece of sunshine up their ass, and they can't wait to tell someone because information is how you determine your place at the trough. Press is supposed to be the connection between the WASPs and the real world. Except Press has never stepped foot in the real world. What does he know? He knows the banks will go up four percent a year until the sun dies. That oil will go up then go down. That people will believe in equities because they believe there is belief. You take away that infrastructure, that brilliant vacuum that people walk into, and there in the centre is Jesus with his wallet out, then the whole religion is ready to take a leap." Ebbetts stared at his empty glass. "And that is one scenario that benefits no one."

Harry remembered Press from a party decades ago. A cocktail in his hand, flirting with someone's wife. One of those silver-haired guys who look like they scored the winning touchdown.

Their lunch arrived and they ate quietly for a few moments.

"Sampson is the sharpest knife in the drawer," Dick said. "Poor bastard has cancer. He might have two months."

"My father was essentially broke when he died, Dick."

Ebbetts stared upward into the soft gloom of the restaurant. "That I can't imagine, Harry. I'd check those accounts. He might have been cleaned out, but you want to see the paper on that."

"How hard is it to manufacture that paper?"

"People do it."

His father's death hadn't done any of the things Harry had hoped it would. It hadn't given Harry a fresh lease, or delivered a mid-life epiphany. It hadn't resulted in a meaningful inheritance. On almost every front, Dale's death had been a disappointment. He pondered this as he was buzzed into his father's apartment. Dixie was still living there and had asked him to come over and talk. Harry assumed she wanted a debriefing on Dale's perverse will or wanted to offer him Dale's clothes before they went to Goodwill.

Dixie greeted him at the open door wearing a black skirt and a tailored white shirt and a bit too much gold jewellery. Her regular features, the residue of a tan.

Dale's apartment had a fabulous southern view, and Harry was always surprised that the city looked like a vast park from this vantage, acres of trees, thousands of them eclipsing the houses that ran down toward downtown. The light caught the first few yellowed poplar leaves in a comforting glow.

"Harry," Dixie said, coming to join him at the window to stare out at the city. "I feel like you're the only one in the family I can talk to. I can understand that your mother hates me." She cocked her head to emphasize the obviousness of this statement. "Maybe it isn't even me. I mean she's going to hate anyone who comes along . . ." Dixie moved her hand around in her ash blond hair. "But I always felt that you and I, we had some kind of connection. You're probably the only one in the family who's always known that what I wanted to do, what I did do, was make your father happy."

Actually, Harry didn't know that. For one thing, it was hard to describe his father as happy, even during the happiest of times. He was a man whose joys were mysterious and internalized to the point where they may have been unknowable even to himself.

He turned to gaze around the large, breezy space, which had last been decorated by a woman who ran with the modernist ball and put in a Le Corbusier sofa and a Mies van der Rohe Barcelona chair in calfskin that Dale had hated. Dixie had inherited the furniture, which his sister, Erin, had assumed would be going to her. As Erin had pointed out in a murderous tone after she heard this news, not only was the furniture the most valuable part of their father's estate, but she, as a designer, appreciated and understood the furniture, while Dixie would sell it for far less than it was worth to some estate-buying creep who would flip it for a profit.

Harry had carried that secret number in his head—the million he would inherit. What had been the number in Dixie's head, he wondered, the number that had surely formed in the early months of her relationship with Dale and, once formed, become something like rosary beads that she could take out and play with absently when she was on the subway or getting her hair done. Harry guessed that her number was around $500,000.

As his companion of almost fourteen months, a woman who had been his rod and his staff, who had discreetly disposed of unfortunately stained underwear, who had cooked for Dale from what Harry guessed was a limited repertoire, had picked up his dry cleaning and ordered from the takeout menus that had print too small for Dale to read, who had been his reluctant but inventive lover: for all this, she deserved more. Her bequest worked out to less than $2 an hour over fourteen months, a calculation she had no doubt made.

They sat in the living room while Dixie made a dignified plea for Harry to make things right. The sums that Dale had left them were so Lilliputian they seemed ironic or whimsical or colossally mean-spirited. Dixie said she assumed there had been some kind of financial sleight of hand—Dale's assets transferred to a family trust in the Cayman Islands or put in the name of a grandchild. As she skirted carefully around the issue, Harry realized she thought he knew where the secret fortune was stashed. She sat beside him, her mascara slightly blurred, her gaze expectant.

Harry felt genuinely sorry for her. Here was a woman roughly his age who was beached by the same tides as Harry, and for some of the same reasons. She managed to convey, without using the word, that she was owed. He reached out and put his hand on her shoulder. "Dixie, I know you did the best you could for my father. And we all appreciated that. His last months would have been so . . . bereft."

"I knew you were the one I could talk to, Harry," Dixie said, grabbing a tissue from a box on the end table. "I just knew of anyone in the family, you were the person who would understand. I mean, your mother probably hates me, and your sister . . ."

"Hates everyone."

Dixie laughed a bit as she sniffled and dabbed at her nose.

"My father, as you know, was a complicated man," Harry said, repeating the first line of his eulogy. "He left you $7,200, which, I agree, is ridiculous."

"Well, I knew you'd see the—"

"But it appears that's all there is."

"There has to be more. I don't understand, Harry."

"Neither do I, Dixie. I'd assumed he was in pretty good shape."

Dixie began to sob, making small heaving noises.

"Dixie, I'm sorry. I really am."

She nestled against Harry then, and he held her, and when she looked up at him, he recognized her expression as the fulcrum of a particular moment, the point at which the future would either remain the same or be radically altered. It might have been better to sprint across the spacious living room, vault over the Barcelona chair and crash cinematically through the floor-to-ceiling window onto the sidewalk twenty storeys down. Instead, they kissed, and Dixie took his hand and said, "Come," and he followed her like a golden retriever into his father's bedroom.

The novelty of touching someone, a new body after twenty-five years with the same person, was like walking into Oz. They kissed again, and Dixie unbuttoned his shirt and unzipped his pants, went down on him and engulfed him expertly. Harry was almost overcome. She gently massaged his testicles and her mouth took him with a hunger and purpose and depth that he had forgotten. She straddled him then, and soon several months of somewhat begrudged near-total celibacy led him to a roaring climax. As he came, the words that arrived immediately, that could have been yelled at the point of orgasm, were: This is how lives are ruined.

Afterward, she laid her head on his chest and toyed softly with the greying hairs around his nipple as Harry looked around the vast bedroom in a flood of guilt. The walk-in closet was open and he could see the neat rows of his father's handmade suits, greys and blues receding into the darkness, suits that had all been made by the same white-haired Italian tailor, who worked out of a tiny storefront on the fringe of the financial district, a man who gave Harry hard European candies when he went with his father to watch him be fitted. One day the tailor's grandson was there, a small, dark boy roughly the same age as Harry, and the two of them sat in silence, eating their hard candy, as Dale stood like a statue and the tailor kneeled in front of him.

"Dixie, when did you first notice the deterioration in my father's mental abilities?"

"You mean, when did he start forgetting things?"

"Forgetting things, getting confused easily."

"Well, I mean, he was pretty forgetful at the beginning anyway."

"But it got much worse."

"There were a couple of pretty weird moments. The first one, I don't know, maybe ten months ago. The neighbour from across the hall, something Stevenson. She knocked on the door and Dale answered and didn't recognize her."

"He couldn't remember her name?"

"No, he didn't know who she was. I think she's lived there for like nine years or something. And one morning I was in the kitchen making coffee, and Dale didn't come out and I went into the bedroom to see what was going on, and his clothes were on the bed where I'd laid them out and he was just standing there, staring at them, like he didn't know where to start."

"You mean he couldn't dress himself?"

"Well, he did, eventually. But it was as if he'd forgotten the order everything went on. I told him to put on his socks and underwear, and that seemed to prime the pump. But it was kind of scary."

Harry wondered if Dale's disease was complicated by dementia or if his confusion was simply part of the brain cancer. He'd had so little contact with his father, he had no idea what his baseline mental state had been. Did it make him a target? Had one of his colleagues seen a wounded animal and culled his money? Harry felt a pang of guilt about spending so little time with his father that his months of deterioration had gone unwitnessed.

"You think maybe someone took advantage of him?" Dixie said. "Someone he works with saw he was losing it and somehow got his money? I mean, how would they do that?"

"I don't know," Harry said, moving her gently aside so he could go clean himself up in his father's bathroom.

"But who would do that?" Dixie called after him.

"Someone who wanted the money."

FIVE

THE MORNING BROKE with that awful knowledge. Sex with his father's nominal widow. It sat inside him, a monstrous growth. When he looked in the shaving mirror, he expected to see Richard III, hunchbacked, withered arm, spitting evil, his moral lapse translated into physical deformity. Dixie would assume they were partners now, both of them on the trail of Dale's money. She had used sex as barter in the past, had used it with Dale, a diminishing commodity that she tracked daily, he guessed, gauging its worth the way investors checked their portfolios on their smartphones, conscious of each tiny dip.

Outside, the late September weather was still golden, the glorious apex between the thick heat of summer and damp misery of winter. Through the window, Harry tasted the cold in the air. He dressed quickly and made coffee, and squirmed in the presence of his wife at the breakfast table. When he left, he leaned to kiss her, but she deflected it to her cheek with a brisk turn of her head. He drove to the BRG offices with his burden.

Harry hadn't been there since he was twelve, when Dale brought him to work and introduced him to Press and August and others long gone now, each of them, he remembered, rubbing his head, telling Dale his son would be joining them at BRG someday, cornering the goddamn market.

Back then, the firm had seemed to Harry to be a powerful and exclusive club, a gentleman's cabal that ran things. This was the hub, and around it were layers of money supplied by retail empires, pulp and paper concerns, developers. Some of the younger generation had decamped, looking for more aggressive approaches to money management. The city changed, and the shape of money shifted. The markets were filled with sharp operators and odd niches and incomprehensible products. Harry assumed that BRG had held on to its core clientele, but he knew it no longer had the kind of presence and influence it once did. BRG had become quaint, safely steering the money of old white people to safe harbours.

Harry checked in with the receptionist, and a few minutes later Prescott strode into the tasteful lobby, glowing with false vigour, his tan impeccable, the whiteness of his shirt almost blinding. Press had expert facial expressions. He could convey all the key emotions: concern, empathy and, perhaps most critically, collusion. His great gift was to make you feel that you and he were part of something secret and successful. When he greeted you, he shook your hand and clasped your shoulder and said something enigmatic in your ear as he stared past you into the crowd. He spoke out of the side of his mouth *sotto voce*, and this manner drew you to him; it made you feel that the two of you were in something together. And this was the greeting Harry got.

"It's a great loss for everyone," Press said, shaking Harry's hand, the other tanned hand folding over top in a grip of condolence. "For you, for Felicia, for Erin, but for all of us here as well, Harry. We lost a good one."

Press led him to Dale's office. "Take whatever you like, Harry," he said, then shook his hand again and left him to it.

His father's office was spacious, a throwback. There was a large, solid desk and a leather couch. There were a few minor trophies—golf, tennis. No photographs of the family or of Dixie. A banker's box filled with files had been placed on the desk for Harry. The cream-coloured folders were neatly labelled, the statements with the company letterhead arranged by year. He filled another with trophies, a crystal Scotch decanter and a leather shaving kit.

Harry's own investments were a vicious battleground, and each monthly statement brought fresh casualties. Ethical Trading stabbed in the back, Global Sustainability hospitalized with asthma, Japanese Growth burdened by its ancient, shrinking population, Global Bond sodomized by its 2.26 MER. Five-Year Reset Preferred Shares and Linked Barrier Notes lay dying as the smoke cleared in a blur of red.

Harry did his own investing, tinkering online with the money he'd managed to put into his anemic, undercapitalized retirement fund. During those years when the market enjoyed one of its greatest historical runs and anyone with a pulse was making money, some small part of Harry believed the gains he made were the result of his foresight and market wisdom (oil would go up because the Saudis were overstating their reserves, and demand from China, India, and Brazil would drive up the price). When everything came crashing down, Harry, like so many, was hard hit and felt betrayed, not just by the market and the banks, but by himself. He estimated that he could finance a retirement of about three years.

During the week, somewhere in the world, regardless of the time, money was flowing, threatening to engulf the London bond market, hitting the Nikkei like a tsunami, spilling onto the parched fields of Kansas and Saskatchewan and snuffing out the engineered promise of ethanol. Electronic fortunes rode on minor blips from the yen or the euro, distress signals that rose from Wall Street and zipped through ten million hard drives like tracer bullets and lit the battlefield as thieves crawled away with gold or growth or emerging markets. The binary commands sluiced through the world's exchanges, and some of that money charging through the ether belonged to his father, belonged to Harry. He was sure of it.

Harry went to Prescott's office and poked his head in. "Do you have a few minutes, Press?"

"Of course, Harry." Press gestured to a leather club chair.

Harry sat and observed Press's perfect head, the Roman profile, sweeping silver hair that shone against the contrast of his olive skin. His handsomeness was reassuring rather than off-putting. Press pointed out the window to the buckling marble veneer of the bank tower across the street. Seventy-two storeys of scaffolding bracketed the building.

"They're taking off the whole facade," Press said. "Forty-five thousand slabs, I don't know how many tons. One hundred million it's going to cost. Same marble Michelangelo used for David. It lasted five hundred years in Italy, thirty-five here. Fucking winter. Some genius picks Carrara marble but doesn't consider the context." He gestured around his large office. "Our world, context is everything. You don't want anything sneaking up on you—hurricanes, banking regulations, new technologies. You invest in something, you consider the context or you leap out the window." Press leaned back in his chair expectantly.

"Press," Harry said. "Look, I need your help with something."

One of Press's hands performed an encompassing wave that meant, Anything, Harry. Anything I can do to help.

"My father's estate . . . it's not what I had anticipated. I'm trying to make sense of it. He left thirteen grand, Press." Harry watched Press receive this news with appropriate solemnity.

"I'd have to see the paper, Harry, but it doesn't make sense."

"You worked with him. What kind of investor was he?"

Press shrugged. "He did for himself what he did for his clients. Took a few more risks. Every once in a while took a shot. That's the usual pattern."

"But conservative. He always told me to do my homework."

"Big on homework." Press's left hand was spread out on the polished wood of his desk, and he examined it.

"Did you notice any change in his personality near the end?"

Press looked up from his hand. "What do you mean, Harry?"

"More forgetful. Or medicated."

"Everyone in this business is medicated," Press said with a smile.

"Would he be trading through some other account?"

"The whole world's online. Everyone's secret vice." Press picked up his phone with one hand and held his other palm out toward Harry. "Helen, can you round up Aug and bring him in here?" He hung up the phone and looked at Harry. "August might know something."

They sat in that lull. Press stared at his hand some more, then looked up. "Hell of a golfer, Dale. Had that swing. Loose as a Vegas hooker."

August Sampson finally entered, his stooped walk. "Harry," he said. August's mournful face had been undone by gravity, his tuberous nose and surplus cheeks pulled south. A mask. His parts were shrinking at variable rates, giving him a mismatched look. His ears had expanded brilliantly. His suit was a sober two-button flannel in a British cut, the shoulder lines drooping, the sleeves an inch too long. August might remember the twelve-year-old Harry, if he remembered anything. Maybe he'd seen Harry a few times when he was college age, parties at the house. And then as a grey, middle-aged man, reading a eulogy. August's own decay was nothing compared to Harry's: from shiny-faced youngster to this.

"Harry has some worries about Dale's estate. He left thirteen grand, which I'm sure you'll agree . . . Anyway, I thought you might be able to help, August."

"Anything I can do," August said.

"Do you know anything about Pathos?" Harry asked.

Press and August glanced at each other, and August's face had a sudden interrogative cast, silently asking a question of Press.

"Oil sands," August finally said. "Flavour of the month. Not this month. But it had an interesting ride."

"Was Pathos something you bought for your clients?"

August shook his head. "People called me about it. It was one of those stocks that had a lot of play. So investors would hear about it. It was going for, I forget, I think something around a buck, then it moved to four pretty fast. People called and said they wanted in. They'd hear the name at a cocktail party, someone would tell them it's going to explode, the Chinese are going to pick it up and move ten thousand peasants up to Fort McMurray, pay them five bucks a day, profit's going to go through the roof. But the fundamentals were never rosy. They hadn't set up the operation; they weren't producing any actual oil. They still haven't turned out a single barrel. So no, I didn't buy it. For those people I couldn't talk out of it, I picked up a few shares. That was it."

"My father bought some."

"For himself," Press said. It wasn't clear if this was a question.

"I think so."

"Well, you can play with this stuff. You know it's going to collapse, but you bid it up with the rest and hope you're first out. Dale was a complicated man."

"Complicated," August affirmed. "Was he under some kind of pressure?"

"I wasn't aware of anything," Harry said. "I mean, there were the health issues, but I can't see that . . . Unless he felt he needed to make a lot of money in a short time and suddenly got reckless. But it would be out of character. Wouldn't it?"

"Completely out of character," August said.

"Dale was all about character," Press said. "Have you spoken to anyone else here, Harry?"

"No," he said.

Press glanced at August.

"Is there anyone you could suggest I speak to? Someone who might know something?"

"We'll ask the troops," Press said.

The carpet in Press's office was massive and worn. A ray of sun sliced through the room and lit the wood of his desk in comforting amber tones.

"How many clients was he dealing with?" Harry asked.

"Well," Press said, "most of his workload had gone to others. Natural scheme of things. He still did the Thorncliffes, Teddy and Ella. By the end, most of the larger accounts had been moved over. Dale was half-time, not even. As you know."

Harry didn't know. He didn't know how much time his father had been spending at the office. He didn't know how Dale spent his days. Or his nights.

Harry smiled. "I wonder if I can get some help with those boxes."

"Boxes," Press repeated.

"My father's effects."

"We'll get someone to carry them out for you."

Press and August held their expressions of sympathy for a longish moment more. Harry was curious to see what they would be replaced by. He met August's mournful gaze. How far had his cancer advanced? His face was an ancient rune, and Harry imagined that if he could decipher his expression it would tell him something revelatory. Harry looked over at Press, who glanced quickly at August, his eyes the only thing that moved. Harry finally stood up, shook hands and left them both.

When he got home, he went through his father's files. He followed numbers through prescribed mazes, hoping to see Dale taking shape, like the faint outline of the Virgin Mary on the wall of a Mexican restaurant that got half a page in the paper: a sign, a miracle.

SIX

Harry met Erin for lunch at Arancia. She was wearing a vaguely Japanese collection of expensive knitwear, autumn tones that blended and flowed. Her dark hair was short. She was forty-eight years old. She carried the killing gene, handed down from Felicia, that gift of verbal dissection, a few deft lines that left lasting wounds. Her two daughters had it too, a trait that followed the feminine bloodline. Erin's face also held traces of their mother, the bright eyes that photographed so well. She surveyed the restaurant and waved to a woman who looked, more or less, like herself.

When Harry told her about his meeting with Dick Ebbetts and the possibility that their father had been swindled, she just shrugged.

"They're a bunch of thugs," she said. "I'm not surprised." She stared at the woman she'd waved to as if she wasn't sure she actually knew her.

"But someone may have that money," Harry said.

"Maybe. Maybe Dick was wrong and Dad just didn't get out in time. Maybe money didn't look the same to him anymore, Harry. You're near the end, you can let loose a bit. He's old, feeling impotent, he takes a flyer. Anyway, how the hell would Dick Ebbetts know what Dad was trading on his personal account? It seems odd."

"You don't think it's odd that Dad's estate was worth less than $20,000?"

"Remember Charlie Evans?"

"The Jaguar." When they were kids, a neighbour had gone into the garage with a bottle of bourbon, closed the door and sat in his Jag with the engine running. The rumour was he'd lost all his money on the market.

"God, I wonder whatever happened to that family." His sister picked up her wineglass by the stem. "Why did you go to Dick Ebbetts? He's such an awful man. Twyla Spence told me he spends half his income on prostitutes. No one pays a hundred grand for the missionary position."

His sister's witch-like intuition and eerie store of information unnerved Harry. "How would Twyla Spence know—"

"Why didn't you go to Prescott, or August?"

"I did. But I went to Dick first to get the lay of the land."

"So what does Dick think?"

"Who knows. These guys make their living being opaque. I don't really trust Dick, but I don't trust Press or August either."

"It would be a stretch for Prescott to steal Dad's money. I wonder if he's smart enough. And August is probably too ethical."

"August has cancer. He must be eighty. He's on his way out."

"Which isn't exactly a motive."

Left unspoken was the fact that Erin didn't really need the money. She was still venomously angry that Dixie had gotten all of their father's furniture, but Erin could easily afford to buy whatever she wanted, and wouldn't have had room for any of it, anyway. Whatever her husband, Ty, did, whatever dark corner of the banking world he inhabited these days, it was clearly profitable.

"Erin, I think we have to make an attempt to find out what happened."

"What, you mean hire someone, a detective? Don't you think the money is long gone, Harry? If there even was any. He wouldn't be the first person who lived beyond his means."

Harry absorbed this subtle assault. "What if there is money, Erin? There might be $8 million floating around out there. Even if it's just $2 million . . . "

"You could afford a divorce, Harry."

If there really was no money, it occurred to Harry, they might need to sell the house. It had been the first of his investments to disappoint. Real estate was supposed to be the bedrock, but his house had proved to be the foundation of his debt. Every detail of the house's inflated price, ongoing disappointments and lawsuit-threatening renovations was etched in his mind. Harry had stayed awake and brooded over it for years, off and on, replaying his decisions. The first problem was that he and Gladys had bought at the top of the market. Perhaps it was the day the market peaked. They had paid $522,000 back in 1989, far more than they could afford, but the reasoning was that, at the time, the housing market was going up between six and nine percent annually. "Your house is your savings account," the real estate agent had said. A trim, petite woman, Del drove a BMW and wore flared dress pants and heels. "This is land. They're not making any more of it," she said. "In history, historically, land goes up. A dip, maybe, but up, always. Harry, I pride myself on knowing what my clients are *not* saying. And what you're not saying is, *I love this place!*" This was partly true. Harry loved the southern exposure, the light it spread through the house. He was nervous about the electrical system and the ancient furnace. And he was fearful of the bidding war that would surely take place. He had already lost six bidding wars, and it was emasculating, and Del had a real talent for subtly reinforcing this idea and suggesting—without actually saying anything—that Harry was wasting her time with his small-dick offers.

The house was listed at $458,000. There were five bidders. Because of the interest, there would be no house inspection report, no handsome binder that told you whether the house had termites or corroded lead pipes that leaked dangerous chemicals into your drinking water, causing irreparable brain damage. They had to take their chances. Del gave him The Talk. "Harry, you have to understand what this house means to you. I don't mean bricks, parking pad, breakfast nook, whatever. I'm talking about its meaning. Because that is what you're buying. You try and put a dollar figure on that meaning. What it is. And that dollar figure is based on what, Harry? People think it's based on what they can afford. And they live with that regret every day of their lives. Twenty-five years ago, this house sold for $27,000, and some poor immigrant and his wife, they looked at each other and said, 'Jesus, we can't do this.' And now its listed at $458,000, and it'll go for more than $500,000. There are four other people out there, Harry. And some of them have already lost. They haven't even put in their offer and they're gone. They think, Well, why not go a few thousand over asking? It's worth a try. Not in a field of five. They'll go two, five, maybe ten. They don't deserve this house. You know what an extra fifty grand is over the life of a mortgage, Harry? Two grand a year, six bucks a day. A cup of coffee. But one of those bidders, maybe two, they don't mind a little blood. We only get one shot at it, Harry. Do you deserve this house?"

As it turned out, he didn't get just the one shot. He and Gladys stayed up most of the night, discussing it without really coming to a decision either of them was comfortable with. So they bid high because they had come this far and the thought of dragging themselves through this again was too dispiriting. That initial blood-chilling bid of $511,500 was close to another bid, Del said. So close the agents felt the only fair way was to have the two competing parties go back and put in a second, higher offer—a process, Harry dimly noted, that would benefit both agents.

"This is poker, Harry." Del said. "This is you sitting on your new deck eight years from now, telling your friends how you couldn't afford to buy it if was listed now. The way to stop bidding is to close. You go in hard and send that bastard home, Harry. Or next week, you are going to be going through this same shit again."

They went with $522,000. It seemed excruciatingly high. It meant a load of debt he hadn't remotely anticipated. But they had their house.

The first headline arrived a month later: "Cracks in the Foundation?" Within a week, a second: "Unreal Estate." Then they were a fixture: "The Last Bidding War?"; "The Bubble Has Burst!"; "A Pox on All Your Houses."

Within a year Harry's house was worth approximately $360,000. The furnace that was manufactured by the J. Grantham Co. in 1951 chose a December evening to quietly expire. The pipes were, indeed, lead. The electrical system, a knob and tube network of fire hazards placed cunningly in the uninsulated walls, had to be replaced in order for them to get insurance. In their second summer, the basement flooded, 18 inches of act-of-god water that ruined the contents of their storage room. They lived with his mother for a tension-filled week while termite poison was drilled into the foundation by a gap-toothed teenager.

Later, they took out a second mortgage to renovate the second-floor bathroom. Then, five years ago, they hired an architect to redesign the kitchen. Gladys had found him, a German named Fassblut, with dramatic glasses and close-cropped silver hair, who sprawled on their couch, ignoring the coffee Gladys set in front of him, pretending to listen to their needs.

"One of the things we desperately need is more storage space," Gladys said. "I know there's too much . . . junk, and I'll be getting rid of some of it, but now, as you can see—"

"Cooking is the desire for salvation," Fassblut said in his slight Germanic accent. "An attempt to fill the empty space with sacrifice."

"And a larger counter. I think I'd like the counter to be a focus."

"You must have confidence in the negative space. The void left by God is a gift that settles into convention. And we must reject this."

"Mary Oglethorpe had glass panels on her cabinets," Gladys said, talking to both Fassblut and Harry now. "A hint of green in the glass. It was very clean-looking."

"The deconstructing of the boundary," Fassblut said, getting up and approaching their kitchen—its eighties-era peeling maple veneer and off-brand appliances, "is only a temporary refuge. Look here," he said, his hand cutting the air near the drying rack. "Here we have an exodus from the mythology of appetite. The emphasis, always, is on the materiality of truth, which comes, of course, in many guises. Is this an impression, or is this the fabric? Every kitchen is an argument with itself, yes?"

The oddest thing about Fassblut was his hold over Gladys. A pragmatist in most things, she held on to the notion of his genius for a surprising stretch. She had looked at hundreds of kitchens, both in magazines and in people's homes, and this immersion had set something in motion: she deconstructed them into their myriad components—black-coral quartz countertops, Philippe Starck brushed nickel faucets, Next Generation refrigerators, ironic plywood, AGA stoves, Brazilian rosewood cabinets—and then into an almost Foucaultian exploration of their meaning, a maze of signifiers and collapsing semiotics. And it was into this particular and somewhat European moment that Fassblut appeared. She had gotten his name from a woman in her book club who swore he was a genius, and said he had reinvented not just the kitchen but the idea of the kitchen.

"I think we'd like pot lights," Gladys said. "Something subtle that disappears, almost."

Fassblut nodded and looked up at the track lighting that had looked modern only sixteen years earlier and now looked like shag carpet. He took two short steps and stood in front of the refrigerator, a wheezing nineteen-year-old Troublefree Frosty.

"The refrigerator, of course, will go," Gladys said.

"Stand here," Fassblut said, gently guiding Gladys to a spot at the centre of the room, the place she wanted a butcher's block island.

"Here?"

"A bit this way." Nudging her slightly.

Gladys stood as if waiting for a photograph to be taken.

"The spacing of the geometry so often ignores the human."

This seemed to comfort Gladys. She wanted something singular and arresting, yet ultimately functional. And she didn't want it to be too cold. She wanted hints of Mediterranean warmth. Maybe a playful colour in the backsplash. Their orange Le Creuset cookware on display.

"There's something in a magazine I'd like to show you," Gladys said. "It's not what I want this kitchen to be, but I think it caught something that I'm trying to do." She fetched the magazine and Fassblut ignored it.

Fassblut stared at their erratic DesignerStyle dishwasher. "There is the unspoken aesthetic that haunts," he said. "The animals that are unmourned on our plates. Of course, blood is the ritual, but not the result. You need transcendence. Look at Formica. It took the American kitchen into gleaming servitude. It constituted a mystery of ignorance that fed the masses."

"We had Formica in our kitchen when I was young," Gladys said hopefully.

Fassblut said, "Every kitchen is filled with death."

A week later a courier dropped off Fassblut's drawings. The epic counter was, in fact, Formica, a classic white with tiny squares of black and beige sprinkled on it. In the centre of the kitchen, where Gladys had wanted her island, there was a single block of wood, a piece of redwood that was seven feet long, three feet high and three feet wide (and cost $11,600). It was symbolic, an altar. Untreated, the exposed wood would absorb blood and juices, and it would be "a testament to both life and death [and bacteria] under this roof and a living portrait of all that sustained the Salt [sic] family." This was in the short essay attached to Fassblut's $83,000 estimate.

In the end, he settled for a $4,000 kill fee.

Harry later discovered that Fassblut's entire career was built on unconstructed kitchens, bathrooms, houses and buildings. None of his designs were built: not his windowless corrugated-tin farmhouse that was a rejection of the pastoral myth;

nor his stainless steel bathroom that was a witty take on the hygienic fallacy; nor his suburban sod huts made of living grass ("the breath of conformity transposes content into history"). And especially not the synagogue that was to be built entirely below grade, the only evidence of its existence a massive twenty-foot periscope sitting on a spacious, otherwise empty gravel site ("a stone witness that weeps for all antinomies"). The name of the synagogue was to be spray-painted onto the gravel and remain subject to wind, rain and snow. And for all this, Fassblut was well paid.

In the end, Gladys got blond oak veneer cabinets from IKEA and an expensive polished Tyndall stone countertop that looked, Harry thought, both clean and functional. The slate floor was heated. The backsplash was rectangular matte glass tile in Cherokee red, and there was far more space for their pots and pans and less clutter, and the kitchen was a wound in Gladys's heart that would never heal. It cost $27,000, all of it put on their line of credit.

Harry's world was unspectacular and unpaid for. If he had lived entirely within his means, if his consumption pattern had taken on the literal mien of a Mennonite farmer who arrived at the Ford dealership with $23,000 in twenties to buy the new F-150, what would his world look like? Who is content to live in the world they can afford?

SEVEN

HARRY DROVE SLOWLY through the quiet streets of Rosedale on his way to his mother's. He had grown up here, surrounded by the nation's bankers, brokers, politicians, fixers, touts, lawyers, industrialists and heirs, a fountain of money that shot out of the ground, and in the gush of afterbirth came the nannies and cooks and gardeners who made multiculturalism such a success.

He had incorporated the neighbourhood into his lectures on political history (Revolutionary Toronto, 1826–1841), had in fact incorporated his life into what he feared was becoming a distracted personal narrative rather than an educational opportunity.

Harry felt the city's aspirations, its longing and timorous steps, its distrust of grandness, the vestigial stump of its Protestant start. Toronto didn't want to draw attention to itself, yet it wanted to shine. He saw himself in lockstep with the city, a victim of decreasing budgets and poor planning, bewildered by the future.

In the Biblioteca Nazionale Marciana in Venice, which Harry had visited several years earlier, doing research for a book on civic politics that still hadn't entirely taken shape, there was a globe made in 1683 for Louis XIV by the cartographer Coronelli, and on it, plainly written in cursive script on the north shore of Lake Ontario is "L. Taronto." Sometime before 1600, the Hurons and Petuns who lived on the site now occupied by the city packed up their settlements and moved north. The inventively savage Iroquois then occupied the site, looking to control the fur trade. Before the turn of the century, the confluence of trails had become an established village that hosted Senecas and Mississaugas and French explorers and British soldiers, all warily circling the notion of ownership. The Sulpicians set up a mission near the Don River, which teemed with salmon, rather than sewage, and they watched the Senecas spearing fish at night by the light of torches, and claimed their heathen souls for the king.

In 1793, Alexander Aitkin, a planner of limited talent, laid out the city's relentless grid. It expanded in three directions—east and west along the shoreline and northward, orderly lines that incorporated the old trading trails. A rare exception to the grid was Rosedale, which was laid out according to the winding horse trails that rose up from the ravines. It was here that Mary Jarvis, wife of Sheriff William Botsford Jarvis, used to ride. They were the neighbourhood's first residents, and it was Mary who named it Rosedale. The predictable civic grid was abandoned, and its streets wound in a concentric maze that deterred intruders.

Rosedale wasn't where the wealthy first settled. But the grand homes to the south were too close to the water, finally. All the unhealthy things that arrived on ships crept up on them. Prostitutes and rats and drunkenness. Some of those massive Second Empire houses had been torn down or turned into rooming houses. The elegant park still had its greenhouse, a reminder of the nineteenth century. At night, teenaged prostitutes now patrolled, their midriffs bared to prove their youth, their feral small-town faces registering hope and fear as each car slowed.

His mother's house loomed into view. It wasn't as big as some on the street. Its grandness was understated, stable in its limestone and oak. He parked in the driveway and walked to the back door, which was open, and went in.

"Mother," he called.

Harry checked the empty kitchen. "Mom?"

He took off his coat and draped it over a chair.

"Harold."

He turned to see her behind him, wearing bright blue rubber boots and pristine gardening gloves. Dressed to go out and tend to the leaves or bulbs. She gave him a kiss.

"I'll make some tea," she said. "Or would you like something stronger?"

"Tea is fine."

His mother was a slight woman, not tall, the same proportions, maybe even the same weight she had been as a debutante almost sixty years ago. Her face was lined, her hair expertly done and dyed a shade that deflected any criticism: not grey, yet not an obvious blonde, or even a pedestrian ash, but some undiscovered note on the visible spectrum that gave her a look of vitality without any hint of forced youth.

She moved around the kitchen, putting the kettle on. "Harold, I must tell you something."

"Mother, are you okay?" he asked quickly. Perhaps it was her hip. She'd had it replaced and there had been complications. Had an infection crept in?

"I'm moving, Harold. I'm getting out of the house."

He was dumbstruck. His mother was so intimately tied to the house it seemed inconceivable. Not just the house, but the neighbourhood, its tensions and drama, its stores and experts, the sellers of artisanal cheeses, the helpful girls in the liquor store.

"I've found an apartment. It's very pleasant. Near St. Clair."

"St. Clair?"

"It borders the cemetery. Charming and private, and I could use both of those qualities."

"But your whole life—"

"My whole life has been carrying burdens that were not of my making. I am laying those burdens down, Harold."

It was true that the home was far too big for his mother. Not to mention expensive to maintain. What could the taxes be? But he'd grown up in it, its four dark bedrooms, its splendid yard, the rose bushes, the grand, underused dining room. The kitchen was its most winning feature, renovated expensively to his mother's specifications, with a black granite countertop nine feet long. This wasn't the kitchen that Harry had known as a child. That was before kitchens were spectacular showcases, back when they were utilitarian and still occasionally populated by the help. They had breakfast there every morning, his wordless father searching the newspaper for market epiphanies, the room a bit dark, despite its southern exposure. It hadn't yet been opened up to the yard with the two nine-foot glass doors framed in rosewood and custom-made in Germany, and installed, if Harry remembered correctly, by actual Germans. The doors pivoted on stainless steel rods and were opened with steel cranks. His mother was a good cook—had become a good cook, anyway. He didn't recall her being much of a cook when he was a boy.

"Who's going to sell the house for you?" Harry asked.

"It's already sold. A private sale."

"Who bought it?" Harry asked numbly.

"An awful little money man."

"I hope you got a good price. Why didn't you get something closer, though, one of those apartments near the ravine?"

"I need the distance, Harold."

"What about Trish Halpern and Amy McPhail . . . all your friends?"

Felicia's diction grew especially crisp. "Trish is so toxically self-involved it's impossible to be with her for anything more than the occasional lunch. She's been seeing a therapist for forty years and all that's left of her is ego. And I've been listening to Amy talk about her marriage for even longer. I'd happily kill Arnie McPhail just to change the subject. I'd like to move to Tuscany, but I lack the courage."

His mother had gone to Tuscany for a few months, renting a villa with Amy and Trish and another friend. Was it ten years ago? Maybe fifteen. When she got back, she redid all the colours in the kitchen in the orangey tones of Siena, and had the back patio redesigned to look like a small piazza.

What would she do with all the furniture, the paintings? While his father had no interest in art, his mother had bought a couple of large Pratts that Harry had always liked. "What are you going to do with all this?" Harry said, gesturing around him.

"Clarington's, thank god. They're going to take it all." She looked at him, anticipating his question. "This furniture is much too dark for you, too heavy. Gladys would be mortified. It would be like dragging a corpse into your house."

"The Pratts . . ." Surely they would bring in something.

"You need a wall for them. You don't have a wall."

———

To have the contents of her house sold at auction, to be perused and judged by neighbours. Worse, perhaps, to be bought by them. His mother was going through some kind of repudiation, like St. Francis.

"It's a dreadfully big, dreadfully expensive home," Felicia reiterated, meeting his eye. "And not all the memories it contains are a joy, frankly."

The night she and his father were out on the front lawn, arguing drunkenly at two a.m. What were they doing on the lawn? Secrecy above all, that was the (secret) motto they all lived by, the whole street. Then his father's quick right hand (the left holding a drink) and his mother crumpling onto the grass, Dale bending down to say something—an apology, a threat?

Harry had watched from his bedroom, his body limp with fear and tense with hatred. Across the street, his friend Jimmy Carson was watching from his own bedroom. Harry lay awake, plotting revenge, driving a sword through his father's guts.

The next day had been a Sunday, his father nowhere to be seen. Erin was at camp, so he and his mother went to see Pinocchio on their own. The ten-year-old Harry had been frightened of the whale. He felt the coldness of that dark, ribbed room, the most desolate thing he'd ever seen. Afterward they took a long walk. It was a nice day, his mother wearing a white head scarf and her Ray-Ban tortoiseshell sunglasses to cover her black eye. She bought him a licorice whistle from an old corner store that still had wooden floors and penny candy, an anachronism even then. She held his hand and explained that a young man walked between the traffic and his escort. It seemed suddenly a brave thing to do, protecting his mother from the passing cars, holding her light, girlish hand. This was the universe that boys occupied with their mothers, one of amnesia, hope and subtle wooing, and then you were thrown into the ring to kill your dad.

Sunday was still a day of rest back then, most of the big stores closed, the city empty in late summer, Erin at camp. Instead of going home, they had dinner in a greasy spoon and sat in a booth of faded red Naugahyde. Harry felt they were surrounded by gangsters, but his mother seemed oddly at home, smoking and making jokes with the cook, a large man with a sweeping pompadour and a stained white T-shirt who stood behind the counter flipping thin steaks on the flat steel grill. There was a small jukebox at every booth, and she flipped through the thick plastic pages and played corny country and western songs and old Buddy Holly tunes, and they sang along together to the ones they knew. They walked back through the university campus. Students played touch football in the pleasant dusk while Harry protected his black-eyed mother from the sparse Sunday traffic. When they got home, the house was still empty. His father came back three days later, and the following morning the unheard pitch of their breakfast silence was different, the tone of that vacuum changed.

Maybe his mother simply didn't want to be reminded of age and hopelessness, Harry thought. It's what she would see if she looked into the Botoxed mug of her friend Trish, a mask that moved like a marionette's hinged wooden face. Trish, who believed her legs were her best feature, gaunt sticks cloaked in stockings like a schoolgirl, was marooned in the culture of youth, a culture she had neither understood nor enjoyed when she was young, Harry suspected. When he was a teenager, Trish had come to a party at their house, wearing a geometric print dress. She smoked Craven As and did a blueblood version of the Twist in their living room. When her husband started having affairs, she said they had an "open relationship" and tried to look bored. Harry remembered her coming into his bedroom at two a.m. and kissing him when she was drunk, and here, suddenly, was his fifteen-year-old fantasy (a version of it, anyway—it had always been Amy he'd thought of) landing in his bed, her tongue moving inside his mouth like a lamprey. He and his erection both lay rigid with fear. Then she stopped kissing him and began to weep, holding onto him as she fell asleep. Harry extricated himself and went to the guest bedroom.

"I've given up the club as well," his mother said.

"Mother, you love tennis."

"No. I enjoyed it. But no one plays anymore. They stand out there in their whites and meet up at the net and gossip."

His mother had played competitively, and it had always frustrated her when people didn't take the game seriously. Perhaps the best rapport his parents had had was on the tennis court. She was Dale's match—lacking his power, but with better strokes. When they played against one another, the sublimated rage made for glorious competition.

His mother got up and took a bottle of gin out of the cupboard and poured an ounce into her tea. If this were a movie, Harry thought, the camera would move in for a slow-motion shot of the gin tumbling out and splashing dramatically into the tea, a shot that foreshadowed what was to come. At a certain point in her gin intake—Harry and his sister had calibrated it at roughly nine ounces—Felicia could become mean-spirited and eerily articulate, and would turn on people and exploit their weaknesses with pinpoint accuracy. A few months earlier, when Harry and Gladys had dutifully attended one of their mother's lawn parties and his mother was on her third martini, Missy Walsh had walked over a little gingerly in her heels, glassy-eyed in the afternoon light, a mannish, handsome face shaded by an elaborate hat, and pointedly asked,

"Why is it, Felicia, that you don't like me? I mean, I've always wondered why you've been such a perfect bitch for—what is it?—four decades now."

His mother turned to her with that cobra smile. "Why? Your husband made a pass at me the week you moved in. Perhaps he mentioned that. You'd been married a month. Jack was drunk, of course. I imagine he still is. It was that cocktail party at the Harrises, and Jack said you were like the Queen Mother in bed and he needed an outlet. Such a romantic word, don't you think? 'Outlet.' And here we are, forty years later, and by remarkable coincidence you look like the Queen Mother, especially with that hat, and Jack, by the look of him, I'm guessing no longer needs an outlet. So it's all worked out, and we're all friends, thank goodness."

Harry had witnessed dozens of speeches like this, delivered to his father, to his father's business associates, to neighbours, to concierges in European hotels, to police officers. Felicia never raised her voice, so you had to move closer to hear her, and of course everyone did. And when a woman with such an emasculating tongue is cut loose from her marriage, two things happen: some men want to sleep with her and others want to avoid her. After Dale left, they did both.

It occurred to Harry that the reason his mother was moving might be that she had snuffed out the last flicker of friendship in the neighbourhood. Maybe one final gin-fuelled speech had killed the last spark of affection in her last friend. If that was the case, then the house would be a prison, Harry thought, parts of it still as dark and gloomy as a crypt. She would have alienated everyone, an impossible task she had embarked on forty-odd years ago and had finally completed.

Or she had tired of her flawed friends. Felicia had a gift for unearthing weakness, for discerning moral lapses, and perhaps this knowledge had become too great a burden. It occurred to Harry that she knew Dale's former colleagues far better than he did. In the early years of the marriage, there had been a lot of socializing with them. And some of them she would still run into, or at least hear things about.

"How well do you know Press?" Harry asked.

"Press? God, I've known him for forty years. Since Dale went to work there. Ruthless man. I slept with him, but that was when I was married."

His mother was adept at giving him news he'd prefer not to have. "Do you trust him?"

"No one trusts Press. They would like to. His silver hair, that fine patrician head— but he's ruthless. Though, of course, at some point in a woman's life, that's quite sexy. His poor wife. I can't imagine. Why do you ask about Press?"

"I just wonder about Father's estate. Dick Ebbetts told me Dale did well in the market in his last year, before the hospital."

"Dick. God, another thug. At least he looks the part. How would Dick know, I wonder. I suppose it's all on computers now and you can find out somehow. If there is a way, Dick likely knows it. He shops for prostitutes on the computer. It's like paging through the old Sears catalogue, apparently."

When Harry left, his mother walked out with him in her blue rubber boots and waved goodbye as he backed his Volvo out of the driveway.

He drove up to St. Clair to scout his mother's new apartment. It was in a cul-de-sac that dead-ended at the Mount Pleasant Cemetery, a lush, peaceful park filled with the famous dead, Harry's grandfather and now Dale. Harry parked and approached the nondescript brick apartment building. What was inside? A student apartment with a fold-out bed? It was impossible to tell from the exterior.

He passed through the iron cemetery gates. There were a few dozen people wandering the grounds. A small group was gathered in front of the Eaton crypt. Timothy Eaton had built an empire based on department stores. When he was a boy, Harry and his mother had sometimes gone to Eaton's to buy clothes: corduroy pants and durable wool sweaters. The empire Eaton built had trickled away after 130 years, the last stores now gone. His competitor, Robert Simpson, was also somewhere in the cemetery, his empire gone too, though Harry couldn't remember the circumstances. Those two grand stores used to face one another across Queen Street. And now the two men communed with one another, conversations that snaked through the damp roots and moved among the rhododendrons and violets. You see how fleeting an empire is, Timothy? I didn't have any sons, and I look at your offspring and think perhaps that wasn't such a terrible thing. Your Irish blood, carrying those temptations. We fought one another all our lives, and now we lie forgotten in this pleasant grove.

Eaton, still unsettled after a century of death, buried in a black wool suit from the men's department (goods satisfactory or your money refunded), answers, But I was a giant, Robert.

Harry walked past Glenn Gould's grave. He had all of his Bach recordings and still found comfort in them, in Gould's fluidity and eccentricity, the creaking of his favourite chair that could be heard in the background. He had seen Gould on television once, hosting a show about the city, and was surprised to find him so normal-sounding. He had expected a twitchy genius. Though Gould had looked like a homeless man with that overcoat and tweed hat.

Harry stopped briefly in front of his grandfather's crypt, then finally came to his father's grave, which still seemed fresh. The loss of the house was the final pillar of Harry's childhood to topple. The comfort of his father's money was gone, and now the refuge of his mother's house. His line of credit had been murdered by the bank, and, of course, there was Dixie, that moral quicksand he had willingly jumped into. His father lay beneath him, with his many sins. How had he managed to carry all that?

"Dixie called for you," Gladys said when he got home. "Your father's . . . what do we call her now? Widow?"

In his head, Harry reacted as if Gladys had crept up behind him and yelled in his ear. He hoped he hadn't looked startled. "Ex-girlfriend might be more accurate."

"She left a number."

Gladys's tone was neutral. Was it calculatedly neutral, or genuinely neutral? Harry couldn't tell. Her face didn't offer any clues, and into this void, Harry projected a terrible feminine knowledge.

What could Dixie want? Was this a threat? Or was she just registering her presence, her dangerous proximity? Like thugs loitering casually at your children's school, just to remind you of what you're risking.

"What do you suppose she wants?" Gladys asked.

Harry shrugged. "Who knows? What we all want."

EIGHT

HARRY PUT OFF CALLING AS LONG AS HE COULD, which was just under twenty-four hours. Any longer, he felt, and Dixie would call again. There was no possibility of good news. She would either want to get together for another guilty coupling (or she would make it clear she didn't want to, which somehow wasn't good news either, another affront to Harry's potency), or she would want to formalize their mutual effort to find Dale's money.

"Dixie."

"Oh, Harry, I'm glad you called me back. Look, after we talked, I was thinking that we owe it to Dale to find that money."

"Well, if there is any."

"But he must have had more money. I mean he couldn't have only had that."

Dixie's options were few. She was an attractive woman of a certain age, unattached, listlessly working in the travel business, now largely the province of the Internet. Once it had been fun,

Harry guessed. Endless trips to sunny places. The kind of job you do because it has the promise of adventure. How many times had she visited Mexico? How many margaritas? None of the tanned men she had flirted with at beachfront bars, who spent the night licking the faint salt tang on her skin, tasting the ocean between her legs—none of them had lasted. A life lived in the present.

"Well, if there is money, we should definitely find it," Harry said.

"But, I mean, where do we start, Harry?"

Harry twitched uncomfortably. "I'm going to make some calls," he said, noncommittally.

"Let's check in a few days from now, then."

"Give me a week."

There was an awkward silence before they hung up, a few seconds that contained their coupling and its messy, unstated aftermath.

He went downstairs and sat in his Volvo and turned the key to complete silence. There wasn't even the discouraging sound of the engine sluggishly turning over without catching. The last repair bill had been $1,438. The car was eleven years old. Perhaps it was dead this time, another Swedish suicide.

If the car was dead, they'd have to buy a used one. A new car was out of their range. A used car was out of their range. It would devastate their budget, if they'd had one. The notion of a budget had loomed on their horizon for years. It sat like a threat, an organizing principle that they both suspected would somehow diminish them. And there was, in their marriage, as in most marriages, the instinctive shared knowledge of what the relationship could bear. Harry knew they had reached a threshold of disappointment with their lot that was best left unstated and undefined. A budget would establish borders that they could not comfortably live within, so it existed as a code word for the reality that they had to spend less money. The reason they had to spend less money was so they could avoid ever having to sit down and make a marriage-destroying budget.

Three days later, the Volvo irrevocably dead, he and Gladys stood in the toasty showroom of the Toyota dealer, looking at the Camrys.

"This is the one I drive," the salesman said, opening the door of a gleaming XLE. The features went by like he was a child reciting the books of the Bible in Sunday school: Leviticus, Numbers, Deuteronomy, Smart Key, Blue Tooth, Dual-Zone Climate Control with Plasmacluster. He listed the automotive awards it had won, the sterling resale value and the safety record, which, despite recent setbacks that may or may not have been politically motivated, was now even more unimpeachable than it had been before the recalls. "You drive into a wall, no kidding, this is the chariot to do it in." The salesman wore a grey sports jacket. His face was as wide as a prairie wheat field, his eyes separated by an unfortunate span. His teeth weren't up to salesman standards.

As a child, Harry had believed that Cadillac manufactured a superior luxury car (the Eldorado). He had believed in God and the Maple Leafs, and that the X-ray glasses advertised in his Aquaman comic would allow him to see his grade three teacher's nipples. And he had watched in sorrow as those beliefs had joined St. Nick on the scrap heap.

Harry remembered going to the Cadillac showroom with his father, who bought a new Eldorado every two years. He did it for decades before switching abruptly to Lincolns without explanation. The salesman knew Dale by name and would expertly steer him toward the new Eldorado and recount the amazing innovations that had been added in the previous twenty-four months, as if a team of engineers in Detroit had spent all that time trying to figure out what Dale Salter might want or need two years down the road. Inside the trunk would be a revolutionary new strap that lashed down his golf clubs so the Ben Hogan driver wouldn't rattle around. They would drive away in the new car, the warm September air rushing in and meeting the new car smell as Harry tested the electric windows until Dale told him to stop fiddling with it or you'll break it.

But he and Gladys weren't looking for a new Camry. The showroom spiel was simply the standard, fruitless prelude before the trudge outside into the unseasonable October cold and the particular bitterness it held, to look at the used Camrys lined up at the edge of the lot. Glad had collated the stats and reviews from Consumer Reports and three semi-authoritative online sources on all four of the cars they intended to test drive that day. A two-year-old Camry with low mileage was the Holy Grail. They wanted to buy from a dealer, despite the obvious markup, because they would have recourse if things went wrong.

Harry looked south through the spotless showroom windows to the stream of traffic on the highway, new vehicles speeding toward downtown. He had gone to Shenzhen, China, two years earlier to deliver a paper at a conference on the future of cities, and the traffic there had left a lasting impression. Not just its volume, but its extraordinary variety. Large trucks, Buicks and Volkswagens shared the road with tiny Chinese-manufactured cars and thousands of scooters and dirt bikes and old women on ancient black bicycles with four feet of Styrofoam strapped to their backs and braces of soft dead birds draped over the handlebars. The traffic in Toronto was approaching that level of chaos, a Third-World mélange of scooters, motorized bicycles and inline skaters weaving through stalled cars.

"Now, I don't want to steer you away from what you want," the salesman, Dick or Dirk, said. "Believe me, that is not what we are about. We want you to leave here with what is right for you." They stepped outside to where the used cars were. The air was hard and carried the iron tang of industrial pollution. They walked up to a Camry that was on the list Dick/Dirk carried with him. "Let me just get the keys," he said, and walked briskly back toward the showroom.

"Is it Dick or Dirk?" Harry asked Gladys, staring after him.

"It's Robert."

Gladys was wearing a wool peacoat and a flowing silk scarf that might be too light for this weather. It was grey near the lake, with a thin line of light near the horizon as if to mark where the edge of the world was. They stood out there in the wind, waiting for Robert to return with the key.

"It seems fine," Harry said, assessing the car. There was a time when he recognized every car on the road. Now they all looked the same. He simply wanted something reliable and inexpensive, and he was already bored by the act of shopping for a new one, even though this was their first stop. He was prepared to buy the beige two-year-old Camry SE they hovered over.

Gladys had pages of notes in her purse, annotated in neat schoolgirl script, with boxes and arrows and asterisks. She had printed out a list of Tips and Necessary Questions, and pulled it out now, trying to memorize the important ones before Robert returned. An organized woman, admirably, unbearably.

Robert half-sprinted toward them, still in his sports jacket, and handed Harry the keys.

They drove east along the lakeshore and Harry was neither happy nor unhappy with the car. "It's got the best ride of any car in its class," Robert said from the passenger seat. "The engineers at Honda have been taking it apart for years trying to figure out why."

Harry pulled over into a supermarket parking lot and told Gladys she should give it a try. They switched places, and when Robert turned on the radio, Gladys reached over and turned it off. One of her tips warned her against this old salesman's trick, to get you to listen to how fabulous the six-speaker stereo was so you didn't hear the wheezing engine. Though neither of them would be able to identify engine trouble by anything other than it stopping.

Gladys drove east, both hands on the wheel.

"The handling, they modified the Formula One," Robert said. "I mean, it's for the city. But the technology, basically . . . it takes some getting used to, because it handles *too* well." He gave a laugh that was intended to be conspiratorial, as if all three of them were now part of the Toyota family, and god have mercy on those poor Honda people.

This couldn't be easy for the man, Harry thought. Robert didn't know which of them to address with his flurry of specs: 2.4 litre, 158 hp, 15 cubic feet cargo. Harry was distracted, and Gladys held to the script she had tucked back into her purse. It seemed to Harry that even the manufacturers had thrown in the towel and that was why so many cars looked alike, why a Lincoln and a Honda were almost indistinguishable. How many cars were sold in China in the time it took Robert to describe the safety features of the SE? A hundred? A thousand?

Robert should move to Guangzhou. It had been more than a generation since the car had represented a romantic notion in the West, since it had embodied a form of freedom (not just mobility, but sexual freedom for the sixteen-year-old Harry).

But China was just arriving at that moment. It was, Harry reflected, a good time to be a sixteen-year-old in China.

"The extended warranty—listen. You're going to find a lot of people pushing this on you. Between us?" Robert waved his hand and made a soft blowing noise that indicated, Harry assumed, nothingness. "Waste of money. You did not hear this from me."

When was the last time Harry had sat in the back seat of a car? He felt like the oversized, unsuccessful offspring of the two adults in the front seat. On the way home from the cottage on Sunday nights when he was a kid, he and Erin would fall asleep in the back of the Cadillac. There was a particular kind of silence in the interior of their car at night, a muteness that incorporated the subtle hum of the engine, the feel of the tires. The back seat was huge, like a private palace. If they were stuck in traffic, they sometimes played games with the cars beside them. Once, Erin took the crayons and construction paper that Felicia had given them to occupy themselves and wrote HELP, WE ARE BEING KIDNAPPED and held it up to a woman in a white Thunderbird who was stuck beside them. The woman looked alarmed, but didn't try to save them.

Back at the dealership, Robert tried to close, a creepy, nice-guy-no-pressure kind of pressure that was easy to resist.

By mid-afternoon, he and Gladys were in a Starbucks, considering their options, Harry sipping an ill-advised espresso, Gladys drinking herbal tea. The Mazda was peppy and handled well. The Passat was precise. The Honda was Toyota-esque, the Honda salesman intent on becoming their new best friend. By the time they'd driven the Mazda, Harry could sense that Gladys's interest was flagging too, but she bravely pressed on, asking the short, bewildered salesman with the unpronounceable name if the front brakes oscillated during low-speed turns, checking her notes to see if she'd gotten the question right.

Harry felt that not buying a car this afternoon would be failing at something that was already, unto itself, a failure. Shopping for a used car indicated a failure to evolve. Twenty-five years on, he and Gladys were still students wondering if they should buy that used Corolla with 270,000 kilometres on it from the guy who said fuck engineering, he was going back to the Punjab.

"Which way are you leaning?" Harry asked.

"The Toyota and Honda have the best resale."

"But it's a used car—we probably won't resell it. We're the ones paying that premium. We'll just drive it until it dies, like the Volvo. Which one is most likely to die first?"

Gladys consulted her notes, which were spread out on the small table. "I don't like the Mazda's chances," she said. "What did you think of the Passat?"

Harry was thinking he could take it or leave it, but said, "There's something about the Passat. Like you can hear the machinery ticking or something. It's not as fluid, maybe. I don't know. They all drive better than our old Volvo."

"I didn't like the Honda salesman. I don't like it when they tell you all about their family." Gladys took a sip of her tea. "I'm not sure he even had one. I think he made them up."

"You think he pretended to have a son in university?"

"If we'd said we'd adopted eight kids, he would have had eight adopted kids."

"So we can scratch the Honda."

Harry thought of how Dale used to just drive to the Cadillac dealer and pick out the colour. Years later, Harry found out that the same guy bought Dale's old Cadillac every time he traded it in. Dale took care of his cars. This guy made a deal and he picked up Dale's old car hours after Dale drove away in a new one. Sometimes the guy was there and saw Dale drive away in the car he would be buying two years later.

Harry sat in the cramped, caffeinated interior of Starbucks and tried to think of this purchase as a new beginning. Like on a road trip with their parents, when he and Erin used to restart their game of finding cars in alphabetical order (Acadian, Bel Air, Chevrolet, Dodge, Econoline, Falcon) every time they got stuck, with one of them saying, "Starting now." It suddenly seemed critical to come out of all this with a car. This would be the new beginning. Starting now.

"The Camry. I think that's the way we should go," Harry said. "They're still hungry after that big recall. The service is going to be good. It doesn't handle as well as the Mazda, but it scores higher on reliability. I like the safety specs. It's maybe the largest car company in the world, and at this moment, maybe only at this moment, they have the power that comes with scale and they are humbled by the recall. We should climb on now. He wants eighteen; we offer seventeen and be prepared to walk if he doesn't drop down five hundred bucks and throw in a one-year warranty on everything, drive train, all of it. We tell Robert/Dick/Dirk that it's our way or the highway, then drive off into the sunset."

"So, the Camry, then."

They sat in the silence of this decision for a few minutes, then Gladys said, "You're still wondering where the money went."

"You're not?" Harry raised his cup to his lips to find it empty. "I just can't believe my father died more or less penniless."

Gladys shrugged. "I think it's a shame that Ben didn't benefit. But your father hardly acknowledged him when he was alive. I think I would have felt more settled if he'd left something to

Ben." She looked out the window at the students milling in front of the college across the street. "It might have opened up Ben's options."

Outside on the sidewalk, a woman pushed a stroller filled with twins. She made that face, the rhetorical talk-to-your-baby face one makes, that Harry had made. Who's a sweet baby?

Ben's options were an ongoing topic. His chief gift appeared to be for renunciation. Any child could grow up to be prime minister, but not every adolescent. By the time they got to Ben's age, only a handful truly had a shot. This was life's essence—a narrowing of possibilities until the final choice: another breath on the respirator or endless sleep.

If Gladys found a job, it would help. Gladys had worked as a librarian, and as the libraries were hit by budget cuts and gradually became more automated, she accepted a retirement package that had seemed like a windfall at the time but had quickly gone to the mortgage, credit card debt and a holiday. She still had a little money left, and used it for the odd luxury. She had taken an editing course and occasionally got work editing textbooks or a cookbook, but it was uneven, uninteresting and low-paying work. For a while she had talked about going back to school, but every plan invited unpleasant math: If I'm out in two or three years with a teaching certificate/law degree, I'll be over fifty. Who will hire me? Why not take the energetic twenty-five year-old—why not integrate those perky breasts into the system?

"Did I tell you I talked to Dick Ebbetts?" Harry said, knowing he hadn't.

"Dick Ebbetts?"

"From BRG. Short, troll-like. I think you met him once. Or at least at the funeral."

Gladys made a doubtful expression.

"He thinks Dad had money. He apparently made a big score on an oil sands play."

"So what does Dick Ebbetts think happened to that money?"

"I didn't press him. I'm not sure I trust anyone at BRG."

"Isn't that the cornerstone of their business: trust? Anyway, can't you pretty much do anything with computers these days?"

"I'm thinking of hiring someone to try to find it. The money."

"Could someone even look without drawing attention to the fact that you're basically accusing the company of taking Dale's money? Why don't you talk to them first, Harry? Just mention that it seems odd. Maybe there's a perfectly logical reason."

"I did talk to Prescott Lunden and August Sampson. They didn't have a perfectly logical reason."

"You don't think they were involved, do you?"

Harry shrugged. "Who knows. They're an odd pair." And now they knew that Harry was looking for that money.

There was a squeal of brakes and a soft crunch. Across the street, a BMW had collided with a parked car, damaging the bumper. A man emerged from the parked car and pulled out his cellphone and began taking pictures of the mess. A woman in a short dress and heels got out of the BMW, holding her cell, and began taking pictures of the two cars from different angles. She took a picture of the man, who took a picture of her. They moved closer and snapped aggressively like paparazzi, leaning to get new angles, thrusting their phones out for close-ups, bobbing and weaving like boxers. They walked backwards to their separate vehicles, still shooting, then got in and closed their doors.

Harry and Gladys took a cab to the Toyota dealer and collected their prize.

—

When they got home, Harry went up to his study and called his brother-in-law, Ty, who had begun his career in investment banking and was now a financial consultant of some kind. It was never entirely clear to Harry exactly what Ty did. But he had once mentioned a forensic accountant he knew, some guy who was brought in to analyze a high-profile scam that was in the papers for a week.

Erin's husband was a serious basketball fan, and Harry could hear the game on in the background. Ty had once taken Harry to a game, where they stood in someone's corporate box and idly watched the home team get shanked by the prison-yard Knicks.

The sound of the game suddenly disappeared, Ty pressing the mute button, Harry guessed, but still watching. "This is our destiny," Ty said. "We get a new superstar every four years, and around him, our faith builds. The new Messiah. We finish twelfth. We're in a rebuilding phase. We finish thirteenth. The superstar gets traded to New Jersey. This is the business model. This is how you get twenty thousand people paying to witness futility."

"Ty, the reason I called—"

"Christ, you're making six point two and you miss a fucking layup? Sorry, Harry."

"You once told me you knew a forensics guy. He was brought in for that Emptor Inc. thing."

"Tommy Bladdock. They had like fourteen gnomes on that twenty-four/seven. There were twelve hundred boxes to go through. But these guys, it's amazing. Tommy told me you have enough paper on a guy, you can see his soul. You know more about him than his wife. What do you want with Tommy?"

"Is he discreet?"

"Discreet? That's basically his job description. While we're sleeping, guys like Tommy are chewing through paper. They're like termites. You don't know they're there until the house collapses."

"What do these guys charge?"

"I don't know. One fifty, two fifty an hour."

"You think he'd work on commission?"

"Like a percentage of recovered monies?"

"Yes."

"I suspect it's cash on the barrelhead. They're not called accountants for nothing. But maybe you can work something out."

"Risk/reward."

"Right. This is about Dale, I assume. Erin told me there might be something there. Tommy probably needs some kind of retainer. Why do I watch these idiots?" Ty asked rhetorically. "You've got some paper, Harry. That's half the battle."

"But you have to figure that anything that's incriminating has been shredded by now," Harry said.

"That's the beauty of forensics. There's always something missing. These guys see what isn't there. They see the negative space between two numbers, and in that space they see a mistress or a gambling problem or a crushing mortgage. It's like a seance. They bring back dead numbers and talk to them. It takes some kind of brain, some kid who grew up reading Sherlock Holmes under the covers with a flashlight. Anyway, Tommy's a star. You want me to call him?"

"Yes."

In the morning, Harry woke up feeling bloated and unsure, had a hasty, unsatisfying shower and came downstairs. Gladys was sitting at the breakfast table, her face sleepy, something that Harry still found oddly sexy.

"Ty told me about this forensic accountant, a friend, sort of. I'm going to hire him to look for Dad's money."

A piece of toast was poised near her mouth. "What do you think he's going to find?"

"I don't know what he'll find. But if there's money missing from my father's estate, some of that money is ours."

"How much would we have to pay him?"

"I don't know. These guys aren't cheap. One fifty an hour, maybe."

"According to whom?"

"According to Ty. He knows this guy."

"Ty the money expert," Gladys said.

"I'm going to call him."

"How long will he take?"

"I don't know. He probably needs to see the paper before he can give us an estimate."

"At $150 an hour."

"I can't see it being more than a day."

"A $1,200 day."

"Look, Gladys, if this helps us find that money, it's a small, an infinitesimally small price to pay. It's not an expense. It's an investment."

His debt took issue with this and made its presence known, a sudden high-pitched squeal from a Dantean hog slaughterhouse.

NINE

PERHAPS, HARRY THOUGHT, as he drove north to visit her in her new place, his mother was simply part of the ongoing demographic lurch. The city was on the march, the tectonic shifting of a dozen immigrant cultures. The Italians had long cleared out of the east, and the Greeks had filled the empty space. The Jews kept moving north. The East Indians looked to the exurbs; the Chinese filled the fringes. In their wake, they left Chinatowns and Little Indias, and the owners of those stores and restaurants commuted in from the suburbs every morning. The rich had started the perverse migration away from the lake. Now the waterfront had been abandoned to generic condos, to childless couples with $3,000 bicycles. The carcinomic clusters of high-rises formed a wall between the water and the city, a bulwark against invaders, a wall too listless to declare its intent, to spell the actual words: Fuck You.

His mother's apartment was larger than Harry had suspected from the outside. There were two bedrooms and a surprisingly spacious living room. The building was built on a slope, and her apartment was at ground level at the back and opened up onto the cemetery, which appeared as a huge forest; both criminals and spirits could easily wander in. He had offered to manage the move, but his mother declined. Harry wanted to reassure himself that his mother was fine in her new place, the way parents wanted to make sure the university dorm their child was in was sufficient. Gladys was at her book club, and so Harry had invited himself over for dinner.

Felicia answered the door dressed in pants and a long cashmere cardigan that closed with a clasp. She took the flowers and wine that he'd brought. "Harold, I'm making myself a martini. Would you like one?"

"That would be good." He guessed it was her second. Her deft, practised movements, shaking the gin and vermouth and ice in the silver shaker and pouring into two martini glasses.

"Santé," she said, tipping her glass toward his. "To new beginnings. Take a look around. Dinner will be ready in ten minutes."

Harry walked out the screen door and strolled up to the steel mesh fence of the cemetery. The trees were magnificent. Old-growth oaks, maples, birch, Japanese flowering cherries, elms, a dozen kinds of conifers. A two-hundred-acre park devoted to the dead. The perfect neighbour, though Dale was there, which couldn't be a comfort. Felicia's father was contained in a modest crypt. Harry had visited him when he was a child, holding his mother's hand. His grandmother had been with them, in memory a crone no taller than young Harry.

His mother's repudiation of her past life was even more complete than Harry had imagined. She told him she had gotten a library card, her first. She took the subway now. Harry suddenly wondered if she had given all her money to a battered women's shelter or a food bank. Her father had been a famous philanthropist; perhaps she wanted to continue his work.

As a child, Harry had spent a lot of time with his mother. He'd gone to camp for three weeks every summer, an expensive place with a Native name, bad food and a *Lord of the Flies* philosophy. The rest of the time he was at the cottage with his mother and sister. On weekends, Dale came up from the city, arriving on Friday night, the highway clogged with fathers smoking in their Buicks with the windows down. One Friday at midnight, Harry crept out of his room to see his parents dancing drunkenly, his mother's arms around his father, her cigarette burning in her fingers, crying as he carefully patted her head.

In fall, the mothers and children all returned to the city, and there were family dinners, cocktails with neighbours. Harry was reunited with his friends and went back to the familiar rhythms of school. They burned the autumn leaves as a pagan ritual. His father disappeared into work.

He went back inside, where his mother was setting out two plates of Argentine short ribs on a bed of spiced wild rice.

"Mother, Erin and I are a little concerned." This wasn't true. As far as Harry knew, Erin wasn't concerned about anything. "You've basically renounced your life."

"Harold, you come to the end of things. Love, money, sex. It dissipates over time."

"You're still active. You're still attractive to men."

"I'm still attractive to precisely the kind of men I don't want anything to do with. Old men who need a nursemaid, witless retirees who want a companion, entrenched old roosters who have seventy years of dull stories waiting."

His mother's ruthlessness extended to herself. She wasn't one of those people who sit deluded in their apartment, hoping for salvation, carefully retouching their highlights in case they met someone in the supermarket. She had calibrated her future precisely and would take steps to occupy it with as much grace and interest as she could muster.

Harry remembered that she and Dale had once gone to New York for a weekend with a few other couples. Erin and Harry had been left with someone. Back then, you could leave your children with anyone. His parents went to see Ella Fitzgerald at Radio City Music Hall. Afterward they all went to the Plaza and drank martinis. Nat King Cole was sitting nearby and they didn't register his presence, they took him in stride. It was this fact that came up repeatedly when his parents told the story of that weekend. We didn't even notice him. And it was this casual proximity that made them feel that they were part of something.

But the whole city had shifted beneath their feet, subtly moving away from them. He remembered when he would see neighbours in the society page of the paper. Now there was only beauty and celebrity. No one recognized money anymore.

"Eventually you find yourself on the edges," Felicia said. She drained the last drop of her martini and poured a little of the Malbec into her wineglass. "There is no defense against being marginalized. Perhaps talent, but so few have it. Money isn't much help. Not as much as people think, anyway."

Harry wondered if his mother was marginalizing herself before she could become marginalized, her need for control.

"Harold, there's something I need to tell you. Your grandfather, as you already know, was a force. He gave away, I don't know how much land—all that land where the hospital sits. He donated land to the university, to the Anglican church. He fell in love with giving. It became his mistress, I think. One of them, anyway. His fortune was impregnable. Certainly that is what we thought when he died. My brothers and I. Philip hired his own lawyer, you know. Frightened that Prentice and

I would somehow conspire to disinherit him. How could we? In any event, there wasn't much to disinherit. He left me that house. My mother didn't want it. I was a woman, vulnerable, he thought. I would need shelter at some point. The money went to my brothers. They each got something like half a million dollars. Not an insignificant sum in those days, though a fraction of what they expected."

Harry remembered his grandfather dimly. Occasionally they all went to dinner at Barton's house, seated at the oversized table, his grandparents at each end. His grandmother, a small, faded woman in an antique dress, silent and attentive, still carrying the nineteenth century within her, slowly disappearing, like the Cheshire Cat. Barton, a big man who smoked cigars and laughed outrageously, always wore a vested suit. He was a man of American appetites, and that's where he went to play, renting a suite at the Pierre and entertaining impressionable actresses. Harry remembered being asked to read aloud at the breakfast table from a newspaper article that outlined one of his grandfather's charitable acts: "Barton McClary Donates Land to Church."

He had made much of his money in real estate, a fortune built on luck (and perhaps some bribery, it was never clear) when the corporate boundaries of the city expanded to include farmland he had bought for a horse operation. The city engulfed the last of his rural properties, increasing their worth twentyfold, but he didn't have any other tricks. The various enterprises he got into after that had mixed returns. There had been some nasty business in New York as well, a girl he had gotten into trouble, who may or may not have died while having an abortion. Part of the family mythology.

"So I had the house," his mother said. She poured a little more of the wine. "When I married your father, we both had the expectation of a substantial sum being passed down. Instead, there was the house. Dale had some money, of course. But most of what we had he earned. We were a pretty good couple. Better than you remember, I'm sure. We weren't good at the end, of course. And we weren't good at times in the middle. When we divorced, I kept the house for the simple reason that it was mine. Dale gave me some money, but not as much as you would think. Everyone assumed I had my own money and I was only going after Dale out of spite. But I needed the support. Even then, it wasn't enough. So I sold the house."

"What did you get for it? I would put it at somewhere near three million, what with—"

"No, Harold. I mean I sold the house seventeen years ago."

Harry sat stunned for a moment, then took a sip of his wine. "Seventeen years ago," he repeated dully.

"The market was still flat. That lull after the housing bubble burst. I sold it for $760,000."

"My god. But you've been living in it."

"I was renting."

"From . . ."

"Dick Ebbetts. He bought it and rented it back to me for $3,000 a month. At least, that's what I was paying when I left. It was less at the beginning."

"Ebbetts. Jesus."

"He was in love with me. He's always been in love with me. He knew he couldn't have me. Not even with a gesture like that. But it was the next best thing for him. A boy from East York who now owned a house in Rosedale and the heiress in it."

So the house had been long gone. Harry attempted a quick calculation of what she had paid in rent over the years. In utilities. What did it cost to heat that pile of stone? "Did Dad know?"

"No. Dick would never have told him. And I certainly didn't."

"You said Dick was a thug."

"He is."

He mentally went through his lunch with Ebbetts.

"So I've got the proceeds from the Clarington's sale," his mother said.

"The Pratts."

"The Pratts were a disappointment." Felicia took a sip of her wine. "Harold, I have enough money to live comfortably if I'm careful. Frankly, to be rid of that world is a relief. I've been holding my breath for the last decade, and now I feel like I can breathe."

His father's money was gone, and his mother's money had never existed. The hum of his debt was suddenly louder, high-pitched, a car being driven too hard, the engine singing on the red line.

But his mother could still be charming company. Their second bottle of wine was a modest Chilean Merlot. They chatted for forty-five minutes. She liked going for walks in the ravine, she said. She was going to Italy in early spring. She opened a third bottle of wine as a precaution.

"Harold," she finally said, "I told you this so you can make the appropriate plans. I know Dale's estate was a disappointment. Mine, when it comes to it, will be as well. But at least you've been warned."

They drank more of the wine and Harry felt like he was underwater, moving slowly through a sea of fresh debt, the wine heaving within him.

"I've had too much to drink," his mother finally said, "and so have you. I'm going to bed. You certainly can't drive yourself home. Call a taxi, or if you prefer, take the guest room. Good night."

Instead of heeding her advice, Harry poured the last of the wine into his glass, took it outside and walked down to the wire fence that bordered the cemetery. He peered through the conifers at the undulating rows of headstones. Barton McClary was there somewhere, sealed in his modest neoclassic crypt with the four Ionic pillars. Had they only visited once? When Harry was a child, walking on a Sunday afternoon as his mother identified the famous people. Frederick Banting, one of the discoverers of insulin, was buried there.

Harry tried to fit a toe into the crossed pattern of the wire, but it slipped out. If he could get a leg up, he could probably heave himself over. He held onto the bar and kicked one leg up, the way he had done as a child, his face going from heart attack red to violet. His arms shaking with effort, he hoisted himself up and teetered there and fell on the other side, ripping his sports jacket on the wire, landing on the hard ground. A distance of only four feet, but he was dazed and winded. Jesus, the blunt force of this earth.

Clouds scuttled by the pumpkin moon in dirty bunches. The cemetery looked like a Greek ruin, oak leaves drifting against the crypts. One hundred and seventy thousand lives—the eternal city—their final sighs leaking into green-walled rooms, their addled regrets muted by morphine. He scrambled up the ridge to where the bronze lions lay guarding the Eaton crypt. The road wound around late blooming asters and the brown remnants of impatiens, of Dicentra, Tiarella and Baptisia. Glenn Gould was playing *The Goldberg Variations*. It was the version he had recorded in 1981, sombre and mathematical. Harry could hear Gould's squeaky chair. Had he been buried with it? The perks of genius.

Harry's vision was unreliable. When he put his hand to his face carefully, it came away bloody and he stared at it without surprise.

Harry walked toward the looming mausoleum, a beautiful

Georgian building, his head filled with keening voices. There were shapes moving among the oaks. Romanesque crypts rose out of the mist, and hydrangeas drooped near the path. Grey headstones quoted Donne. It took twenty minutes to find his grandfather's crypt. Ezekiel 3:14 was carved in stone on the lintel: A spirit hath lifted me up, and doth take me away. A winged angel perched on top.

You've come to visit, Harry, his grandfather said. *This is a surprise.*

The money, Barton, where did it go?

Two visits in forty years and you want to talk about money. It doesn't come up in conversation around here much. I made some money, mostly by luck. I enjoyed it while I had it. I gave most of it away to good causes.

And the bad causes.

There were a few.

Did that girl die?

A terrible thing. The doctor was no back alley butcher. But something happened. Who knows what?

You weren't with her.

Don't judge me, Harry. It was a different time.

She had a family.

In Texas. I sent them money.

How old was she?

How old? I don't know. Those girls were all the same age, seventeen going on thirty. Look, Harry, everyone here is haunted by something. Two hundred acres of regret. No one rests in peace. Even Banting, the saint, had mistress problems. He discovered insulin and saved lives. Some of those lives he saved are buried here, dead of something else. There's no vaccine for death, and if there was, who would want it? You get tired, Harry. Better to leave it to others. Anyway, you have demons of your own; otherwise, you wouldn't be here in the middle of the night.

Felicia lives at the edge of the cemetery now.

I wonder if I'll see more of her. She's been twice on her own, both times drunk.

It hasn't always been easy for her.

Compared to whom, Harry?

Harry looked over to a plot of sunflowers, Russian Mammoths, seven feet tall, husks now, their frying pan heads bowed. There were thirty of them, a dead congregation.

But you wanted to talk about money. Why do people want money? As a unit of measurement. A certainty that God was never able to duplicate. I had few gifts, Harry. But I recognized money for what it was. People think it's a medium of exchange. It isn't. It's a river we all swim in, and it flows to the same place in the end. You have money problems, Harry. Everyone does, just not the same ones.

Harry shivered. It was cold; perhaps it would snow. The first of the season, a white Halloween, the children wearing masks and parkas. He had once dressed as the Monopoly character who wore the top hat and tails and appeared on the Community Chest cards. None of the neighbours guessed who he was—a magician? his grandfather? After an hour of frustrating explanations, he came home and went up to his room and sulked in his formal wear and ate his candy, then threw up a rainbow of colourful dyes.

Your money bought you distance from your family, Barton. If you'd been poor, you'd have been stacked up like cordwood in a railway flat with nine kids. It bought you sex with chorus girls. Another kind of distance.

It gave me a chance to give to others, Harry.

A girl dies and you give land to the Anglican church. Penance? A bribe in case there's a God? You loved the love of strangers, Barton. Isn't that what philanthropy is?

What would you know about philanthropy? You can't even get a loan. Look, Harry, we didn't think we could fix everything back then.

I knew my sons wouldn't amount to much. Felicia was the smartest of my children, but she didn't fulfill her potential and it soured her. I exceeded my potential and that's what made me happy. So much is luck. But what is it you want, Harry? You're getting cold.

Harry wasn't sure what he wanted.

And don't say "closure" or any of those other claptrap expressions people use these days. If I had a nickel for every time some ninny stood over his father's grave asking for "closure," I'd still be rich. It never closes, Harry. Life can't be resolved. If it could, it wouldn't be life. Relax, Harry, laugh when you can. You don't get another shot at it. So, what is it you need?

What was it he needed? Harry had no idea.

What do you hear from Dale?

Never cared for the man. A father wants what's best for his daughter. Dale had appetites.

He was too much like you, Barton. Now his money is gone too.

There's a difference between carelessness and philanthropy. It's late, Harry. Go home. Get some sleep.

I'll sleep when I'm dead, isn't that what they say?

Another lie, it turns out. I can't remember the last time I slept.

Maybe your conscience won't let you.

Oh Christ, Harry, you drunken halfwit, who are you to be such a sanctimonious prick?

Harry stared at the crypt, where the cement angel flapped its wings, unable to lift off, like an injured pigeon. He turned and walked down the path. Was this the way he had come? His legs were heavy, a mammoth's legs. There was a fog coming off the creek. A rush of shapes in the pines. No longer playing the subdued 1981 version of *The Goldberg Variations*, Gould had reverted to the one he recorded in 1955, the audacious bebop interpretation that had made him famous. He was wailing now, sounding more like Coltrane than Johann Sebastian. The voices were louder, the whole cemetery out of sorts. Even Banting was yelling about something as Gould crashed on his piano like it was a set of drums. If Bach could hear it, he'd have a Germanic fit. The sunflowers swayed in beatnik rhythms. A snowflake fell, landing on Harry's nose, the first of the season. Wraiths crashed through the trees. The gravestones sang a hymn. The forest was on the march, the armies of dead sobbing in their graves. Ashes swirled and snow fell softly, a quiet blanket to lay everything to rest.

TEN

IT WAS LATE MORNING when Harry woke up, his head muffled and thick, a larva about to give birth to something lifeless. He recalled the cab trip home, half-conscious, bruised, going past the klieg lights of a movie set, the trailers lining the street. Harry spent a longish time in the bathroom, then walked gingerly down the stairs, his debt a high-decibel buzz saw in his ears.

Gladys was on the couch with the newspaper. "How was your charming, alcohol-free evening with your mother?" she asked sweetly.

"She told me she's been renting the Rosedale house for the last seventeen years."

"What? From whom? Your father?"

"From Dick Ebbetts."

Gladys folded the paper and put it down.

"She sold it for $760,000 way back when," he said.

"It has to be worth more than two million now," Gladys said. "Maybe three."

"Not to us."

Gladys processed this information, another door slamming shut. "Where's the car, Harry?"

He'd left it at his mother's. "Safe," he said. "Safe and sound."

He was almost catatonic for the rest of the morning. At noon he took the subway to his mother's and picked up the car, then drove to the gym. He entered his code into the machine at the front desk, then placed his hand on the biometric scanner and waited for the click that meant the automated gate would admit him. It took three tries. How many codes and passwords jostled in his brain, proof of his existence, of his poverty and security, and how long before a number from the gym code invaded his ATM code, or the ATM number displaced the security code, his memory grasping for some mnemonic that would grant him access.

He was there for the hot yoga class, a recent experiment. He changed quickly, then walked to the small studio and opened the steel door and stepped into a sudden Mumbai heat wave. There were a few women already there, lying on their mats, eyes closed. Within ten minutes their yoga clothes would be lightly stained with perspiration, damp maps that flowered around their openings, all the places Harry wanted to be.

He moved through the poses for seventy-five minutes, pouring sweat. The instructor, a lithe Asian woman, finally directed them to shavasana—the corpse pose, Harry's favourite. She dimmed the lights and Harry lay there drained, near sleep. What he thought about wasn't the soothing blankness that the instructor said he should seek, a nothingness that pushed all thoughts aside—*invest in the stillness.* Instead, he thought about sex. Dixie had given him a concrete fantasy, and she returned in all her lascivious glory, anticipating his fantasies with courtesan-level knowledge. They moved together, a blurry image in an indeterminate landscape as Harry edged into actual sleep. The dreamscape became a beach, but the light was off; the sky looked like a charcoal painting and the sand was grey. Harry was alone, then a speck grew until it took the form of a woman. A siren perhaps, though when she got close Harry saw that she was talking into a cellphone. She passed without acknowledging him. The sky was streaked with red. The ocean threatened. The waves came in hard. Fish rained down onto the grey sand, writhing, those glassy eyes. He ran, but the sand made it difficult. Each step was heavier than the last, like jogging in peanut butter. He was exhausted. "That's enough," he said.

When Harry woke up, the room was empty. He got up unsteadily. How long had he been asleep? He walked dully to his locker, situated in a short row that dead-ended at a large floor-to-ceiling mirror. Sitting in front of the mirror was a man of seventy-five or so. He had wild, angled, snowy hair and was staring at his naked reflection, his buttocks flowing over the small metal stool like a Lucian Freud painting, his skin the consistency of drywall mud. Moles spattered his back like one of those children's exercises where you join the dots and an elephant appears. His face was only three inches from the mirror, the fluorescent bulbs above lighting him in shades of grey and peach. What was he looking at? Harry wondered. He left the man to his examination and took a shower and shaved, and when he returned, the man was still there. He hadn't moved. His eyes looked lit from within, bright and blue, a rheumy hint at the corners.

Harry edged closer. "You okay?" he asked as breezily as possible. What if he'd had a stroke or a seizure and one finger could topple him?

The man didn't respond.

Harry got dressed, then stuffed his wet yoga clothes into his gym bag. He glanced at the man once more as he left the locker room and in the lobby suddenly felt he was abandoning his responsibility as a citizen. The man clearly wasn't well.

"There's a man in the change room," Harry said to the bored woman behind the front desk. "I think he's having a . . . I suspect he's having a problem."

"Like with his lock or something?"

"No, a health problem, I don't exactly know . . ."

"You want me to call an ambulance?"

"Yes . . . well, no . . . wait, hang on." Harry went back to the locker room, bouncing up the stairs two at a time.

The man was gone. He checked the sauna, which was empty. He checked the bathroom, but there was no sign.

Harry returned to the front desk and the girl looked at him expectantly. "He's not like dead or anything?" she asked.

"No, no, he's fine. The patient made a full recovery."

Harry emerged into the ugly maw of rush hour. All hours were rush hour now, it seemed. On the sidewalk, a man pushed a shopping cart filled with scavenged metal. He was wearing a military greatcoat, a dirty toque and what looked like children's mittens; on top of the cart was a rusty sheet that was maybe six feet square, too long and wide to deal with comfortably. He needed to hold it down with one hand while he pushed with the other. A wonky wheel spun uselessly. His face was hollowed, and beneath the beard Harry could see that his skin was deeply pitted. The man was walking at roughly the same pace as the traffic, in lockstep with Harry. He looked to be roughly Harry's age.

Harry's cell rang. He picked up and heard Dixie's voice and immediately realized he'd forgotten to call her. Not that he had any news.

"I know, Harry," she said. "Do you understand? I *know.*"

"Know what, Dixie?"

"Dale's estate. I know it was worth a hell of a lot more than $13,000."

"How do you know?"

"That's my business," she said, with a sudden girlishness. *None of your beeswax, mister.* "And I have a lawyer, Harry. You knew there was more. A lot more."

"There may be more, Dixie. But if there is, I don't know how much or where it is."

"But you withheld this information from me."

"Dixie, I don't know if it's true even, let alone how much there is. It could be two million, it could be nothing. It could be that eight million was taken and we'll never find it."

Harry glanced over at the man with the scrap metal. With his long coat and beard, he looked as though he was on a pilgrimage. The neighbourhood was a mix of industry, poverty and gentrification: a gold mine for scrap. Washing machines were set out to be cannibalized. Front porches held rusted dryers and Slant-6 engines. Every third or fourth crack between the sidewalk pavers jarred or stalled the man's cart, and he shoved it with his chest, getting lower and using his legs for power. His gait was like a very complicated limp.

Dixie's voice broke the silence. "What do you think is fair, Harry?"

"I don't know what's fair, Dixie."

"My lawyer says that two-thirds is fair. That three-quarters is not out of the question. There is a precedent, Harry, and the law is based on precedent. Dale left me more than he left you and your nightmare sister put together. And if my lawyer can prove that you withheld information, that you withheld actual money, then that would be a crime, Harry. That could be jail, the whole nine yards."

A welcome anger began to rise in Harry. He had regarded Dixie sympathetically, and had been feeling guilty about the sex. He thought she was a woman who was a bit opportunistic and who hadn't made ideal life choices—a plight he empathized with—but he felt she wasn't a gold digger per se. Now Dixie was leaning on him like a gangster.

Were her fourteen months of occasional sexual sacrifice worth more than his and Erin's years of paternal neglect? It seemed to Harry that decades of Dale's epic silence had to be worth more than Dixie's few months of minor nursing. And who was Dixie, anyway? She filled the hole that Tess left. Dixie was what Dale settled for, a serviceable companion who had just enough awe of his apparent wealth to make the relationship work. On this front, Dixie was a minority stakeholder.

"The first thing I'm going to do, Harry," Dixie said with some force, "I'm going to get my lawyer to start working his magic."

"The first thing you want to do, Dixie, is talk to your gospel source. A lawyer isn't any help unless there's a crime, unless there is evidence. If you're the one who's going to benefit, if this two-thirds or three-quarters is rightfully yours because of the fourteen-month hiatus you took from an otherwise rich and rewarding life to care for my father, then you should phone the police, hire a forensic accountant, set up a surveillance team, do whatever you need to do to find that money." Harry didn't like being muscled. "The first thing you do, Dixie, is fuck that reliable source until he gives up the goods. That's the first thing you do."

"I don't think we need this to get any more complicated than it is. Now that you've brought up fucking, Harry."

The unstated threat—she would call Gladys. But Gladys would despise Dixie. She would be disgusted with Harry, but she would terminate Dixie with extreme prejudice, would assess this tacky shakedown, then banish Dixie with a goodbye as chilling as a Taliban death threat.

In the silence on the line that followed this threat, Harry imagined Dixie sitting on the couch in Dale's living room. Her highlights were fresh. There were lines around her mouth where the possibly precancerous UVA radiation hadn't penetrated.

"Call Gladys if you like, Dixie," Harry said. "I don't care. I wish you and your 'source' luck. Let me know if you find any money."

He hung up and felt a lurching nausea, immediately regretting his angry ultimatum. He couldn't imagine that she would actually call. Surely she was shrewd enough to realize that the possibility of it gave her leverage, while the reality would only leave scorched earth.

As Harry drove past the ancient distillery, a sprawling collection of brick buildings from the nineteenth century that was used by film companies to approximate a dystopic Europe, his cellphone rang. He picked up, optimistically thinking it might be Dixie calling back to reconcile already.

"Harry, it's August. I didn't really have a chance to talk to you at the office. So I'm just calling to say how much I thought of your father. He was steady as a rock. All those years."

August's voice was monotone, as if he were reading from a script.

"It's good of you to call, August. I appreciate it."

"You know, Harry, you were in the office, talking about your father's estate . . ."

"I don't know that you can call it an estate."

August was silent, not quite long enough for Harry to ask if he was still there.

"Was there something you wanted to tell me, August?"

After another pause, August said, "You know, about thirty years ago we went on a fishing trip, down to Florida. Me, your dad, some clients. Fishing for tarpon. We were out in this boat, fishing and drinking in that sun. We weren't having much luck, and we left to find another spot. We were moving pretty fast over the water, and Bennett Cain, a client, he'd been drinking quite a bit and he fell off the boat. Like hitting cement at that speed. This was before everyone wore life preservers all the time. Your father was about half a second behind him. Jumped over the side and swam to where Cain was already sinking. Your dad saved him."

Harry turned up past some pawnshops and August's voice was suddenly distorted.

"I'm having trouble hearing you, August."

"I just want you to know that this business wasn't always like this, Harry. Your father, he was a good man. We were all good men."

Static sounds.

"What?" Harry said.

August said something that sounded like Dale susceptor.

"I'm losing you," Harry said.

Why had August called? Harry wondered. A deathbed confession, perhaps. He pushed Redial. There was no answer.

ELEVEN

ON HIS WAY TO THE UNIVERSITY, Harry pondered the unfairness of his life. He hadn't been unsuccessful, had worked as a reasonably well-known journalist for a formerly prestigious public television station, was employed as a professor (albeit untenured), had a lovely wife who he still wanted to fuck after more than twenty years of marriage, though she didn't seem to want to fuck him back. Still, he chalked up his desire for her as an accomplishment of sorts. Maybe the sterile patch they were mired in at the moment was only a temporary and inevitable phase in a long relationship. His one indiscretion still put him in what he guessed to be the top tenth percentile for morality in this city.

But it was irksome that without what he had come to regard as his rightful inheritance, his modest success looked for all the world like failure. He had called August Sampson again, but had been unable to reach him. He wondered if August was in a hospital.

While it wasn't entirely a relief to be back teaching after his condolence leave, it did give him some comfort to feel employed again. Though his mind was on money as he surveyed the faces of his students and absently guessed at the student loans they carried, what their chances were of paying them back before they turned forty (slim), what kind of job market waited for them (cramped, confusing and competitive), what kind of post-sexual revolution lurked.

Harry's students had the glossy, drugged faces of privilege. Today's lecture was on the Family Compact, the group of families that had controlled Upper Canadian politics for decades in the nineteenth century, the cozy exclusion and casual corruption of Protestant Tories. That arrogance had led to rebellion. The people rose up! Would these students rise up, Harry wondered, this generation that had a statistical voter turnout of twenty-eight percent? What would galvanize Briscow in his FUCK THE WHALES T-shirt, or Melanie, whose hair appeared as a new sculpture every week; what would incite them to take up arms?

"Imagine you're a citizen of this city in 1828," Harry began. "A sexless city in black and white, a colonial outpost with airs and cholera. The legislative assembly has no real power; the elected officials are empty suits. The power still comes from London, and it is apportioned to Anglican Tories, who use it like a sword.

"It was William Lyon Mackenzie, a Scot, who coined the term 'the Family Compact.' He was denounced as a reptile, a combustible redhead. The sons of Toronto's finest families dressed up as Natives and broke into the office where Mackenzie printed his newspaper and smashed his printing press and then threw it into the harbour. Mackenzie sued and won and got a new press and began a larger newspaper operation. 'To die fighting for freedom is truly glorious!' he wrote. 'Who would live and die a slave? Never never never!'

"Does this remind you of anything?" Harry asked the class. "Briscow? What are your thoughts?"

Briscow was on the brink of sleep. "Yes?" Briscow stared at him, blinking.

"Mackenzie. Rising up against the rich and powerful. What does it bring to mind?"

Briscow's blank, helpless face.

"Well, the Occupy movement." This from Verma, one of the few bright lights. She was wearing a modified sari and leggings and a wool watch cap. "It's basically the same scenario, isn't it?"

"Have you been down there," Harry asked, "with the protesters?"

"I've spent a little time."

"What do you think the impact has been so far, Verma?"

"We brought attention to a critical problem."

"And what was the result of that attention?"

"You're going to say that nothing has changed," Verma said.

"It's a bit early, perhaps." Harry said. "An inequity that has existed for centuries was highlighted. Grievances were aired."

Verma said, "We've had coverage in the media every day."

"But will it lead to change?" Harry asked. "For a revolution, you need two things. You need preconditions, and you need a precipitant. It's not enough that people are oppressed. Something has to set them off. Who starts revolutions? The people? That's the myth, isn't it? They rise up as one. They're tired of being cheated, being hungry, whatever. They rise up and overthrow the corrupt regime.

"But the great gift of the people, the great sad gift, is their ability to adjust to almost anything. So they endure. They live with the horrible inequities, the mouldy bread, the shortages, the unfairness of it all. They trudge home and make dismal Russian jokes, or pray to a flinty Highland god, they pay the soul-destroying taxes.

"What makes a revolution is someone coming along and making people believe that things could change. You have to understand that the idea of change isn't just foreign, it's inconceivable. There is no model for it, either in their restricted worlds or in their restricted imaginations. Someone has to create that world, they have to draw the outline and colour it in and then sell it to thousands of people who are without hope and ammunition."

"But the people *are* rising up," Verma said.

"The issue is whether they'll subside again."

"You're saying we shouldn't do anything?"

"Not at all, Verma. It's admirable to join in. But in the end, when you all go home, will anything have changed? The dogs bark and the parade passes."

"But it is something."

"It is. But what is it? You have the head of one of the major banks coming down to the site, a man whose annual salary is just south of $12 million, offering public support for the protesters. Maybe his media coach recognized it as a good PR move. But he's still making $12 million."

"What are you saying?" Verma said. "That there has to be blood in the streets? We have to burn the banks down?"

"Mackenzie promised to burn Rosedale," Harry said. "At the time, it wasn't a neighbourhood, simply a house, the house of William Botsford Jarvis, Sheriff of the Home District and staunch defender of the Crown. But it was a symbol.

"Mackenzie hated Jarvis; Jarvis hated Mackenzie. Most revolutions get personal at some point. But a colonel in Mackenzie's army—Samuel Lount—said he couldn't do it, he couldn't burn the house. Jarvis's wife, Mary, and two of her sick children were inside at the time and he couldn't torch it: he would not fight women and children. Lount was later hanged by Jarvis. Hanging the man who spares your wife. Maybe their marriage wasn't going brilliantly."

Briscow put up his hand now, but Harry galloped ahead.

"Mary Jarvis used to ride her horse in the mornings. Perhaps she rode as distraction. She was lonely. It was a great century for loneliness in this country. For a while, theirs was the only house in the neighbourhood. Maybe the love was gone and she rode slowly through the ravines thinking of ways to cook her husband's heart."

His students obliged him with a titter.

"Mackenzie sits in our history as a hero. But how much actually changed? The elasticity of the ruling class is epic. They make a few concessions and regroup. The Occupy movements are widespread, but there hasn't been any change in banking policy or tax policy. After the crash of 2008, there weren't any indictments; the one percent is still the one percent. The people have been heard and the regime is intact."

The occupation of St. James Park reminded him of an anti-nuclear march he'd participated in as a student. That sense of solidarity when hundreds walked down Yonge Street, blocking traffic. A feeling of righteousness and malicious glee at bringing the world to a halt. That brief confederacy, the promise of sex. But the nuclear world marched on regardless.

"Here is an exercise. You'll all go down to St. James Park and talk with the protesters. Gauge the mood. Is this a revolt? Is this simply posturing? What do you think will be accomplished? Go on your own if you have a chance this week—who knows how long it will last? And then, for our next class, we'll meet down there, beside the gazebo."

Harry looked up at the clock. It was 11:20 a.m. Another forty minutes before the students would stand up and their faces would go by in a blur of ennui, leaving him alone in the starched fluorescent light.

After class, Harry walked to his office and called Tommy Bladdock. He had already dropped the files and whatever he'd found in Dale's apartment off at Bladdock's office and was surprised to see that the accountant was a muscular man in a tight polo shirt. He had expected a human mole.

"Tommy, it's Harry. Just checking in. Was there anything in that paper?"

"The paper isn't much help—it's been scrubbed. But I found his other trading accounts. And we may catch a break. Word is, the Securities Commission is looking at BRG. I have a guy there, and I'm hoping he'll share."

"I don't know how much more cash I can—"

"We can work that out later. First, your father. There are two trading accounts. Dale was heavily into Pathos, as you mentioned, but it looks like he got quite a bit out before it cratered. You can see here, there is $1,287,321.80 in cash in one account. There was still a pile of Pathos, pretty much worthless, and almost two million in bank stocks, utilities, gas, all dividend. In July—"

"He was in the hospital then."

"In what kind of condition?"

"Dying, suffering from dementia."

"Well, in that condition, he allegedly cashed out what was left through different trading accounts. The total would be just north of three million."

"Where did it go?"

"We don't know. But we will. Maybe someone was operating a Ponzi out of BRG."

"That seems unlikely, Tommy. BRG is very quiet. Old money."

"What are they spitting out for their clients annually, forty, forty-five million?"

"Bit more, maybe.

"Anyway, there's a trail. A little thin, but . . ."

"Well, thanks, Tommy. Keep me posted."

"You'll be the first."

He had paid Tommy a $1,200 retainer, and the meter was running. It was like buying five hundred lottery tickets. What were the odds? But action, Harry reasoned, even expensive and fruitless action, was still preferable to inaction.

When he got home, Harry went online and checked his anemic retirement account. He might need to plunder it so he and Gladys could get by. Financial people said that was the single worst financial move you could make. The money taken out would be taxed, for one thing. And the fund was already woefully inadequate for his retirement. But what were his options?

When Harry was fifteen, he took the money that was in his bank account—the accumulated birthday cash from his grandmother, mostly, almost $1,900—and invested it in the market. The three therapists Harry had briefly seen since posited that he was either trying to win his father's approval by entering Dale's arena and excelling, or he was trying to kill his father by making money at the very thing Dale made money at, thus sending the message that Dale was redundant and Harry was now the man of the house.

He put all of his savings in an asbestos mine, on the vague advice of a broker he'd talked to while bartending at one of his parents' parties. It was high-risk, high-gain, the man said. Harry heard only the high-gain part. With the windfall, he planned to buy a Jaguar when he turned sixteen and impress Jennifer Summers when he gracefully wheeled into the school parking lot wearing leather driving gloves with holes at the knuckle. He would show his mother-hitting father that making money on the market was child's play. But asbestos chose that moment to go from miracle substance (It's fireproof! It's light! It's cheap!) to carcinogen.

Since then, Harry had been mildly unsuccessful as an investor. The banks had reliably climbed, but he'd been gutted by mining fraud. Conservative and diversified—this was the philosophy he had been born into, and he had attempted to embrace it, though a part of him still held to the One Great Stock theory, the idea that a substantial (though not suicidal) leap into a brilliant start-up would be his deliverance. He had tried it twice since his asbestos adventure, with hydrogen fuel cells (O HydroDyne, you radical purveyor of cutting-edge poverty) and pharmaceuticals (BioNute, you opaque ethical sewer). So he was skittish. Still, he now found himself hovering around a Chinese manufacturer of solar panels, the familiar logic nagging. First, it was Chinese, a synonym for growth and technology. Second, it was on the right side of history. However fossil fuels ended—bang or whimper—eventually they would end, and something would replace them. Evidently not the hydrogen fuel cells he had bet $27,000 on. But if the Chinese government willed SunRise Inc. to rise up, it would rise up. It was traded on the New York exchange and had almost doubled since it had come onto Harry's radar two months ago, going from $5.12 to $9.81. You want to be on that rocket when the Chinese government dictates that the future is solar.

Solar power would give China independence from foreign oil sources—untrustworthy Arabs, flaky Venezuelan socialist dictators, African nations that could collapse by brunch. It would give the immoral Chinese moral and (yet more) financial leverage over the amoral Americans. Cheap, abundant energy would keep its 1.4 billion restless citizens in line and would feed the insatiable domestic economy. And solar was green: the heavy blanket of particulate smog that covered most of Shandong Province, resulting in an estimated 770,000 lung disease–related deaths a year (the UN's admittedly dodgy stats), would gradually dissipate. This wasn't a stock that was, in any real way, driven by market forces. And these, Harry knew from the bitter experience of not owning them, were the best kind.

What if he put twenty grand into SunRise and it went up tenfold? This still left him with a disappointing number. If he put in fifty K and it went up twelvefold? This was better. Six hundred grand. Sixty and fourteen—and he would cut the fantasy off there.

While he waited on SunRise, Harry was betting on the apocalypse. It was a strategy that was freighted with obvious ironies. The world had to approach collapse—it had to resemble a Bosch painting—in order for Harry to profit. His first move had been to put money into the Goldman Sachs Commodity Index Fund, a safe haven. The index was based on the price of several food staples—beef, coffee, corn and wheat among them. He reasoned, as all investors in the index must have, that we would always need food. Populations were growing, and the price of food would go up. It did, in fact, go up. Food was more expensive than it had been since 1854, the year its cost was first calculated. In 2008, the number of the world's hungry, which had been on the wane, increased. The reason for this was attributed to the false economy created by the various commodities index funds, which had made some people a great deal of money but further impoverished others.

The details blurred. He wondered how much of this was true. The media was prone to drawing crude causal lines between events, then pronouncing with authority.

His other hedge was water. Bread and water, that prison metaphor. What is more elemental than water? Our bodies are made up of it (oddly, men's bodies have a greater percentage than women's; perhaps all the tears women shed). Here was a necessary commodity (unlike that imposter, gold), and a diminishing commodity. It was transparent and familiar and increasingly politicized. Several aquifers had collapsed in the U.S., and the Americans were quietly looking north, not for the first time. California and Texas could be approaching End Days in terms of looming water shortages. The Ogallala Aquifer, which gave life to the Midwestern agricultural belt, was shrinking rapidly. When this reached a critical mass, there would be a destabilizing period when water would be much more valuable than oil or gold. Harry had done his homework, as his father had once instructed him. Rainfall in the Brazilian rainforest was down more than twenty-three percent over the last sixteen years. Worldwide, desert habitats had encroached on more than 1,682,000 square kilometres of vaguely arable land in less than twenty years. The Athabasca Glacier, the hydroponic apex of North America, which fed three oceans (Pacific, Atlantic and Arctic), had lost half its volume since 1844 and was retreating by more than two inches every day; you could actually stand there and watch it disappear. There was a tour group in Banff that organized gourmet lunches at the base of the glacier so you could watch it go. There were more than a dozen countries where political stability was already tenuous and water shortages were imminent. You could plot on a graph where these two lines would meet and suddenly there would be madness on an unimaginable scale. China's wheat belt was disappearing due to pollution of groundwater and the accelerating usage by rampant industry. The situation was likely much worse than China admitted. Las Vegas could return to desert as Lake Mead continued to evaporate and the Colorado River continued to shrink. In the north, the Athabasca River was being plundered by the oil sands and could disappear in a decade.

The more Harry researched the world of water, the more frightening it became. It took hundreds of litres to irrigate enough cotton to make a single pair of blue jeans. The average North American woman over the age of seventeen owned nine pairs. On the conspiracy websites, where he wandered late at night, secret deals had already been made among various Knights of Malta to keep Opus Dei members in water. A cell within the American government had achieved secret control of the Great Lakes.

So Harry bought into a hedge fund called Spectre Island that was heavily weighted in water. It invested in a company that used Icelandic icebergs to make bottled water, then sent those bottles to Dubai, where drought was a fact of life. The company had a bottling plant in Maine and was poised to move, according to two analysts he semi-trusted. Spectre was the odds-on favourite to be named "Hedge Fund of the Year," and that would attract more institutional money and the price would move up.

For Harry to thrive, the world had to fail. But it was already failing. He wasn't contributing to its collapse, or even profiteering. He was seeing the world for what it was—a series of bad bets made by mankind.

TWELVE

HARRY WAS MEETING HIS SISTER for an early dinner at Umlaut. Erin arrived late, wearing boots that he guessed cost $800. The restaurant was done in a subdued grey palette and resembled a first-class airport lounge, a contrast to its heroin-addicted Belgian chef, who had recently died of a deliberate overdose. He'd been found in the kitchen, according to Harry's morbidly informed sister, with a sheaf of recipes on precisely how to prepare his unappetizing, heroin-ravaged corpse. It was titled "The One-Metre Diet."

After they ordered, Harry asked, "When did you know?"

"Know?" Erin repeated.

"Mom. Ebbetts. The house."

"Oh. The house. Mom told me." His sister had a gift for evasion.

"But, I mean . . . Christ. Ebbetts," he said.

"I actually think she's happier now, Harry. She's been trying to kill that world for forty years, and now it's finally dead and

I think it's brought her some peace."

"I worry about her getting lonely. Maybe she'll have lunch with Amy or Trish once in a while at least."

"I don't know. Dad had an affair with Trish. Like thirty years ago. Amy, too, for all I know. But Trish for sure."

"You know this how?"

"I saw them," she said. "I used to go into Mom and Dad's closet with a book and read with a flashlight. It was my private retreat. I'd lie in that oversized laundry basket they had, the clothes smelling of Dad's aftershave and Mom's perfume. She changed about three times a day; nothing ever got dirty. I heard something and got up and looked through the wooden slats. Trish was bent over the dresser and he was fucking her and spanking her and Trish was reciting something. It was in Latin, Harry. A novena, I think. All the handy uses for Catholicism. After the initial shock, I thought, So that's how it's done." Erin laughed her big laugh. "A formative moment, you might say."

Harry sat, stunned by this news. Their dinner arrived and Erin pushed a piece of asparagus around her plate like a broom, then lifted it to her mouth.

"You watched this," he finally said.

"Hmm, uhmmm."

"Jesus."

"Well, time, a little therapy . . ."

"You didn't . . ."

"Tell Mom? Develop a taste for discipline?"

"Jesus, Erin."

"Mom already knew, I'm guessing. Probably not the details, though don't be too sure."

Harry pondered the circle of expertly charred vegetables that surrounded the duck breast on his plate.

"Her new place, though," he said.

"I think it's cheery. It's manageable, anyway. That house was a burden passed on from her father, really. Then it became a different kind of burden after she sold it to Dick. Sold it *for* dick. What did she get, $760,000? God. But the point is, she has a chance to be happy now. I don't think she did in that house. I really don't. Around those people."

"She's seventy-six," Harry said. "She goes for a walk, shops for groceries, mixes a martini. Then two more. What's she going to be like in January? What's going to fill her days?" The winter darkness, the vengeful winds. His mother was almost incapable of watching television; after ten minutes, she began arguing with the people on the screen.

"We'll have to spend more time with her, Harry. I've asked the girls to take her to New York. It would be nice. Just the three of them, without me. Take matricide out of the equation. She'll relax."

Erin's daughters were self-absorbed beauties who had inherited a great deal from their grandmother. Maybe not the ideal travelling companions, though it could be fun.

"Isn't there anyone she can salvage from the wreckage? There must be some friend she could still see."

Behind Erin was an open kitchen with smoked glass dividers that allowed the seated diners to see the head and shoulders of the chefs. Flames leapt up every few minutes, like a crude effect in a school play that announced the arrival of the devil.

"She should play tennis again," Harry said. "It would be good for her. She'd meet new people."

"Since her hip operation, I don't know. I mean, she can probably still play, she just can't win. So . . ."

"What about moving in with you and Ty? The girls are gone—you've got room."

"We'd kill each other, Harry. You know that." Erin examined Harry's plate. "I should have ordered the duck."

"I hired a forensic accountant," Harry said. He hoped that Erin would offer to chip in and pay half the fee. "Tommy Bladdock. A wizard, apparently."

"Ty told me. What do you think he's going to find? People usually don't recover anything from these things, do they? The money's always gone."

"You don't think it would at least bring some peace of mind?"

Erin shrugged.

"I talked to Dixie the other day," Harry said. "She's hired a lawyer. She thinks there may be more."

"And just how, I wonder," Erin said pleasantly, "would Dixie know anything that didn't have to do with rack rates at Mazatlan? I'd say she's the prime suspect."

"She says she's going after two-thirds."

"Two thirds of what?" Erin said. "I hope Dad spanked her. Though I can't imagine he had the energy."

Harry stared at his sister, who was busy quarantining carbohydrates, pushing them to one end of the white rectangular plate, near the lightly nibbled chicken. There was a very faint hint of grey at the roots of her part; otherwise, her hair was a rich, brownish black.

"Bladdock says there was about $3 million in Dad's accounts three months before he died," Harry said.

"Does he know where it went?"

"Not yet. He also thinks there may have been something going on at BRG."

"Like what?"

"He doesn't know. Apparently the Securities people are taking a look at them."

"And Dixie the helpful travel agent wants $2 million of this," Erin said caustically. "Because she was his soulmate."

Harry heard a familiar voice he couldn't place.

"Erin! Oh, Harry!"

He looked up to see Trish Halpern, the lucky bent-over recipient of his father's affections so long ago. An unwanted image. Trish was wearing a red swing coat, which had probably looked festive in the store but in this light made her look like a sad child. Thin and sagging, no longer game for the surgeon's knife. Her eyes, those final windows, still gleamed, though.

"I didn't see you two. We were eating in the corner, a few of the girls."

"How are you, Trish?" Harry said. If she'd come for a late lunch, she'd lingered over the wine for four hours. She weaved slightly.

"I'm well," she trilled. "But we don't see anything of poor Felicia. How on earth is she coping?"

"Never better," Erin said.

"I mean she simply disappeared."

"I think she needs some time to herself," Harry said. "A retreat."

"But I mean, she must be desperate, all that time alone."

Erin's smile tightened.

"She's left the club even. Posey Dault thought she'd died. She didn't believe me when I told her." Trish was swaying slightly now. Her face had the smudged look of afternoon drinking. "Amy thinks she's simply trying to make a point. I don't even have a phone number—it's as if she joined a cult. If there's something I should know . . . I was only her best friend for fifty years. I mean, everyone assumes—it's obvious, isn't it?—but to try and keep it from her friends? I'm certainly not going to judge, and we don't even know which clinic, not that they're allowed visitors or anything. I remember when Posey was drying out—"

Erin interrupted, "And here you are still drinking wine all afternoon with the girls, Trish. You naughty thing. *Malus puella*. It's lucky no one's left to give you a good hard spanking."

Trish's smudged face looked puzzled, as if she'd misplaced her keys and was mentally going through all the places she could have left them.

"It was lovely to see you, Trish," Harry ventured gently. "I think the girls are waiting for you."

Trish looked blankly at the three women standing by the door. One of them offered a Queen-like wave. "Yes," Trish said. "Yes. It's late."

Harry and Erin sat in silence for a few minutes after Trish had limped off, concentrating on their dinner, the artful use of pomegranate in the quinoa, the splash of mint.

As a child Erin was precociously self-assured, Harry remembered, and that self-assurance, in its coolness, its surety, that sense of malign confidence coming out of that unblemished face, had looked, for all the world, like evil. It was precisely the quality that casting directors sought when they needed a child actor to play the devil. Innocence is much more chilling.

Once, Erin had disappeared. "In the ravine," her breathless friend Dorothy said. "We were in the ravine." And suddenly that extensive maze of forested troughs that had been gouged by glaciers was no longer a place of bike trails and leisure. It was a dark Grimm's wood filled with bullies, gypsies, escaped convicts, coyotes and feral dogs, a place of unspeakable menace. They all went out looking, his mother biting her hand, saying, "Oh god, Dale," his father calm but walking quickly, almost running, calling Erin's name. A few neighbours helped. It was autumn and the trees were stunning, a few fiery maples amid the gentle yellow of the poplars. The leaves on the ground hadn't dried yet and yielded underfoot with a spongy feel. They passed a mouldy plaid blanket on the ground. Two condoms and an empty package of Export As were beside it, and the fourteen-year-old Harry registered all these things, along with his mother's ratcheted anxiety. It was cool in the trees as they scrambled along the uneven ground, careful not to articulate their thoughts. After two hours they found her in a small clearing, sitting on a fallen tree, looking like Alice in Wonderland. The tree was grey and smooth, and ten-year-old Erin was calmly observing the ants that moved along it in an undeviating twelve-foot line of black. When they walked home, they were a family, overjoyed to be intact.

"I think Press may have been involved," Harry finally said.

"Press the idiot."

"Ebbetts says Press is a fraud; he's got one foot in the abyss."

"So Press stole Dad's money?"

"Why not?"

"The problem, detective, is that stealing three million requires at least some financial wit. I don't know that Press has that. Plus, it seems out of character. He's an ass, not a thief."

"Maybe he needed the money."

Erin signalled for the check.

As Harry was driving home, a squirrel darted across the road in front of him, choosing just that moment to end its life. There was a sharp thump and Harry slowed and looked in his rear-view mirror. He had had one glass of wine too many and pulled over carefully. He got out and walked back. The squirrel was in the middle of the pavement, its guts coming out of its black fur like toothpaste squeezed from a tube. It was still alive.

Harry stared at the squirrel's face. In its small eyes, he could see fear. It knew it was dying. There was nothing to be done. But he couldn't just leave it there. It was suffering horribly, twitching, waiting for the comfort of death. What if the next car swerved, as it likely would? Was there something to kill the squirrel with?

The retaining wall of a nearby house had loose stones in it, built in the style of the rural Irish. From the wall, he pried off a stone, a jagged, uneven bowling ball, and walked to the squirrel, checking for cars. Harry briefly imagined joining the squirrel, his own guts leaking, the cars not stopping, the bank manager, Ms. Remnick, walking toward him with a rock. He knelt and lifted the stone higher than necessary and brought it down hard. Not a direct blow to the head as intended, but a glancing one as Harry instinctively turned away. He tried again, this time succeeded and slammed the rock down again before standing up. A woman on the other side of the street stared at him. Harry dropped the rock and walked back to his car.

It was nine p.m. when Harry got home. The house was dark. There was no sign of Gladys. Harry poured himself a glass of wine and drank most of it, then went into the family room. Ben and Sarah were there, curled up on the couch in the dark, watching TV without the sound on.

"I didn't know you were home."

"We're just watching TV," Ben said.

Sarah was wearing her trademark look of defiance.

Harry listed slightly, wishing he had stayed in the kitchen. On the screen a man pulled out a large automatic weapon. Die fucker, Harry thought reflexively. Payback time.

"Ben and I are getting married," Sarah announced. Her tone made it sound like a taunt.

Harry was stunned at the news. Ben, he noticed, seemed a bit stunned himself. Marriage, Harry thought, how curiously old-fashioned. Sarah would certainly write the vows, a manifesto of some kind.

"We're going to adopt," she said, answering a question Harry hadn't even thought to ask.

No reading to fetuses for Ben.

Who would pay for diapers, daycare, swimming lessons, the right jeans? Where would they live? What kind of messy parting awaited when Ben's natural passivity finally incited her to murder, or Sarah's doctrinaire rants showed no sign of flagging after four years of marginal employment and Ben decided he had had enough? And what of the child? Would Harry be left to care for this imported thing, a refugee from the Urals or a Chinese orphanage; would the infant, fleeing poverty, only re-embrace it with the grandfatherly Harry?

The man on the TV kicked in a door and moved his gun like a semaphore flag, looking for danger. He inched through the living room, then kicked open the bedroom door and silently emptied his clip.

"Congratulations," Harry finally said.

Ben stared up at him with his expectant face, the face Harry remembered from the football field a decade earlier, that teary stoicism. Save me, it said, save me from all this.

THIRTEEN

THE AUTUMN MOOD HAD DIED. Dry leaves swirled in vicious eddies, the deadened trees against a grey sky. He and Gladys were already late for their dinner party but were still standing in the clever lighting of Je Ne Sais Quoi, looking for a suitable appetizer. Harry checked his watch and saw 8:02. Gladys was asking about the wild boar pistachio terrine. Was the boar truly wild?

"Totally wild," the girl behind the counter said. "Nuclear." She might have been twenty, a small crucifix bolted through the flesh above her left eye.

"It's just that what is sold as wild boar often isn't."

"As far as I know," the girl said.

Gladys assessed this to be not very far and after another five minutes of browsing and questions, picked a duck, hazelnut and Calvados terrine that cost $26. She moved down the long, gleaming glass case and examined an ash-covered monastery goat cheese. "And the ash is . . ." Gladys asked.

The girl hesitated. "Organic Japanese maple?" she offered.

Harry looked at the terrine and the cheese and calculated their cost as a percentage of his savings account; it amounted to almost forty percent. It was understood that this was an expensive and off-limits shop, but Gladys was using her own money in order to make the right kind of impact with the friend who was hosting the party.

Faced with the bleak economy that Felicia's confession had reinforced, Harry had engaged in a flurry of cuts. He had cancelled the absurdly priced cable, gotten rid of their land line, vowed not to take taxis and avoided the organic butcher shop with the cheery map that showed the source of their meat, local farmers appearing in earnest headshots with their names inscribed in blue script beneath. He had tried every one of the wines listed in the wine columnist's "Best Buys on a Budget" feature. He walked more, cancelled the newspaper and all magazines, renegotiated his cellphone plan with a chipper Bangalore resident. His monthly savings from all these measures, he figured, was somewhere in the $400 range. He was careful not to compare this modest gain with what he was paying Tommy Bladdock.

They stopped at the wine store and picked up a Côtes du Rhône that had been recommended by the same columnist who had steered Harry to the bargain bin. In the car they were silent, listening to the comforting FM. The dashboard clock said 8:17.

"We should stop and get flowers for Paige," Gladys finally said.

"We're bringing appetizers and wine. I don't know that flowers are necessary."

"It's her birthday."

"I thought that was a month ago."

"Technically, but this is a dinner party birthday party."

"We're already late. If we stop and get flowers . . . I don't even know where you're going to get them—some convenience store that's selling shit roses for eight bucks? It's going to look like an afterthought."

"I think we should bring flowers, that's all."

"But we should have got them from a florist two hours ago. We're late and bringing the appetizer. People will be eating dinner by the time we get there."

They drove in silence for a few minutes before Harry said, "I don't have a good feeling about Ben and Sarah. Who gets married these days? It seems so old-fashioned. Don't you think they're too young?"

"We were young."

"Not that young."

"Anyway, it's just an engagement. They probably won't get married for at least a year."

"Long enough to realize the sex isn't that great. I don't imagine it is."

"I haven't given a lot of thought to that, Harry," Gladys said. "She might be good for him."

"I think his innate passivity will make her homicidal. If they adopt, as she threatens to—and almost everything seems to be a threat with her—their marriage will turn into a civil war."

"I think you have to have a little faith."

It felt odd to be arguing against the union. Usually it was Harry who was laissez-faire and Gladys who was the pragmatist. But that was before his conversion, before Dale died, before he saw life as a series of missteps that lead, finally, into a blind alley filled with poverty-tinged regret.

"What if we're left to raise the baby?" Harry said.

"I can't imagine Sarah would abandon the child."

"She could eat her child. She barely has a pulse."

"Harry."

"It would be a burden, Gladys," Harry said. "Another burden."

They arrived at 8:37. The duck terrine in the cloth bag dangling from Harry's hand felt heavy and lost. Four faces smiled hello.

"These are for you," Gladys said, handing the discount freesias to Paige.

"Oh, Glad."

"Nothing really."

"No."

Paige and Gladys had gone to school together and after a long hiatus had renewed their friendship. Her husband, Newton, a school principal, walked toward Harry with his hand extended. He was slowly rounding into the shape of a teardrop, his gait awkward, swishing.

"Harry."

"Newton." He offered up the wine, cheese and terrine, and Newton gathered them and trundled to the kitchen, calling over his shoulder, "Harry, this is Satori and Dean. Dean, Satori, Harry."

Dean was a glum leftie in his fifties, dressed for a trade school dance. Satori was indeterminately Asian. They all shook hands.

Newton came back and handed Harry a glass of inexpensive Chilean Merlot. "Harry, we were talking about the New Poverty."

"I was just getting used to the old kind," Harry said.

"Dean thinks everyone's going to be poor. We're headed back to the barter system."

Dean was a sculptor, an environmental scold who made unlikable shapes out of bicycle parts and discarded laptops.

Gladys had shown Harry Dean's website before they left the house. The home page was a photograph of Dean's backyard with his sculptures in it, aggressive steel shapes with titles like *Scheherazade Forgets the Words* and listed at $9,300 per. The New Poverty would be inclusive and levelling, Dean said now: lawyers would take in laundry, doctors would perform vasectomies in exchange for homemade wine, investment bankers would labour over backyard vegetable gardens.

"What could you trade, Harry?" Dean asked. "What is it you do?"

"I teach political science."

"Well, there you are," Dean said. "We'll always need political science."

We've never needed political science, Harry thought. "We barely have politics anymore," he said. "Half the electorate doesn't vote."

Dean ignored the rebuke. "The old systems have broken down," he said. "Newspapers, TV, music, books, banks—it's out of the hands of the corporate beast. The whole animal is dying and there is blood in the streets, and that's a good thing."

Satori looked at her husband when he talked, but her face didn't reveal whether she was absorbed or appalled by his facile rant.

"It's post-production," Dean continued. "Innovation. The artist rules."

Harry thought of asking Dean how he was ruling exactly, but the pre-dinner conversation balkanized, and Harry was stuck with Newton and Paige and the quiet Satori, while Dean chatted with Gladys in the living room. Newton was talking about the school system's imminent collapse, betrayed by lack of funds and vision, the classrooms filled with dolts. Harry nodded and watched Dean and Gladys.

Dean's head went back in a theatrical laugh. He would be laughing at something he had said, not something she'd said. From a distance, without the audio, it was like one of those nature shows where they run a montage of mating dances done by various species: Jaggeresque preening, intricate salsas, parts of birds and lizards puffed up for effect. Dean was in full display. His hair was outrageously thick, quills that sprouted, greying heroically, reminding Harry of a porcupine.

Harry had once seen a program on the mating ritual of the porcupine. They mated once a year in a stunning performance that had rarely been filmed. They were solitary and territorial animals, but in mating season, the male went in search of the female, and often two or more males would end up in the same area. They were too slow to move on; mating season would be over by the time any of them found another mate. So they stayed and preened and fought for the female's attention. The male stood on its hind legs, displaying its erection. Unlike humans, with their fallible, abused members, the porcupine's erection could last for hours. The males fought one another for this rare chance at sex, and afterward, bloodied and insane, carrying the barbs of their enemies—a hundred quills stuck in their faces!—they danced for the female, waving those reliable boners. Who would love her like she'd never been loved?

The lucky winner first showered the female with urine, then, as she flipped her tail onto her back, he mounted her delicately from behind, his front paws resting on her upturned tail, protected from her quills. They had sex repeatedly until the female broke it off and retreated to a tree.

The voiceover was done by a British actor, who spoke in a hushed, educated tone. "Sexual contact ends," he said, "and is followed by hostile screaming."

He watched Gladys laugh and put her hand on Dean's forearm. Gladys was the kind of woman that men were usually attracted to after dinner rather than before. Her beauty was subtle; her soft wisdom took a while to penetrate. But Dean, the artist, had discerned her qualities immediately. As he flirted openly with Gladys, Harry shot a quick look at Satori, who was slightly older than Dean. She had registered the mood in the living room with a single glance. Harry guessed this was a familiar scene.

Paige announced that dinner was ready. "Come and sit, everyone." She set two bowls down on the table. "Butternut squash soup with toasted pumpkin seeds and nutmeg," she proclaimed.

"Oh, how lovely," Gladys said. "So autumn."

Dinner marched on. Dean drank and pronounced. Satori was soundless. Newton laughed heartily at everything. Paige and Gladys caught up. Harry drifted in and out of conversations. He was the negative space in an expressionist painting, the blankness that surrounded the main subject; he filled the uncomfortable dining chair and picked at the farfalle con funghi. His marriage was disappearing, eroding like a glacier, helpless against the sun. He wondered about Dean and Satori—what was the nature of that relationship? He examined them for clues. Dean the serial philanderer and Satori the constant he returned to? Paige and Newton seemed unmysterious, middle-aged in the way middle age looks to children: solid, uninspired, sexless. But who knew?

"Harry. Harry? What's your view?"

Newton's face was poised across from him, waiting for an answer to a question Harry hadn't heard.

"I think they should all be shot," Harry ventured.

Newton laughed uproariously.

"Oh god, Harry," Gladys said.

Harry noticed that Dean had gone from being cinematically drunk—filled with toasts and rants—to being almost comatose. In repose, he looked like one of van Gogh's potato eaters, hollowed and blank, slumped in his seat.

The cake was finally served, a smallish mango mocha tart with a single candle in its centre, surrounded by blackberries. Dean had slumped farther in his chair, as if the air was slowly leaking out of a balloon. From Harry's perspective, he was framed behind the small cake and single candle, and Harry thought he would make a brilliant photograph. There was the unplanned juxtaposition that photographers seek, that immediate visual irony. Seeing Dean publicly crumble made Harry feel he was somehow a little further ahead.

Paige blew out her candle and they ate the cake, though Dean didn't touch his. And after the briefest possible gap that was still within the bounds of dinner party etiquette, Satori excused herself and came back with Dean's coat and draped it over his shoulders like he was a damaged fighter.

"Thank you so much, Paige," she said, kissing her on both cheeks. "It was wonderful to see you both. Happy birthday." She turned to Harry and Gladys. "And it was a pleasure to meet you."

On the way home, Harry wondered if Satori had led Dean away out of love or solidarity, if his collapse was something that happened on a regular basis. "How do you suppose they met?" Harry said.

"Newton and Paige?"

"No, Dean and Satori."

"Art school would be my guess," Gladys said.

"How old do you think she is?"

"Older than Dean. I gather all she does is yoga."

"She was the exotic beauty and Dean was the *enfant terrible*," Harry said. This had once been a game of theirs; to make up a history for everyone they met. "He had a long scarf and smoked Gauloises and said everything Picasso did after *Guernica* was shit. It must have been fun, don't you think?"

"Less so now, I'd say."

"Now his only joy comes from flirting with other people's wives."

"He was hardly flirting."

"You were enjoying it. You were laughing."

"It isn't against the law to laugh at a dinner party."

Gladys was driving, due to the large cognac Harry had accepted after Dean and Satori had gone. He stared at her profile, framed in passing bleats of light as they drove toward the ravine. She had both hands on the steering wheel, as they taught in driving school, placed at ten and two o'clock. In the ravine they were the only car going east, the steep, forested hills rising up on each side, the elegant bridge decorated with bloated graffiti letters. He wanted to see someone dangling up there with a can of spray paint; he wanted to see it actually happen. The city was decorated with the insistent signatures of idle youth; banal, self-referential, though you had to admire their initiative. How did they paint the side of a bridge? Dangling from harnesses? Held by the ankles by trusted friends?

The trees went by in a comforting blur. It reminded Harry of childhood car trips, when simply driving through the night was filled with mystery.

FOURTEEN

HARRY FIRST NOTICED THE DULL, NAGGING PAIN IN HIS lower abdomen shortly after the dinner party. When it persisted, he immediately suspected something serious. One of the benefits of the Internet was that it could confirm your worst fears about anything. Deep into a series of hyperlinked sites that demonstrated a causal link between cancer and negative thoughts, using pie charts and testimonials from doctors identified only by initials, Harry was convinced he carried the disease. These days, he *only* had negative thoughts.

He hastily scheduled a prostate exam, blood tests and a colonoscopy. The first had revealed normal swelling, the second came back clean, and the earliest colonoscopy appointment was months away. Then a cancellation allowed Harry to jump the Soviet-length queue, and now he sat in the endoscopy waiting room, that dismal casino. As he flipped through a dated magazine, he recalled the odds that someone had of developing colon cancer: a very promising seven percent if you were under fifty (which he almost was), had no obvious symptoms (no rectal bleeding) and no family history. He hadn't been in a hospital since his vasectomy five years ago. He recalled the pleasant, middle-aged nurse washing his freshly shaven testicles in warm soapy water as they talked about funding cuts to hospitals, though the encounter ended with the soldering iron and the smell of his burning flesh.

This colonoscopy had already required two days of abstinence (no alcohol), fasting, laxatives and purgatives, which had left him feeling both empty and enlightened, in a religious state, ready to receive the spirit. He put on two hospital gowns that were so thin from a thousand washings they hung like gossamer. The first gown was open at the back, the second at the front. When we put on the uniform of the old and infirm, he thought, we inhabit their world. His exposed white calves were complicit: thin and hairless and vulnerable.

Led to a gurney and instructed to lie on his side, Harry contemplated the equipment hanging from the ceiling, de Sade–like and dated, like the waiting room magazines. The paint had peeled on the walls, and there were water stains on the acoustic tile ceiling. The anesthesiologist introduced herself—Marta?—an austere woman with narrow hips and a slight paunch that protruded under her scrubs. She put an IV into his hand and Harry watched something drip into him.

"What is that?"

She listed a handful of unfamiliar drugs.

"Are those morphine-based?" he asked.

"Morphine," she repeated noncommittally.

Harry was already agreeably, effortlessly high. He wanted to engage this woman in conversation. He wanted to buy her a drink. A sign came into focus on the far wall—a small homemade sign that said, REMEMBER THE OXYGEN!

"That isn't a good sign," Harry said.

"What?"

"Remember the oxygen."

"Oh," she laughed. "It isn't what you think."

"That's your story?"

"And I'm sticking to it."

Harry was floating just above this woman and wanted to bring her along to where he was going. Perhaps he called her name (or what might be her name). He found himself in a darkness that was comforting, like floating in warm salt water. There were shapes just beyond his reach. Something crawled up inside him. The gate had been breached, a snake sliding in, stealing his secrets.

Few things are as elemental as the colon. You consume, you process, you excrete; this is the essential biology of the living. Whatever else you do is up to you. You procreate, if the mood strikes you.

When he used to bathe Ben, the happy, splashing baby, there was a comfort in the way those tiny hands held onto him like a marsupial. The perfect harmony that exists before language complicates everything. But he saw this scene from Ben's perspective now, the looming shape of Harry over the bath, the looming shape of every father, large in their presence, larger in their absence. Harry's face leaning down, young though not youthful, the smile and sounds that were reserved for children. And Ben's (his own) arms reaching up.

Harry floated onward. Though he wasn't alone in this; the world was unanchored—cut loose from history, free of the church, the nuclear family lurching into the sunset. What binds us now? Debt, all of us chained to the same rock, our livers being delicately gnawed at eighteen percent compounded annually.

The other shapes around him—were these people? He couldn't tell; the light was so dim, the air so thick it was more like liquid. His limbs were moving, but he made so little progress. He could hear voices. Maybe it was only one. It was slowed down like a tape recorder with dying batteries. The vowels were drawn out, elongated into soft sounds.

Aaaauuuuglaahh.

What?

Harry, did you need it all? The voice was suddenly clear.

Did I need . . .

So much was unnecessary. The indulgence. All that wine. Pecan pie.

It wasn't that much, really.

You've lost track. But not me.

Harry kited through the amniotic fluid, floating, arms out. Lost track, he echoed in a musical voice.

I remember every chocolate-covered espresso bean, every cognac, every woman you tasted, everything that passed through. I can't forget.

Was Harry talking to his colon?

Now look at me. A camera. I guard my privacy, Harry.

Your fifteen minutes, Harry said. *You should be happy for the attention.*

I'm not happy, Harry. I wasn't expecting company.

But look at you! I'll bet you're pink as a newborn, as fresh as lavender.

Harry, I don't deserve this.

Harry suddenly had a bad feeling. It crept through the fluid, infiltrating his druggy dream. *Have you betrayed me?* he asked.

I betray you? I'm not capable of betrayal, Harry. I'm just a factory worker. I take what I'm given. You're management. You betrayed me. You make the decisions and we all live with them. Try to live, anyway.

What the hell do you mean by that?

—

The room came into focus slowly, a different room. An old man lay on a bed next to Harry's. Like Harry, he was on his side. A druggy groan came from him. Harry was still enviably stoned. He thought of the few drug experiences he'd had, the one time he took LSD, with Jonah Freedman in university. They went to the Army Surplus store and wandered the dark aisles, among the faded green jackets and heavy boots, and fell down laughing. They found everything in the store hysterical. Jonah tried on a helmet and looked into the cloudy mirror, then laughed so hard he peed his pants slightly. The owner berated them in an accent so thick they couldn't understand what he was saying. Jonah tried to buy a switchblade knife at the counter, but the owner wouldn't sell it to him and told them to leave. They stood on the suddenly bright street laughing, the world seen with what seemed to be absurd clarity. They counted their money four times before convincing themselves they had enough for a movie. It took three hours to decide which one and then find the theatre. It turned out to be one that both of them had already seen.

After five minutes, Harry was helped onto a lounge chair, where he sat beside a woman with a sleepy grey face, wearing the same gowns as him. They chatted drunkenly. A nurse gave him a small cup of apple juice and handed him a form. On the top, written in blue ink, were the words "seven polyps (small)."

Harry got dressed shakily, then was ushered into Dr. Nathlett's office, where he began to focus. Dr. Nathlett had a small head, a ring of ginger hair, a freckled face that looked unhealthy, a heaviness that spread over his chair.

"We found something," he said.

"Seven polyps."

"We took them out. They'll get looked at."

"What if they're cancerous?"

"Well, let's wait on that. They're small. It's lucky you came in when you did."

But seven—such a precise number. Harry wondered if there could have been eight, or nineteen. Did they find everything? What could you see in that underwater camera, that searching eye that crawled along his scourged bowel? Don't we have sixty feet of large intestine? Or is it more? The colon was only part of the intestine, though Harry wasn't clear on that relationship. How could you check that expanse? It would take a crew of technicians, a Cousteau expedition.

"We should have some results in two weeks."

"But if the result is positive? If they are cancerous?" Harry was suddenly sure they were.

"Well, we have options."

"Options."

"At this stage, with their size." The doctor held his thumb and index finger a millimetre apart to indicate smallness.

"You'll call, then."

"Better that you check back in two weeks. Call my receptionist."

Harry left the hospital and got into a cab. He watched the east-end houses go by, modest bungalows built for returning World War II veterans. He passed the halal butchers, the impromptu mosque, the cutely named organic café, the Greek clubs with men sitting outside in the cold air, smoking and gesturing, filled with solutions. The drugs were regrettably wearing off, leaving him bereft. A group of boys spilled along the sidewalk, slapping, laughing and grabbing one another. Two weeks to wait for news. Hope for the best, prepare for the worst. It was someone's motto.

FIFTEEN

"You don't see it. That's the beauty. It's invisible. It's moving through this room right now, millions, the molecules traceless. It's silent, and everywhere it goes it takes something. It moves like the plague. That's how you tell it came through. You count the dead."

"But it gives something."

"Money's a dark gift, Harry."

"You bought my mother's house."

"I'm putting it on the market. It's too broody for me. All those old bricks. They're like tombs, those places. I've got a condo, windows on three sides. You wake up you know it's morning. In those old places, you wake up, its 1912. You want to buy the place, Harry? It's yours if you want it."

Dick Ebbetts punctuated this offer with a shrug. The considerably padded shoulders of his tight suit didn't come back down with his shoulders but stayed up around his ears. He was framed by the pewter-coloured banquette. Above that, a million dollars' worth of climate-controlled Burgundy. They were sitting in Crux, amid the animated lunch crowd.

Harry considered the imbalance between himself and Ebbetts. Harry was burdened by debt and colon cancer (he was increasingly convinced), and unburdened by sex. This troll was rich, from all accounts had inventive sex with beautiful escorts and was, as far as Harry knew, disease-free. These comparisons with other people had become involuntary for him. He had invited Ebbetts to lunch in the hope of getting more information on BRG in the wake of Tommy Bladdock's news that the Securities Commission was looking at the company.

Harry stared at Ebbetts' stubby manicured hands. Ebbetts the thug. So thought his mother and sister. Perhaps they were right. But Ebbetts was the only one at BRG who wasn't tied to the company through the daisy chain of bloodlines, intermarriage, and racquet club memberships. The meeting was awkward because of his mother and her house, though Ebbetts' purchase of it was chalked up, nominally at least, as an act of charity.

"How did BRG come out of the subprime crash?" Harry asked.

"We're far enough from the killing floor that we didn't get any blood on our shirts."

"But they didn't see Lehman Brothers coming."

"No one saw Lehman. You figure banks are the bedrock. Then you find they're basically the big, disruptive dummy in the back of the class who gets pushed through the system because no one wants to deal with him."

Ebbetts's plump hands described tiny circles in the air. "Look, the whole thing was going to topple anyway. More people got in, they started working the margins at first. For a long time you could do pretty good just eating after the big cats were full. But this clusterfuck between the bankers and the carnies, they gave birth to that monster: a million subprime mortgages hustled to single mothers in Florida that are going up three points after year two. You take that debt and roll it up with Russian oil and student loans and the Vegas line on whether Tom Cruise is gay, and you dress it up so it looks like a bond and sell off slices in London and New York, and pretty soon even you don't know what you're selling. You're the guy selling the air inside Yankee Stadium, and everyone is thinking, Well, we have to *breathe*."

Harry looked around the restaurant and made a rough calculation of the accumulated net worth of the people who were eating lunch. He came up with the unscientific figure of $314 million. But who knew what kind of debt was eating these people? A developer who was overextended, his suburban mega-mall project stalled because of skittish banks or retail saturation. A banker with a gambling problem. A lawyer on his fourth marriage. Hopefully there was some tragedy amid the caramelized sea scallops in truffle sauce ($48) and the 2008 Puligny-Montrachet ($465).

"Is it possible that Press is under some financial pressure, Dick?"

"You mean personally underwater?"

"Taken a hit somewhere."

Ebbetts waved his knife, a speck of blood on the serrated blade. "You want to map Press's progress, just look at the declining value of his girlfriends. Fifteen years ago it was that former skater, did PR, I think she medalled in Sapporo. Four, five years ago, the spokesmodel what's-her-name, back-combed, braindead. Now it's a Russian, she has about eight words of English. You're a technical analyst and you throw those girls up on a chart, you can see he's basically 1929."

"Could he have been desperate enough to take Dale's money?"

"It's a leap, Harry. He would have to be standing on the ledge."

"Do you know for sure he wasn't?"

"Nothing is for sure. Look, all the money is concentrated at the top. But it's never enough. How do you make more? In another five years, brokers will go the way of travel agents. You can buy stocks on the Internet for five bucks a trade. Half the time you've got the same information as your broker. They're on TV giving away their so-called expertise for free."

Ebbetts took a quick bite of his steak, chewed it rapidly and started talking before he'd swallowed. "The rich got rich by fucking the poor, but now the poor don't have anything left. So the only people left to fuck are the rich. The market looks like that soccer team that crashed in the mountains. Everyone's eating each other." Ebbetts stared upward. "Look, Harry, there's something you should know."

"What's that?"

"Well . . . Look, I'm not saying this is anything that happened, but the market, you know, the whole thing is held up by rumour and bullshit. So here's the deal. There is a rumour, and I emphasize the word 'rumour,' but there has been talk that Dale had his hand in the till. Somehow."

"What?"

"Like I said, there is not one shred of evidence. This is talk. But talk is talk, and when you're dealing with whoever, you should have this in your pocket is all."

"If my father stole money, then why would all his money be gone?"

"Well, the theory is that it's one of these I-got-burned-so-how-could-I-be-the-guy-who's-doing-it things. He takes his own money, parks it wherever, they find out he's been ripped off, and he's a victim rather than a suspect."

Harry suddenly wondered if the Securities Commission was investigating his father.

"Press thought my father was embezzling?"

"It came to his attention."

"My father knew his clients. They were friends of his. He played tennis with them. He wasn't going to steal their money. Even if he could, he wouldn't. Even if he had some kind of latent criminal bent, even if he had motive and opportunity, Dick, he couldn't do it. For him, the social stigma would be unbearable. And it would last generations. It would be his legacy. He'd never have risked that."

"Harry, you don't need to defend Dale to me. I'm just telling you what to expect."

"What to expect," Harry repeated.

"Maybe Sampson knows something. I mean, the guy's on his way out. I don't know the prognosis, but it's weeks at this point. Maybe you can get a deathbed confession out of him."

Harry thought about August's phone call. "How close are August and Press?"

"They don't see each other outside the office, but there's almost fifty years there."

The waiter came over and stood in that attentive way that stopped conversation, and they ordered coffee.

"Watch out for Press, Harry, I mean it," Ebbetts said after the waiter left. "He got caught in the last downdraft. He's on his way out and he's full of shit, but he's a wounded lion."

"And why are you leaving this wonderful game, Dick?"

"You're thirty years old, the market seems like the centre of the world. But from where I'm sitting, it looks like a dying planet." Ebbetts tore into the remains of his cold steak, cutting off small pieces that he stabbed into his mouth. He reminded Harry of a heron, stabbing frogs in the shallows with its deadly bill.

"The shareholder is god and the shareholder is an idiot," Ebbetts said, "and we live in this splendid paradox. Generally, Harry, we're dealing with two things: shit no one understands, and shit everyone understands."

Their coffee arrived and they drank it slowly, chatting aimlessly about baseball.

When the check came, Harry made a slow-motion reach for it, but Ebbetts thankfully picked up (he was the one who had chosen Crux) and resisted Harry's token protest. They worked their way out of the booth and shook hands as they stood outside the restaurant. Behind them were Mies van der Rohe's stirring towers. Beauty in simplicity. A version of the buildings existed in New York and Chicago, a template for the modern world. A courier zigzagged across the busy street, weaving among BMWs.

"Harry, you know why Deutsche Bank got screwed on those subprime bonds?" Ebbetts said. "Because they're Germans. They believe in rules. They think there are rules. They believe the ratings agencies did their homework. But no one does any homework anymore. And there are no rules. Look, Harry, I'm sorry about this thing with your dad. I don't know what happened there. But you should be careful. I don't have a dog in this fight anymore. But it's a lot meaner out there than it used to be."

They shook hands again and Harry walked to his car. The downtown air was percussive. Noises came from every direction. City life was disguised as harmony, but it was warfare. People wanted what you wanted. They bid against you for houses, got up earlier than you to enroll their children in enviable summer camps, took the last daycare spot. Criminals were easier to deal with. They took what you had. They broke into your house and stole your stereo and shit on your Persian carpet. Harry wasn't sure he wanted what he had. But other people—almost everyone, it seemed—wanted what he wanted.

SIXTEEN

HARRY SHOWERED THEN SHAVED, first with the grain, then against it. He rinsed with warm water, then cold, and applied some of Gladys's expensive moisturizer, then gave his cheeks a nostalgic slap, as men had done in the age of after-shave, the sting of alcohol and violence before going out to threaten the world. He put on jeans and a black polo shirt that flattered his torso.

He had $119 in his savings account. His Visa bill was comfortably into five figures, gently testing the $20,000 threshold, his maxed-out line of credit holding steady. The dull buzz of his debt sounded like a cheap air conditioner, rattling and wheezing, though at the moment safely in the background. He smiled carefully at the mirror and went downstairs.

Gladys was sitting at the table, drinking coffee. When he'd told her about his colonoscopy, he added a few polyps to bring the number to eleven, and said they were large, hoping to make an impression. Neither of these tactics had the desired effect, and so he added that the doctor "didn't like the look of them." He used the word "biopsy." She remained maddeningly pragmatic, saying there was no use in worrying until the results came back.

Harry made himself an espresso and sat down. "Ebbetts says my father may have embezzled from the firm," he said.

"Really? Why on earth would he say a thing like that?"

"He thought I should know so I wouldn't be blindsided if it came out in an investigation. Apparently, Securities is looking at BRG."

"I can't imagine Dale taking money," Gladys said. "Especially near the end. He was in no shape to do anything clever. Maybe someone is using him as a scapegoat. Blame the dead."

"Maybe."

"Maybe it was Dick Ebbetts himself. Isn't he leaving the business?"

"I'm hoping Tommy Bladdock can shed some light. He wants to meet this morning."

"Tick tock," Gladys said.

Harry wasn't, in fact, meeting Tommy Bladdock. His true mission filled him with shame, and he especially didn't want Gladys to know he was going to a financial seminar that had been advertised in the paper, especially one with the slightly squishy title, "Personal Profit, Personal Loss: Finding Balance." It was offered under the auspices of a financial think tank that dealt with global oversight, but the main attraction was Peter T. Horst, a television personality whose appearances veered toward the evangelical.

Gladys would have sensibly suggested going to one of the free seminars offered by the bank. But the bank seminars had prosaic titles ("You and Your Savings") that Harry felt were simply shills for the bank's own investment vehicles. The decision to go to the seminar had been made at a moment when the sound of Harry's debt had filled his ears like metal shearing off a defective jet engine and pierced the natural cynicism he had always held for this kind of Dale Carnegie self-actualizing whatever.

He had felt that he needed to do something out of character, but now that he was on his way, he felt he should have obeyed his natural distrust of all mankind. He felt depressed and leery of his mental health.

It was an overcast Saturday, the wind coming hard from the west. He walked briskly across the park. The splendid, unifying park filled with wealthy socialists, professional dog-walkers, lesbian soccer players and teenagers in search of calamity. In front of him, a woman loped uncomfortably behind her Bernese mountain dog. November was a dismal month, a palette of greys and bitter winds.

Harry took the subway. There was a surprising number of people on it, given that it wasn't a weekday. He examined the women around him. As adolescents, Harry and his friends used to manufacture their dream creatures: Elizabeth Taylor's high-heeled, tipsy, feminine menace combined with Anne Bancroft's legs and lascivious smile. He glanced carefully at the women on the train and mixed and matched.

The seminar was in a venerable, still mostly grand hotel. Harry took a seat in the large meeting room, among three hundred or so people who were drinking coffee and finding their place in the rows of metal chairs draped with bunting. He was neither encouraged nor discouraged by his fellow seminar-goers, people who had also paid $275 for three hours of Peter T. Horst's time. He hoped, though, that he wouldn't run into anyone he knew.

Horst was introduced by an attractive woman in impressive red heels who described him as "an investment luminary" and a man who "has integrated the personal with the financial" and who had "helped people just like you" in seventeen countries. Harry wondered if the woman travelled with Horst, and if this was her only duty.

Horst was of medium height, with carefully combed, gleaming black hair. He wore a blue suit and a large watch that was visible when he solemnly grasped the edges of the podium. He had a sleek headset on, and stared out at his crowd.

"You have lost something," he stated right off the top, pausing for effect. "You've lost money. Perhaps you've lost your way. You don't know where to turn. How will you live? This is the central question. I'll repeat it: How will you live? The answer is: You will live the way you choose to live."

Horst left the podium and paced the front of the room. "When you woke up this morning," he asked, "did you think about what you were going to do? Did you make a list that said: 'Open my eyes. Get out of bed. Brush teeth. Get dressed. Make coffee. Read paper.' No, you didn't. You did the same thing you do every morning: you got up, got dressed, brushed your teeth, made coffee and read the paper.

"You didn't think. You did what you always do." Horst turned sharply and paced in the other direction. "That's what most people do: They *do* what they always *do*. And yet they expect their lives to change. They expect their lives to get better." Horst stopped and gazed out at them with a preacher's expert pity. "One of the definitions of insanity," he said, "is to do the same thing over and over again and expect a different outcome. My friends," he said, his arms spread wide to include the entire room, "you are all insane."

Harry heard nervous/polite laughter. He calculated what he

could have bought with $275 (ten bottles of Château Maucaillou). Horst talked of Outcomes and Journeys and Claiming the Moment, Planting Your Flag. There was the quiet clatter of coffee cups on saucers. An hour disappeared as Peter T. Horst marched the crowd through foggy syllogisms. Harry drifted. The morning sun caught part of the high windows. The pattern in the carpet was needlessly intricate. The air was stately.

By the time Horst had them break into groups of ten, rearranging their chairs in a circle, a move that Harry should have predicted and that made his heart sink with a sick, leaden thump, he felt betrayed. His money was gone; his morning was gone. He was stuck in this childish exercise, staring into the moondog face of the woman to his right.

Under Horst's hasty guidance, they introduced themselves and stated their mostly redundant reasons for coming to the seminar. They spoke of the specific place they wanted to get to, encouraged to imagine it as a geographical location, to translate the concept of "Less Debt" to a small town that was within driving distance. Harry drifted farther away from Horst's carnival.

The golden age of Harry Salter had never been golden. Now he was faced with ruin and with auditory hallucinations that made him distrust his hearing. Traffic sounded like a private reproach. The deadness of a subway train interior now roared. The city was as broke as he was. It had betrayed and mocked him, reneging on its promise of hierarchy (which he himself had rejected when he thought he was part of the elite). Cuts were coming, the mayor warned. To the bone.

Harry now saw everything in the context of debt. The seesaw of a marriage. Gladys granted him wild sex and he was indebted to her, responding with an intricate dinner (though that particular transaction hadn't taken place for a very long time). And so it went. Divorce was merely the buildup of debt by one partner who had no way of paying it off, no emotional, sexual or romantic capital left.

After they had finished their sharing and had reassembled in rows, a dull man came on stage and read a speech about just how unregulated the financial world was and how it would eventually spell the death of capitalism. He wrapped up his plodding vision of the apocalypse and reintroduced Horst, who talked about how money could rush into the hole left by personal loss, if you gave it permission to. This was at last too much for Harry, and he left quietly, finding relief in the sudden cavern of the lobby.

He walked north along the grand boulevard, his head down. It was 11:17 and the day had cost, he calculated, $319.25 with tax so far. He felt a familiar sense of loss, which he realized might never entirely disappear. He was already hungry for lunch and the north wind blew into his face in annoying gusts. When Harry heard a familiar voice saying "Change?" and looked up to see the man who had ruined his jacket, the man whom he'd bought the hot dog for, his homeless nemesis, he roared at him with atavistic power, "Fuck you, you Fagin fuck!"

In the wake of that adrenaline-fuelled roar, he closely examined the man's surprised face and determined conclusively that it wasn't the same person. Beneath the hood, this man's hair was grey, rather than black. The faces had been battered by the same forces, coloured by the same sun, porous and thickened, Rushmore-like. But this man looked defeated, while the other one had had a breezy insanity. The panhandler quickly moved past him, and Harry stared after his stiff form jerkily moving south, his soiled trench coat flapping, a large flightless bird. Harry should catch up to him and give him money.

"Wait," Harry yelled, walking quickly, his hand going to his pocket. "Hold on, I'm sorry, I thought you were . . ."

The man increased his pace, one arm motioning for Harry to keep away.

"Look, I made a mistake . . ." Harry searched his pockets, hoping for some coins, or even a $5 bill. All he had was a fifty that had come out of the bank machine. He couldn't give him a fifty. The apology without any money wouldn't mean anything, at least not to this man, who was in a half-run now, his right arm pawing the air behind him: Stay back.

"I just wanted . . ." Harry called out, taking a few more half-hearted steps. He stopped, feeling awful.

The man weaved through the light Saturday traffic and now stood on the small island between the north and southbound lanes. He looked like a gazelle that had managed to put a river between itself and a leopard. He stood there, staring at Harry.

Harry turned north and walked past the legislative buildings, dormant on Saturday, the elegant halls unfilled with accusations of economic stupidity and fiduciary betrayal. It would be easy, if he were slightly more paranoid, to imagine the entire city as a vast conspiracy against him, designed to take his money and leave him out on the street with the wretched men he encountered, the dishearteningly similar bums taking his change. And now one or more thieves had taken his father's money, or his father himself might be the thief.

Harry went past the radical architecture and weekend shoppers on Bloor Street as clouds skidded eastward. He felt, suddenly, in the mood to watch a movie. Not something dark and European, but a movie that was explosively American. Harry bought a ticket for a one o'clock show, then went to a café and ordered a smoked salmon bagel and watched the people file by.

He spent the whole afternoon in the movie complex, finally emerging at 8:35 p.m., having seen all of one film and pieces of five others. He had missed a lot of beginnings, joining movies already under way, the show times probably staggered to discourage exactly what Harry was doing: slinking from one theatre to the next without paying. The characters overlapped slightly; the troubled, tattooed love interest in the Scandinavian psychological thriller wasn't all that different from the (almost fatal) tattooed love interest in the action movie. The existential chain-smoking detachment of the Serbian detective occasionally, surprisingly, reminded Harry of the bumbling suitor in the romantic comedy that he saw the last thirty-five minutes of. The various narratives sat jumbled in his head, pieces of unrelated puzzles: a tentative kiss; a decomposing corpse in the woods; a Porsche sailing merrily into a tanker truck hauling propane; a woman wiping tears on a windy beach in autumn; a man farting at a wedding; Neil Sedaka singing as the credits rolled. The careful constructions of a culture sashaying into the abyss. But Harry had seen six films for one low price. He calculated his savings to be $83.75, reclaiming part of the day's losses.

Harry returned home after nine p.m. to find Gladys and Ben on the couch, deep in conversation, a conversation that stopped abruptly (cinematically, he thought) when he walked into the living room.

"I've been at the movies," Harry announced in the tentative silence.

"Which one?" Gladys asked.

"All of them. I moved from film to film. I feel like I got it out of my system. My lack of movie-going."

Gladys and Ben sat on the couch, staring at him.

"How's school, Ben?" Harry asked. The same conversational non-starter he'd been using for fifteen years now. What did you learn today? From the evidence, Ben hadn't learned anything in more than a decade, an unbroken string of useless days. Ben sat silent. Glad was silent. It was, Harry thought, a complicit silence.

"Do you want dinner, Harry?" Gladys asked.

"I had some popcorn."

"That stuff is lethal, Dad. It's a petroleum by-product."

Harry had eaten a bag of it, as well as a bag of red licorice, biting the ends off and using them as a straw in his water bottle, the way he'd done as a child.

"So, which one was best?" Gladys asked.

"Well, I only saw one from beginning to end. But the Serbian detective one looked good. I missed the first forty-five minutes. I'm not sure why he was so depressed and terse. Maybe there was a tragedy."

"Maybe he was just Serbian. That might be enough," Gladys said.

Harry was still standing with his coat on. The living room seemed underlit. Brahms was playing on the radio. The silence was recurring, and he suspected it would disappear as soon as he did.

"Why don't you sit down, Harry?" his wife asked. "Take your coat off."

Gladys's invitation made Harry feel even more like a neighbour who has seen the light on and dropped by unannounced. He hung up his coat and took off his boots. He went to the kitchen and poured a glass of wine. When he came back, Ben was putting his own boots on. His gangly son stood up, unfolded upward, stood tall for an instant before assuming his natural slump. He reached for his coat.

"Anyway, I've gotta be going," he said. "You know, school. Papers. Et cetera."

"Nice to see you, Ben," Harry said.

"We'll talk," Gladys said, ushering Ben out. The two of them stood talking on the porch for a moment until Gladys got too cold and waved goodbye and came back in.

"That's real winter," she said as she closed the door, giving a slightly exaggerated shiver. She brushed past Harry, her hand touching his waist. "I'd better clean up," she said. She went into the kitchen and began filling the dishwasher. She and Ben had had dinner. Harry felt like he'd intruded on an intimacy. These were the kind of moments they had had when Ben was eleven months old, when the sunny-faced baby reached instinctively for his mother and Harry would arrive to find the two of them on the living room floor in front of the fire, hypnotized by their simple existence.

Harry slipped into bed beside the sleeping Gladys, who had been right about so many things. Her providential feminine ethos viewed the world as a series of causal relationships, where Harry saw a night sky filled with improbable fantasies, all of which became probable simply by dwelling on them after two glasses of wine. He settled into his side of the bed facing away from his wife, and was surprised when Gladys rolled toward him, her hand reaching for him, exploring gently, the remembered sequence of touching him, gently massaging, gauging arousal, feeling the stirring, a stirring that surprised him. He glanced over his shoulder; her eyes were still closed. Was she asleep? Her hand moved until he was hard, then she climbed on him in a single fluid motion. She hadn't said anything. Her eyes were open now but staring upward.

Straddling Harry, she massaged her clitoris and rode rhythmically for several minutes. She still hadn't looked at him. Pinned to the mattress, he watched this stranger. She finally rolled over with a slight groan, pulling Harry on top, and he began fucking her. Her face was turned away, her eyes closed. They hadn't kissed, and he thought it was somehow inappropriate now. They fucked vigorously for several minutes, then Harry moved to the side, behind her, into a spoon position, and they slowed down. He remembered a night on a trip to Greece years ago when an otherworldly lasciviousness had descended on Gladys like an ancient spell, and they crawled over one another and fucked with a purpose that left Harry quietly amazed for three days. It was in these moments that a marriage was contained.

At breakfast, Harry felt he should do something to carry the momentum of last night forward. He wondered if it had anything to do with his pending biopsy report. Perhaps Gladys felt she owed him for her indifference to his situation. He made two coffees and brought one to Gladys and sat down. The winter light filled the kitchen, one of the house's graces. The light shone on Gladys's hair. She looked up and smiled at him.

Harry assumed that he knew everything about his wife, the logical by-product of twenty-five years together. Though so much of her story had been told in those first intimate months. Pressed together in bed, telling each other the edited highlights of their childhoods, declaring themselves.

Looking at her now, in the afterglow of his gratitude, he could see the girl who was born of children of the Depression, who grew up on the prairies and carried those withered cattle and scouring sandstorms within them. Her mother saved pennies in Mason jars hidden beneath the workbench in the basement. She recycled paper lunch bags at a time when this was embarrassing rather than laudatory, and the eight-year-old Gladys was ashamed of the stains on the bag that held her liverwurst sandwich and hid it in her desk. She wore a red plaid jacket in the fall, the most beautiful season in the Toronto suburb where her parents had hunkered down in a very modest split-level. If they desired anything for their two children—Gladys and her younger brother, Sam—it was security. They stressed education, vetted their children's friends and strongly emphasized that government was a wonderful place for a career; the benefits and pensions were good and there was always room for advancement (you could become prime minister!). They were well-meaning and smothering, and any imagination they'd once possessed had been left on the prairie. Gladys grew up at least partly in their image. Her rebellions were small (briefly converting to Catholicism, going to Europe with a girlfriend after her undergraduate degree).

Harry had met Gladys at a dance pavilion on the lakeshore, a 1920s-era venue that had once hosted post-war youth—young men in blue blazers and nineteen-year-old women in dresses and pearls who waltzed in front of a twelve-piece band. By the time Harry came to it, in the 1970s, it was sheathed in irony. The band that was thrashing through its handful of chords was called Massive Stroke. Harry would have been more at home with the sailing crowd fifty years earlier. There was no point in approaching the dark kohl-eyed, hard-edged waifs bouncing on the dance floor. After standing at the back and kind of tapping his desert-booted foot to a Ramones cover, Harry went outside, stood on the sand, lit a cigarette and stared at the lake, the primitive pulse of the bass behind him. He saw Gladys standing barefoot on the beach, holding her shoes and letting the water come up to her feet. She looked elegant and slightly mysterious, and walking toward her, he didn't know what he would say. By the time he got to her, the only thing he could think of was, "It's cold, isn't it?"

"I like it. It's so hot in there."

"Hmmm."

She possessed a beauty that was almost Nordic, though her face held a kindness that was absent in the flinty, safety-pinned goths inside the dance hall. Harry recognized that neither of them were in any way hip.

Gladys told him she had grown up on the edges of the city, which wasn't a bad place to be. All the important things came out to her suburb (the Beatles, cable, heavy petting) and fewer of the more confusing things (protests, lesbianism, Frank Zappa). She had finished her degree in library science, had seen a bit of the world with a girlfriend, though at the time she didn't feel worldly; she felt like a suburban girl whose limited French and inherent conservatism was out of place among the tight jeans and high boots of Paris. She'd had sex with a Swedish student who she thought had a somewhat sixteenth-century notion of hygiene, and had met an Italian man with whom she fell stupidly in love and who disappeared on the seventh morning of their affair into the anonymity of Rome.

On their first date, Harry and Gladys drank wine and talked about Europe and complained almost ironically about not being able to find a decent espresso in Toronto.

They kept dating and one night went out for dinner with another couple, Toby and Marsha. Somehow, a discussion between Harry and Toby about whether Martin Scorsese was going to be the American Bergman mushroomed into an ugly argument. Harry took the tack that no American could be the next Bergman; that was the point of Bergman: those spaces and silences were so Scandinavian. In American films, you needed someone issuing a death threat every eight seconds.

"*Mean Streets*," said Toby, an English major who had a store of film and music trivia within him so vast that it had scared away most reasonable women, "is a masterpiece. Period. It's basically Scorsese's *Wild Strawberries*."

"What?" Harry said. "That's ridiculous."

"Both movies are about man's isolation—Harvey Keitel in *Mean Streets*, and Victor what's-his-name in *Wild Strawberries*."

"Next you're going to tell me about Catholic imagery—"

"De Niro and Max von Sydow are basically the same person," Toby said, waving a slice of pizza in the air. "They are who the director sees himself through. Like Fellini had Mastroianni."

"You can't compare—"

"*Wild Strawberries* is *Mean Streets* with umlauts."

"So you're saying *Mean Streets* is derivative."

"Look," Toby said. "Violence is America's métier. And Scorsese gets that, and that's what makes him a genius. In Sweden, people don't kill other people, they kill themselves, but basically, they're talking about the same shit, man. It's, like, universal."

"What about *The Gambler*?" Marsha said loudly. She had an overbite and an annoying habit of holding on to Toby as if she were about to fall over. "You have to admit that was a great movie. And it was completely intellectual. James Caan was sooo good."

"The movie was great," Harry said, "because it was directed by a European—Karel Reisz."

"But it was an American movie."

"Not an American movie per se."

This went on through a dozen more films. By the time Toby declared to most of the restaurant that film was a quintessentially American art form, and that Scorsese was more of a genius than Fellini and Pink Floyd put together, Harry found himself not just getting angry with Toby and Marsha but kind of hating them, and especially hating Toby's annoying trivia-filled head, which he seemed to think was a substitute for intellect. Gladys had sprung to Harry's defense, mustering her considerable logic (if somewhat limited film knowledge). By the end of dinner, the two couples had settled into a quiet hostility that drew Harry and Gladys closer. They spent the drive home deconstructing their night and deconstructing Toby and Marsha and pointing out the many ways they should have seen this coming. When they got back to Harry's apartment, they drank more wine and watched, of all things, Bergman's *The Seventh Seal*, which was the late movie, and which they found oddly hysterical. They laughed so hard they cried when Max von Sydow played chess with Death. Then they made love, and for the first time, Gladys very diplomatically guided Harry's hand to massage her clitoris with a specific light movement and less like he was pushing the button on a vending machine that wouldn't give up his Mars bar. In the morning, they went to a greasy spoon for breakfast, and it was there, in that glare, staring across the stained table as she ate her western omelette, that he fell in love with her.

"I had an affair, Harry."

This was a shock. He had never imagined Gladys in that situation. He had imagined himself having an affair, and in his somewhat Clintonian definition of adultery, he had decided that his one dalliance with Dixie didn't fall under that heading. Mistake, certainly, but not affair. He was, if not innocent, then faithful by most modern metrics.

"It was eighteen years ago," Gladys said. "When I was working at the reference library. Ben was two."

Why was Gladys giving him this news now? First the shock of sex, now the shock of an affair. How calculated was this pairing? Making peace and coming clean as Harry's life spun to its polyp-filled conclusion.

"Why are you telling me now?"

"An unburdening. I think we need a fresh start."

"Who was he?"

"A man doing research. He was writing a book on Audubon that was never published."

Harry nodded, trying to restore some equilibrium, trying to recreate the tenor of that time in their lives together. He remembered visiting Gladys in the religious silence of the rare books room, which was enclosed by glass. The people who came in weren't allowed to make notes with pens; even their indelible proximity was a threat to the collection. It was where they stored the 435 hand-painted prints of North American birds by John James Audubon. Gladys had brought it out like a sacred text to show Harry. He had to wear white muslin gloves and felt guilty turning the pages. The man she'd slept with would have done the same, their heads almost touching, in reverence.

"Tell me about it," Harry said.

"About him?"

"About the affair."

Gladys almost shrugged, a gesture she thought better of. "People always say, 'It was just one of those things.' There's a reason for cliché."

"Was it the sex?"

"No. More the seduction, I think. He would come in twice a week and need something to do with Audubon. We became complicit somehow. First it was a look. Then a touch. Innocent but not innocent. Ben was two. Remember how mired we were, Harry? It was a difficult age for him. For us. We were exhausted, physically exhausted, and tired of each other, tired of being a family, and we'd only started, so that was a bit frightening."

What Harry remembered of the Audubon paintings was that the birds looked so alive. There was something oddly human about them, some of them doomed (passenger pigeon, great auk, Labrador duck). Gladys had told him that Audubon shot them all himself.

"Motherhood came as a surprise to me, Harry, which I know sounds strange. It was like any private life was squeezed out of me. Ben was needy, and you were vague. I'm not making excuses. I'm just telling you what I remember."

"So you slept with this guy. For how long?"

"Three months."

"And you broke it off?"

"He became as needy as Ben. I'd go to his apartment and he'd want me to read whatever he'd just written. I think he needed an editor more than he needed a lover. Or maybe just an admirer. His idea was that Audubon was a perfect metaphor for America. Audubon genuinely loved those birds. Then he shot them and painted them obsessively, got rich, moved to New York, lost his mind and died. In a way he was a perfect metaphor, but Thomas—"

"Your lover."

"Yes. He was struggling with the book. He saw America as this place held together by magic realism and violence and dreams of money, and Audubon embodied that. But he wasn't able to get that on the page."

"So Thomas became another chore."

"Remember how you had to whisper in the rare book room? I think that was part of it. Whispering to one another. I didn't hear his real voice for two months. I think just the private mystery, that seduction, was what was so appealing. He asked me to lunch." This time Gladys did shrug. "Anyway, I would have been happier if it had just stopped there."

"Before it became a chore."

"Before I realized that it was pointless. I wasn't in love with him. It didn't make me feel better—well, maybe a bit, at the very beginning."

"Why did you keep it up, then?"

Gladys toyed with her teaspoon. She stared past Harry. "It was that sudden void with us. I thought I'd regret it if I didn't have the affair, that years later I'd look back and see it as an experience I'd missed out on."

"Sex."

"You keep coming back to that. Sex is the reason *you'd* have an affair, Harry. Perhaps you did have one. Maybe you're having one now."

Harry tried for a blank expression, but Gladys wasn't looking at him.

"It was more the attention, I think," Gladys said. "You and I weren't having sex then. We barely spoke. He thought I was glorious."

"You were."

"You're not angry," Gladys said. It wasn't quite a question.

Harry realized that he did feel curiously philosophical about Gladys's affair: the benefit of almost two decades passing. Thomas was a romantic ghost. What if Thomas had been a brilliant writer? Gladys might have been swayed by genius. As a couple, they were more fragile than Harry remembered. Perhaps everyone is. Every couple is one argument away from divorce. We can all find love around the corner. You need to be careful.

"Eighteen years. It seems an abstraction now," Harry replied.

"It seemed that way then."

We're even, Harry thought. He no longer felt like he owed Gladys for his moment with Dixie. Perhaps he was even owed. At any rate, a debt had been paid.

SEVENTEEN

BLADDOCK CALLED MONDAY AFTERNOON, while Harry was still examining unwanted mental images of his wife being fucked by an unsuccessful writer.

"This just in," Bladdock said. "There's maybe $30 million missing from BRG, my guy at the commission tells me."

"What? Does he know who took it?"

"Well, here's the thing. August Sampson is missing."

"Missing? The guy's dying. Did they check the morgue?"

"Dying?"

"Cancer."

"Well, he's been gone three days. And this pile of money is gone too."

"You think Dale's money is part of this?"

"It's possible. The regulators were following another trail. Some hedge fund that's heading south. But it crossed paths with BRG. And now BRG is suddenly even more interesting."

"They think these things are connected?"

"Everything's connected. Harry, listen, I need another $1,500 to keep this thing going. We're getting close."

"I'll get a cheque to you."

"Much appreciated, amigo."

Felicia called him at work, a rarity. "Harry, I had a very odd meeting with Dick Ebbetts last night. He came to the apartment."

"Ebbetts came to your apartment? How did he know where you were?"

"I left a forwarding address for mail. Anyway, he dropped by."

"What did he want?"

"I think he just wanted to revel in the fact that I was older and no longer the object of his affections. And perhaps there was something else."

"What?"

"To have a clear picture of me in this apartment. In that house, even as a renter, the facade was intact. I think he needed to see what I've come to, somehow. I don't care in the least, of course, but there was something he said that was slightly disturbing. He told me that Press was drowning and he was going to pull people down with him."

"Do you believe him?"

"I don't know whether to believe him or not. Dick isn't a sophisticated man, but there is a shrewdness to him. The line sounded like something he'd rehearsed, and it came out a bit stiff. I wonder if Dick is involved in all this. He's a man who has managed to look guilty his entire life, and he's looked that way for good reason."

"You think Ebbetts took Dale's money?"

"Harold, I think you have to face the possibility that you may never find out. Dick stayed for two hours. Frankly, he made me uncomfortable. I'm not sure a life of paid sex makes for a well-rounded individual."

Ebbetts, Harry thought, would have loved Felicia's mix of hauteur and gutter vocabulary (Harry still remembered his shock when she'd described one of the BRG wives as "an implausible cunt"). And he would have loved her money. Even when he found there wasn't any, he would have loved the kind of money she'd had, which wasn't like the money he had. If you were to be physically confronted with Ebbetts's money, it would be crumpled twenties stored in a damp basement. Felicia's money was cool and airy, and when you opened the vault, you wouldn't see anything at all. That's how subtle it was; that was its true beauty. In her presence, Ebbetts would have felt both hope and crippling inadequacy, and this powerful combination would create an obsession.

"Do you want me to come over?" Harry asked.

"No, of course not. I'm fine. It was just odd, that's all."

Harry decided to drive up anyway. Even without the creepy visit from Ebbetts, he was concerned about his mother. He imagined her afternoons as an unbroken plain she trudged across with her head down against the wind. Making a modest drink and trying on three outfits in the full-length mirror in her bedroom, trying to decide which to keep. Placing the blue wool dress back on a hanger and putting it back into her closet, then taking a sip of her drink.

There would be evenings when she would be grateful for a labour-intensive bouillabaisse: scrubbing the mussels, shelling the lobster, crab and shrimp, sautéing the garlic and shallots. It would give her an hour of mindless work, and she could sip wine and listen to jazz on the French station, dreading that stillness, the sound of her knife as it came to rest on her plate, the sound of her jaws moving.

Harry drove north in the anonymity of the Camry. He parked outside his mother's building, went in through the lobby and knocked on the door. There was no answer. He put his key in the lock and opened up and went in. Felicia was lying on the floor. There was a glass six feet away; the carpet was stained with its contents. She was a talented drinker, so drinking to unconsciousness at seven p.m. was unthinkable. He ran to her and knelt. Her face was a rictus, her leg bent unnaturally. Her eyes were open. A stroke? A heart attack? God. "Mother." He put his lips to her ear. "Mother," he whispered again. She was breathing. He ran to the phone and dialled 911. The woman said an ambulance would be there in eight minutes.

"What should I be doing?" Harry asked.

"Make her comfortable. Get her legs straightened out and her head elevated. Check her tongue. Talk to her."

Harry moved Felicia's leg so it was straight and got a pillow from the sofa and put it under her neck. Stretched out on the floor, she looked like a child. Her face hadn't relaxed, and her arm lay like a piece of wood beside her.

Harry wasn't sure what to say to her, struggled to find some happy touchstone. "Remember that hotel in Rome that served pastries sprinkled with icing sugar at breakfast?" he said at last. "You and Erin and I were there. Dad had to work." It was 1974 and Rome looked like a Fellini film: sharp suits, women in dresses and heels, cigarettes and Campari. He recalled a boy standing by a red Vespa, his black hair combed back. He was wearing a sports jacket and talking to a beautiful dark-haired girl in a sundress who touched his arm and laughed. They both got on the Vespa and sped into the insistent Roman traffic. They seemed so impossibly adult, and Harry felt like a bumpkin.

"Remember that restaurant near the Piazza del Popolo?" he said. "We went into a hotel and there was a huge interior courtyard that went up the hill toward the Borghese gardens. There were lanterns hanging from orange trees on the hill. It was like walking into a secret kingdom. The restaurant was under that canopy, made of some kind of white fabric. There were hundreds of candles." Women leaned forward to have their cigarettes lit, their cleavage suddenly exposed. The candlelight made everyone look glamorous. Felicia was wearing a dress and heels, and the waiter lit her cigarette and flirted with her. Harry could feel men's eyes on his mother. It was almost a physical force, like a wind that blew by him and his sister. Perhaps it was enough for her that she received that attention. It confirmed that she was in the world and that she was desired.

Harry looked at her face, now rigid with pain, the lines deeply etched. "You took me shopping in Rome," he said. "You wanted me to dress like all those Italian teenagers, who looked so grown up." Still no response.

They'd gone to Florence on that trip, then Paris and finally London. They were in Europe because of some particularly ugly marital impasse, and the usual distance of the cottage was insufficient. It was also one of Felicia's rare but determined forays into full-bore motherhood. Harry said, "You wanted us to see the world, to experience other cultures, learn other languages, you said. You thought we should go abroad for a year of schooling. Remember, we visited that school in England and made inquiries. It looked formal and pleasant, and I dreaded the idea of a year there. In London we stayed with a couple that you knew. There was a party."

A drunken dinner party that Harry and Erin watched from the stairs for a while. A man with a moustache and sideburns filled Felicia's wineglass, spilling some and laughing. Later, from the bedroom where he and Erin had been put up, they could hear raucous laughter and glass breaking. There was music and Harry came out of the bedroom to see people dancing, then went back to sleep. At 5:30 a.m. he was shaken awake, opening his eyes to his mother's face a foot away. Her eyes were puffy and bloodshot, and there was alcohol on her breath and the dead whiff of cigarettes. "Pack your things," she whispered harshly. "You have two minutes." Harry got up and looked around at the strange bedroom. The people they were staying with had kids, but they were away somewhere. It was a kids' room that he and Erin were in, with twin beds and a closet filled with formal-looking clothes. A cricket bat stood against the wall. Harry and Erin got dressed quickly. His mother threw their things into suitcases. It occurred to Harry that she hadn't gone to bed at all. They left the bedroom quietly and walked down the carpeted stairway. No one else in the house was up. The dining room was a spectacular mess, and there were stains on the carpet. Bottles were tipped over on the table and an ashtray had flipped onto the floor. Harry and Erin went out the front door behind their mother, who marched briskly up the street. She was wearing sunglasses though it was drizzling rain. It was grey and dismal, and it looked like London had died in the night. She finally hailed a taxi and they got in. She lit a cigarette and stared out the window.

"I'd prefer, madam," the driver said, "if you didn't smoke in my taxicab."

Felicia waited a few beats, then exhaled smoke. "I'd prefer if you drove us to the Grosvenor Victoria."

Harry and his sister spent most of the day playing cards in their hotel room while their mother smoked and stared out the window.

"Remember London?" Harry said now to his mother.

The paramedics came in the open door, sudden and brisk. They laid Felicia on a stretcher and took her out to the ambulance, talking in code to the radios on their shoulders. Harry phoned Erin and told her to meet him at Sunnybrook Hospital, then drove there. He could hear the whine of a siren ahead somewhere, maybe a different ambulance.

Erin arrived shortly after Harry.

"Did they say how bad, Harry? Do we know anything?"

"Not yet."

"Well, didn't you ask?"

"I just got here, Erin. They said someone would come out."

They sat in the fluorescence of the waiting room, on cheerless orange plastic chairs. A woman on a gurney was wheeled past them. She might have been ninety, and her collapsed face was startled-looking, her empty mouth open. How could death be a surprise? Harry wondered.

A doctor came out and introduced himself as Dr. Shakeesh. "You are the children," he said, an odd though not entirely inapt characterization. "Your mother has had a stroke. What is called a transient ischemic attack. So this is the bad news. However, it is relatively mild. Not to say it isn't serious. There is some trauma to her head from when she fell, too."

"Will she be able to take care of herself?" Erin asked.

Shakeesh shrugged. "Of course. You will have to see how she is feeling, what she feels she is capable of. I'm going to put her on Lipitor."

Harry looked at Erin. Felicia might begin reaping the rewards that fifty years of gin (and thirty-odd years of cigarettes) would bring: liver, kidneys, diabetes, a brain withered under the assault. Who would deal with her recovery, which would inevitably feature martinis and recrimination? Which of them would take her in if it came to that? Half of each day would be spent pulling Felicia's barbs out of their flesh.

"The TIA by itself is not that serious." Shakeesh gave a concerned almost-smile. His teeth were unrealistically white, and it seemed as if he couldn't wait to set them loose in a smile. He had thick black hair combed back, a handsome man wearing an expensive shirt. "The greatest concern with the TIA is that it can be a precursor to a more serious stroke."

"You have the statistics." Erin said this as a statement rather than a question.

"A third of TIA victims suffer a more serious episode. This is something you have to be aware of. There are a number of home-care options," he offered.

"When can we see her?" Harry asked.

"Soon. We'll monitor her. Your mother will have to modify her habits."

"Meaning?" Erin said.

"How much does she drink now?"

Harry shrugged, "It's hard to say . . ."

"Between twelve and sixteen drinks a day," Erin said.

"Every day?" Shakeesh said, trying to suspend judgment.

"Today would be an exception," Erin said tersely. Harry could tell that Erin was beginning to dislike Shakeesh.

"She may need to abstain entirely."

Felicia in one of their homes, without gin. They would have to abstain themselves, Harry thought. It would be impossible to have wine with dinner while their mother sat, thirsty and insane, at the table. What would this situation look like after forty-eight hours? After two weeks? It was unlikely that she would quit drinking. It might not even be possible. Though she had renounced so much lately. She might be one of those people who just quietly abandon alcohol without clinics or counselling or confessing to grey strangers in church basements.

"If she doesn't stop drinking?" Erin asked.

Shakeesh shrugged slightly. "We're doing an ultrasound. I'd like to see that liver."

"It'll be a lulu," Erin said.

Shakeesh got up and shook their hands again. "A nurse will bring you to her."

"Thank you, doctor," Harry said. They watched him stride away. Neither of them wanted to start the conversation about caring for their mother. Harry finally said, "Tommy Bladdock told me some money is missing from BRG."

"How much?"

"Roughly $30 million, he thinks. Some of it could be Dad's."

"Who took it?"

"Tommy doesn't know. But August Sampson has been missing for three days, apparently."

"Hard to believe that August took it. He's got to be eighty. He has cancer of . . . what, the liver?" Erin took her cellphone out of her purse and stared at it briefly, then turned it off. "Maybe he was the only one smart enough."

"He called me," Harry said. "Before he disappeared."

"August? What did he want?"

"I don't know. Something."

A nurse came in, a middle-aged woman with a tired face. "Come with me," she said. They followed her down the corridor and through a set of doors and down another corridor that smelled faintly of bleach. She marched through an open door and checked her clipboard and pulled back a green curtain. There were three other curtained beds in the room. There was only one chair in Felicia's cubicle, and Erin sat. Harry peeked through the curtain beside them, where an emaciated man lay motionless, attached to an IV. Harry took the chair there and placed it beside his sister's.

Laid out on the hospital bed, their mother looked heartbreakingly petite, her face dull and colourless, the small lines collapsed in intricate patterns under the yellow light.

"Do you remember when we were in London?" Harry asked his sister.

"When we were kids, you mean?"

"Staying at that house. Just one night, I think. In South Kensington, sort of grand but run down a little. We had to leave early the next morning."

"I don't remember."

"Mom was hungover, poisoned. The place was a mess. I think she might have slept with the host. The guy who owned the house. He had a moustache."

Erin shrugged. "Mom would have been what, thirty-eight, thirty-nine?"

"Remember the next day? It was raining and we stayed in that hotel all day, playing card games, and she hardly said a word."

"Wasn't it always raining?"

"Do you think she can hear us?" Harry asked, and they both stared at her.

They stayed for an hour, rooted by duty. Harry said he'd come by in the morning to be there when she woke up. Erin would come later in the day.

Driving home through the valley, he stared at the river, sluggish and brown, a shallow line of water that hadn't quite frozen. There were tiny snowflakes, a sleety assault carried on the west wind. There wasn't any traffic. Near the ravine he saw something at the side of the road, like a load of clothes that had fallen off a truck. When he got closer, he slowed and saw that it was a group of men, huddled over something. His headlights landed on them, and one of the men stood up and turned into the glare. There was blood on his coat and his face. He was holding a knife. Harry stopped the car, transfixed. He wondered if a movie was being shot, if he had somehow missed the line of trailers.

The man with the knife approached the car. His beard was matted with something, his parka filthy and torn at the shoulder. Behind him, men slashed and pulled. Snow angled in the wind. Another man stood up and also began to walk toward the car, and Harry glimpsed the deer that was on the ground behind him. The other men pulled meat away and cut the tendons. This information came in a horrible snapshot, the details filled in later.

The man with the beard was only a few feet from the car, his dark eyes unreadable. Not anger or shame, but something feral. Harry stepped on the gas and swerved past, and then watched the scene recede behind him.

EIGHTEEN

WHEN HE GOT HOME, Gladys was sitting on the couch, drinking a glass of wine. Harry had called from the hospital to let her know what had happened, to tell her she didn't need to come. "How is Felicia?" she asked.

"I don't know. It was a transient ischemic attack."

Gladys stared, waiting for more information.

"An episode of neurologic dysfunction caused by lack of blood flow." He'd found the definition on his smartphone after the meeting with Dr. Shakeesh. "Basically a kind of mini-stroke."

"God, Harry."

"She'll likely recover completely, the doctor said. The problem is, it sometimes leads to a full-blown stroke."

The same kind of unstated fear that had sat between his sister and Harry at the hospital now entered Gladys's eyes. Who would take care of Felicia? Would she be in their home? How insane would she be? How insane would they be? Gladys and

Felicia had never had a warm relationship. Felicia hadn't overtly disapproved of her, but she had made it subtly clear that Gladys was a disappointing choice. They had little in common. On the other hand, Felicia and Erin had a lot in common and were, after any length of time together, reliably toxic. Harry wondered how any of them would survive this.

"Felicia's renounced almost everyone in her world. She's really quite isolated. What's left?"

"Us," Harry said.

"Let's pray for a full recovery," Gladys said diplomatically. She sipped her wine.

Harry got a wineglass from the kitchen and poured himself some of the Shiraz. "She once told me that she thought she and Dad should have stuck it out. She didn't think it was a great marriage—it was a terrible marriage—but even so, part of her thinks she would have been better off. When it ended, she lost faith in the institution, I think. She saw marriage as a kind of war—you go out and have affairs and inflict pain on one another and don't speak for weeks at a time, but at the end, you're both veterans of the same battlefield. There's a camaraderie. That's what unites you: that pain, those wounds, your shared hell."

"Is that how you see marriage, Harry? A shared hell? Have you lost faith in the institution?"

Harry had lost faith in most institutions. That was one definition of adulthood. "I'll tell you what marriage is," Harry said. "When I was a kid, there was a cheesy museum that was on the way to the cottage. We used to pass this homemade sign for it every weekend, and my sister and I kept asking to go, but we never went because my parents were too anxious to have that first drink on the dock. But one day we decided to visit it for some reason. It was essentially in this guy's house, one of those original log cabins up there. You walked in and there were the skeletons of two moose. They were lying on the floor in a weird position, and their antlers were locked together. It was wild-looking, maybe thirty feet long, prehistoric. The guy who owned the museum said he found them like that. What happened was two males bumped into each other in rutting season. There's a female in heat nearby. They fight for her. They charge and engage those antlers. You've seen them, they're huge. Anyway, they get their antlers locked up. They can't extricate themselves. For a while, they probably keep fighting, pushing and pulling, twisting. But at some point, they run out of gas, they're exhausted, and they realize they're stuck. They collapse and can't get up again. They eat the grass around them. In the morning, they lick the dew. They're still alive when the wolves find them. It's a banquet. Two thousand pounds of meat.

"The wolves gather round and start eating them. These enemies. Are they still enemies? Did they come to some kind of understanding while they were stuck with each other, slowly starving, before the wolves found them? Maybe there was some fraternity when the wolves started tearing their flesh. I wonder how long the female moose stuck around. Three days? Three minutes? Can you imagine? One minute, you think you're going to have the greatest fuck of your life, and the next minute you're being eaten by wolves."

"So who am I in this scenario?" Gladys asked. She poured a little more wine into her glass, then topped up Harry's. "Am I the ungrateful female who abandons them, or is that you and me on the ground, our horns locked, dying."

"You tell me."

"I can't imagine you fighting over me, Harry."

"Would you find that romantic?"

"As an antiquated abstraction. Not a real fight."

"I could take Dean if it came to it."

"Dean?"

"Bang, a fast one right on the beak." Harry threw a half-hearted punch into the air. "Float like a butterfly, sting like an untenured professor. The junkyard sculptor hits the canvas."

"He's one of those narcissists who flirts with everyone. It wasn't personal."

"How about Mr. Audubon. Could I take him?"

Gladys was silent for a moment. "You're not going to use this, are you, Harry? It isn't going to become a thing between us, is it?"

Harry took a sip of wine. Gladys moved into the kitchen, and Harry sat on one of the stools on the other side of the counter.

"How much are we paying Tommy Bladdock?" she asked.

Harry shrugged. "One point six, one point seven," he said facetiously.

"Should we be thinking of selling the house?"

"Tommy might find something."

"He might find himself $5,000 richer. How are we paying for this?"

"We're running a deficit. Governments run deficits."

"We're not a government. Well, maybe the Greek government."

"If Tommy finds something, we'll eliminate both the deficit and the debt."

"If Tommy doesn't find anything, or if there isn't anything, or if he finds that there was something but now it's gone, then he is simply part of our problem."

Harry stared at the wilting flowers in the vase on the counter and tried to recall their name.

"Harry, I have applied for thirty-six jobs in the last six months. I got three interviews, which ranged from discouraging to humiliating. It may be that my professional life is over, that if I want to work it will be as a greeter in a down-market cocktail lounge for minimum wage. I'll come home at midnight, tired and humiliated and near tears, with stories about how everyone at work is a brute."

Harry's stomach lurched as he briefly contemplated the secrets they withheld from one another. "What did you apply for?"

"Jobs I didn't want—school librarian in a rural school district that's a two-hour drive from here, editing government reports. I applied for things I don't even know how to do, Internet and web work that is beyond me."

"Why didn't you tell me you were applying for jobs?"

"For the same reason you haven't told me how indebted we are—we both know we can't bear much more discouraging news."

She opened a drawer and pulled out the large pan and put it on the stove. She took eggs out of the refrigerator, along with some Morbier cheese and fresh basil. She broke the eggs into a bowl and added pepper and a splash of milk and whisked them for an omelette, then took out beets to make a salad. She toasted some pecans and put butter in the omelette pan. As a cook, she moved with economy and instinctively understood the order in which everything had to be done to be ready at the same time. Her movements were sure and balletic, and Harry had always found his wife in the kitchen quietly seductive. Food as sublimated sex. He remembered Alan Bates lasciviously eating a fig in *Women in Love*, Albert Finney tearing into his dinner in *Tom Jones*. Gladys still had a lightness to her movements, the way she glided, the way her hand came to rest on a beet, caressingly, before the intrusion of the knife.

—

Lying in bed, awake, Harry deconstructed his life with Gladys in the kind of detail that can only come in a dark, sleepless room after several glasses of wine. The first apartment they shared was above a crummy furniture store. Harry was in his second year of graduate school, and when he rented it the landlord didn't tell him there was an upstairs neighbour who had no separate entrance and entered through their apartment. The landlord's name was Cecil LeMay, a corpulent former hippie with an unconvincing ponytail. The apartment had been trashed by the previous renter, but the vacancy rate in the city was essentially zero, and Harry got nervous and felt if they didn't grab it they'd be out in the suburbs somewhere, renting someone's basement. But he also saw romantic possibilities in the space. It was large and loftish and in a louche part of town.

Gladys spent four hours cleaning the small, questionable bathroom. They painted the entire apartment off-white (Desert Sunrise). Harry bought two rolls of whimsical pink linoleum and laid it over the decayed brown lino in the kitchen. He replaced four light fixtures. LeMay said he'd pay for half the paint. That was it. "Supply and demand," he said, a trace of hippie whine in his voice. "I didn't invent the system, man."

Harry took the disgusting carpet off the stairs, pulled the nails and staples and did the hot, horrible work of sanding the wood, the mixture of ancient sawdust and toxic oil-based paint settling on his sweating body in the constrained, airless stairwell. He was halfway through painting the stairs an elegant grey (Storm Cloud Steel) when LeMay arrived. "What the hell are you doing?" he demanded.

Improving your slum property, you faux-hippie weasel.

"Where's the carpet?" LeMay asked with mock incredulity.

"I threw it out."

"You threw it out? Man, you do not fuck with other people's property."

"Capitalism 101," Harry said.

"What?"

"Look," Harry said, "it was thirty years old, it was toxic, it wasn't even carpet anymore."

"Well, who's going to compensate me?" LeMay asked. He was wearing a Grateful Dead T-shirt.

"That carpet had a market value of absolutely nothing. It was a health hazard." Harry was aware that he could, with little effort, sound like an entitled university student, but felt that, in this instance anyway, he wasn't. LeMay was a creep, and Harry was improving his property at his own expense, and LeMay's phony counterculture aesthetic irked.

"Well, the value of that carpet might have to come out of your damage deposit."

"It didn't have any value. What does have value," Harry said, "is my labour. Sanding your stairs, cleaning the pigsty that you should have cleaned, painting the walls, installing new floors. How exactly would you calculate that, Cecil?"

LeMay looked up to the iron fire escape that had rusted into an immovable, code-violating sculpture. "I could toss you out on your ass, man."

"No, you couldn't," Harry said. "Have you read the Landlord and Tenant Act? We could stop paying rent and sacrifice live goats in the living room, and it would still take you two years and six lawyers to get us out of here." Harry had no idea what the Landlord and Tenant Act actually said, but recalled a stoned late-night conversation with a guy at a party who said it was more or less impossible to evict people. Harry hoped this was true.

"You are treading on thin ice, man," LeMay said, pointing his chubby finger at Harry. "Do not push your luck with me."

"Fuck you, man," Harry said, the adrenaline pumping.

This was day twelve of their occupancy.

The streetcar ran all night and shook their bed, and the cockroaches survived the nuclear assault of Harry's poison. They had been there two weeks when the upstairs neighbour invaded. They were in bed when Gladys heard the slow horror-film march of footsteps on their stairs.

"Harry, someone's in the apartment." She sat up, frozen.

The footsteps were ominously heavy on the stairs that Harry had restored. Had he not taken the mouldy brown carpet off, they might not have heard him. Harry grabbed a bathrobe from the hook, which he realized was Gladys's as he pulled it closed, and went into the hallway, his mouth dry with anticipation. He was heading to the kitchen to get a knife, but the door to the top of the stair opened just then and Harry stood in that dull, bluish light to confront a man with long dark hair and construction boots.

"Whoa," the man said.

"Get out," Harry said, as forcefully as possible. A simple, visceral command, issued in a woman's bathrobe.

"Oh, you're . . . I guess LeMay didn't . . . Well, he wouldn't. I live here."

"We live here."

"Upstairs," the man said, pointing to the ceiling. He produced a key and held it up, and then fit it into the locked door in the hallway that Harry had asked about when he looked at the place. LeMay had said, "Oh don't worry about that."

"I'm Win Oatley. I live upstairs. Sorry, man. It's kind of late. LeMay should have told you, but, well . . ." He went through the door, and Harry heard the sound of the lock sliding back into place. His first thought was of nailing the door shut. He listened to those construction boots walk up the stairs and move loudly across his ceiling.

Gladys was partly dressed, wide awake. "He lives here?" she said.

"Apparently."

"So he can just come through in the middle of the night? Harry, that is too creepy."

"We have a lock on this door." Harry had wondered why there was a lock for the door to the loftish space at the front of the apartment.

"Harry, I'm never going to be able to sleep. I mean the streetcar, the cockroaches, and now some freak basically lives with us." Gladys was on the verge of tears. "What does he even look like?"

"Some thin guy who listens to Supertramp."

"Oh, Harry."

This catastrophe was largely Harry's fault. He had thought that the location would lend an unearned bohemian quality to their lives, would outweigh the apartment's obvious shortcomings. He imagined going to Emilio's on Sunday for espresso and huevos rancheros, and then picking up the newspaper to see which eventless Eric Rohmer film was playing at Cinematheque. He imagined dinner parties and learning to play an instrument.

In the next few weeks, his battles with LeMay sharpened, and their relationship with Oatley got uglier. The man wrote a music column for a counterculture newspaper that was given away free around the city. So he listened to every new album at concert volume and clumped around in his oversize construction boots like a clog dancer. And Oatley had a surprising social network. A conga line of people who looked sort of like him—thin, disaffected, unhygienic—trooped through their apartment, attracted to Oatley's endless supply of new music, some of it still unavailable in record stores, and his endless supply of killer pot. Harry and Gladys lived like hostages.

"Harry, we have to get out of here."

But they had signed a one-year lease; they were on the hook. Harry's head was filled with revenge fantasies that ended with LeMay and Oatley under the wheels of a streetcar.

After they had been living there two months, their relationship was like sliding down a razor blade. Harry bought all three papers every day and went through the apartment listings with scientific purpose. He thought about all the apartments he coveted: places that friends had, or parties he'd been to. Spacious, cool, affordable. All these things were more or less impossible to find, though everyone he knew seemed to have them. On the eleventh day of his intensive search, he lucked upon a one-bedroom above a deli. It was newly renovated: the blond oak floors gleamed, the appliances were unused. It was small but beautiful, and it was only eighty bucks a month more than the one they were in. Harry signed the lease and gave the woman a cheque that he knew would put him into overdraft.

When he took Glad over to show her, she was overcome with joy. In that first glimpse, that snapshot, she saw tranquility and stability, romance even. Harry saw sex (which had disappeared—the spectre of Oatley killing any possibility) and the clean middle-class world he deserved.

"How are we going to get out of the other place, Harry? LeMay hates us. He'll sue if we break the lease. He told me last week. He wants to keep us there and make our lives hell. He is fucking Satan." Gladys rarely swore, and it bolstered Harry slightly.

"I have a plan," Harry said. "An evil plan."

When he told Gladys, she laughed out loud. "God, Harry, you can't do that," she said in a voice that encouraged him. They kissed and then made love on the pristine hardwood floor of their new place.

On Saturday nights, Oatley always had a party. They seemed to be impromptu, people just drifted over, but they kept drifting, thirty or forty people every weekend, and they smoked pot and listened (as Harry had predicted) to Supertramp, and the noise above them was unbearable and lasted till three a.m.

Harry had tried reasoning with Oatley, had screamed at him, threatened him, and on one sleepless night jammed the end of a broom handle into the ceiling plaster, making fifteen small holes that had no effect on Oatley's party whatsoever. He'd finally called the police, who came and gave a warning that resulted in the new B-52's album being turned down for fifteen minutes, then cranked up to a new, vengeful volume.

But now he was beyond all that. Harry had a plan. On the appointed weekend, he bought rubber door skirts designed to stop draughts and put them on the kitchen door. He peeled back the pink linoleum (which he would oddly miss) in places where he remembered seeing holes that went right through the floor to LeMay's antique store. He lifted the linoleum so the holes were exposed. He took a large bag full of oregano and some glue and mixed the two and poured it carefully into the already slightly plugged drain. He put the stopper in and knocked on Oatley's door, and when Oatley came down, stoned and dim, Harry said, "Look, Oatley, Glad and I are going away for the weekend. Just so you know. We're back Sunday, probably early evening. Anyway, if you're having people over, just—you know."

"We'll be cool," Oatley said. Harry could see that he was already calculating just how many more people he could have over and how much louder the new Wings album could be played.

On Saturday night, he and Gladys made love in their new, shining, hopeful apartment, and afterward she kissed him and whispered, "Public Enemy Number One," and smiled and fell asleep. Harry watched television with the sound down until two a.m. He went onto their deck and smoked a cigarette and looked down to the street and felt like a character in a Raymond Chandler novel. He drove over to the old place and parked a block away, then walked to the rear entrance. Music was coming from Oatley's apartment. It sounded like Patti Smith. He opened the door and looked up the empty stairwell, then quickly ascended to the foyer, where the door to Oatley's was. Their bathroom was already an appalling mess, drunkenly used by Oatley's friends, and he took three towels out of it. He unlocked the kitchen door and closed it behind him and locked it again. He pressed the towels firmly around the bottom of the door, sealing it as thoroughly as he could. He put the stopper in the sink and turned the tap on and watched the sink fill. When it began to spill over, he stood back. The water pooled in the natural dip in front of the sink where a century of standing had worn the floorboards down. Then it moved slowly to the stove, pausing for short investigative forays along small wrinkles in the lino. The water found a hole and gathered around a smaller opening. It spread in logical yet surprising patterns that were bewitching, elegant, inevitable fingers that probed for weakness. Harry opened the kitchen window and stepped onto the useless fire escape. Above him, two people smoked a joint and talked about what kind of genius Rickie Lee Jones was. He quietly slipped through the railing, lowered himself until he was hanging, then let himself drop, landing hard on the patchy asphalt of the lane. He stood frozen for a full minute, but there wasn't any detectable change in the conversation above him. He drove back to his new apartment and slept the sleep of the righteous.

Harry went back at eleven on Sunday morning and unlocked the kitchen door. Water had seeped out into the foyer and into the bathroom. He put the towels on the floor of the bathroom, which had, as he expected, become a much more disgusting mess. The toilet was backed up, a bonus. He went into the kitchen and took the stopper out of the sink and put it on the counter. Looking through the hole in the floor, he could see a minor flood in the antique store below. He pressed the lino back into place, covering the hole. He waited to make sure that the oregano/glue mixture was working as a plug, then disabled the kitchen door lock and used a knife to carve out small pieces of the door jamb. Then he left, with the water still running. He guessed it would be close to two o'clock before Oatley would emerge to go to one of the (many) nearby restaurants that offered all-day breakfasts. He would see the mess and turn off the water. Then he would do one of two things, depending on how stoned/paranoid/wasted he was: he would either phone LeMay, or he would go back up to his apartment and light a joint and try (unsuccessfully) to think everything through and hope that it would all just go away. Harry was betting on the latter.

When he and Gladys arrived at 7:30, coming back from what they decided had been a weekend at a friend's cottage, the water was shut off but there was no sign of LeMay. Harry could hear Oatley padding around above him. He hammered on the door and yelled. "Jesus, Oatley, what the hell!"

Glad was standing beside him, smiling broadly, her hand over her mouth, surveying the glorious damage.

Harry picked up the phone and called LeMay's number and said he'd better get over there right away.

"Why would I come over on Sunday, a day of rest, man?"

"Because there's a flood over here, Noah," Harry said.

When LeMay arrived, Oatley still hadn't emerged from his apartment, though he was pacing overhead. Harry imagined he could hear Oatley's stoned brain going over the events, trying to come up with something that wouldn't make it seem like one of his toasted idiot friends had somehow caused this.

LeMay looked at the wet floors, the apocalyptic bathroom. He quickly ran downstairs and opened up his antique store, and Harry heard his defeated cry from the kitchen. "Oh Jesus. Jesus!"

It was five minutes before he came up the stairs, walking heavily. He stood in the foyer.

Gladys cried out, "We go away for one night." Her eyes welled up convincingly.

LeMay glared at them and then hammered at Oatley's door. "Open this fucking door, Oatley!" All of his soft body was primed for something primitive. He took out his landlord's key and unlocked the door, and Oatley was standing at the bottom of the stairs in his socks, looking like an illustration from a Dr. Seuss book.

"What the FUCK happened, Oatley?"

Harry went into the kitchen to check that he had patted the linoleum back into place.

"I turned it off," Oatley offered.

"You turned it off," LeMay repeated. "Who turned it on?"

"You turned what off?" Harry asked. "The bathroom tap?"

"Kitchen," Oatley said weakly.

Harry walked over to the sink and looked at it. It was full of water. He took a knife out of the drawer, stuck it in the drain and came up with a small blob of the oregano and glue.

"Why were you and your friends in my kitchen?" Harry asked, staring at the knife.

"We weren't." Oatley said. "I mean, I don't know. There were a lot of people."

"We told you," Glad said. "We said, we're gone, keep an eye

out. Jesus, the bathroom is so disgusting I can't even look at it. And the smell."

LeMay looked at the kitchen and the damaged door jamb, at Oatley and up to the ceiling.

"One of your friends emptied his bong in the kitchen sink," Harry said. "That would be my guess. Then he forgot to turn the water off. Didn't you notice when you went to bed? You come down to lock the door . . ."

"I didn't go down. I mean, I crashed. People just let themselves out."

"Christ," Harry said.

"Our place is ruined," Glad said. "Our things are ruined."

LeMay looked at them. "My *business* is ruined. Take a look at the furniture. Take a fucking look."

Harry felt a pang of something for LeMay, but he guessed that the damage was localized and probably only affected a few cheap, shitty things. He'd sell them anyway, and maybe there was some kind of insurance.

The next day there was a fairly rational shouting match between Harry and LeMay, with LeMay finally agreeing to let them out of the lease and refund their damage deposit, and Harry agreeing not to go to small claims court. Harry's argument was that having third-party access to your apartment, particularly when that third party was roofed on Colombian pot, was a recipe for disaster. What if it had been a fire instead of a flood? And there was the fact that LeMay hadn't disclosed that a neighbour had access to parts of their apartment, that they had to lock themselves into their own bedroom at night.

A cloud fell across LeMay's annoying, sparsely bearded face, a sudden sense that, with an argument so well articulated, Harry might somehow have had a hand in this. But LeMay had Oatley to consider, a bud-brained twit whose liability extended to twenty unaccountable friends. Their conversation ended with a stirring chorus of fuck-you's, and Harry walked away with a feeling of accomplishment that had thus far eluded him in grad school.

He walked down the street, thinking he could run for office or put a man on the moon. His relationship with Gladys—framed now by their criminal collusion, their escape from hell and their well-deserved apartment—had never been better. They celebrated with discount Spanish sparkling wine, and he took Glad's hand and led her out to the deck, and they made love on a blanket and lay on their backs and stared at the moon.

And where had all that gone? Who could trace the incremental losses of the last twenty-five years, the tiny defeats, the lengthening silences? What forensic accountant could sift through all that and show them the moment their marriage had tipped into the red? Here, the accountant would say, pointing to a spreadsheet. October 14, 1991. You can see right there, at that moment when your colicky son kept you both awake for three consecutive hallucinogenic weeks, and if you look closely, see right there? That was the moment when what had been exhausted silence took on a tone of resentment.

For one thing, the average cost of raising a child to (relative) adulthood is $243,660. So there is the financial pressure. There are dozens of other negatives: emotional drain, unfortunate genes, discipline issues. There is a physical toll, a psychic toll. Once they are teenagers, they are a threat to everyone and everything. Teenagers end up in the back of police cars. They belong in the back of police cars. They shoplift, burn down cottages, drive your Volvo into a telephone pole. They paint their bedrooms black, steal loose change, water down your

Scotch, follow the herd, dress to annoy and govern themselves according to lyrics written by a rapper who is two years behind on his child support. Teenagers are not mowers of lawns, they are not drawers of water. They use your credit card to order things from the Shopping Channel when they're stoned. They need $200 jeans and unprotected sex. They are unemployable, addicted to video games, believe in the lasting power of graphic novels, speak English as a second language and think life is better in Japan.

Anyway, you can see that once Ben arrives, your Hundred Day Moving Average is a dead man walking, your EBITDA (earnings before interest, taxes, depreciation and amortization) is negligible. You see those small upticks—you can see one right there when you had sex after an almost seven-month post-partum drought. But that was a dead-cat bounce. It fell again before the month was out. See? Right there, it goes down. If you go year to year, you held almost steady, but if you factor in inflation, then in real-dollar terms you were actually losing. And the modest decline we see in this last decade shows that while you are protecting certain core assets, you are not producing anything the market recognizes as valuable. This is a holding pattern, not unusual. If this were a loan covenant (and what marriage isn't?), then it would have been called in June of 1996. Numbers don't lie.

NINETEEN

HARRY DIALLED and a woman picked up. "Dr. Nathlett's office."

"Hi, it's Harry Salter. I'm calling about my test results."

"I'll have to put you on hold."

A Beatles song played annoyingly, an instrumental version of "Here Comes the Sun." "Hi, hi, hi, sorry," the receptionist said three minutes later in her little girl's voice.

"I was in for a colonoscopy a few weeks ago. Some polyps were removed. The biopsy report. Harry Salter."

"Salter . . . Salter . . . Salter. Hang on. No, that's not it. How long ago was this?"

"Two weeks. Two and a half."

"Hang on . . . Here it is. Salter." Harry heard muttering. She was scanning the text. "Hyperplastic," she said. "Wait. Okay, so six of them were hyperplastic."

"Which means?"

"Benign."

"And number seven?"

"Well, this is the odd thing: it's listed as adenoma. So there was some cancer found there."

Harry felt the air punched out of him. A shroud fell across part of his brain. "You found cancer."

"Well, in one polyp, and it was removed. There's a note that Dr. Nathlett wants you to come in for another colonoscopy next year. I can book it now."

"That's it? Are you saying there's no cancer now? That it was removed?"

"Well, there are no guarantees in this business, Mr. Salter. But Dr. Nathlett doesn't think it's urgent."

"But he thinks this is the only sign, that there isn't—"

"Hang on, I have to take this."

Harry listened to the orchestral sweep of "Like a Rolling Stone," though it took a few bars to identify it. The song ended and another one started that he couldn't identify.

"Madhouse. Total, madhouse," she said.

"I'd like to book an appointment with Dr. Nathlett."

"Okay, sure. We'd be looking at . . ." Pages flipped. "We're into February. The fourteenth. Valentine's Day. Ha ha. Three o'clock."

"Beautiful."

Three hours later Harry was walking along the Bloor Viaduct, staring at the darkening valley through the elegant cables of the suicide barrier. It was cold, and he walked briskly toward the centre of the city. At a point in his life when he needed to marshal his resources, when he needed money, patience and wisdom to deal with his various challenges, none of these were available. In their place was a growing fear.

His city itself, he reflected, had been born in fear: in 1793, a threatened American invasion prompted British officials to establish a naval arsenal and build Fort York. The capital was moved from Niagara, which was too exposed to the U.S. border. Merchants arrived to supply the military, and the town grew while the American threat subsided (though never entirely disappeared).

But by 1841, the city was in danger of losing purpose; it wasn't going to be the country's capital, after all. It could have withered then, a cold outpost between a gloomy lake and the endless pines. Yet it survived—flourished, even. Its simple grid grew outward, and more than a century later it was the largest city in the country. Though the nation was slow to embrace cities. Poets wrote about the land; painters turned out forbidding landscapes by the truckload: prairie vistas, naked pines, dark lakes. The collective soul was wilderness.

Still, Harry reasoned, there was hope. He could flourish yet.

Harry walked past the ravine that separated Rosedale from the chaos and public housing to the south. The evening air was a tonic. He congratulated himself on this ambitious trek to meet his friend Bloomberg for dinner. One of the subtle joys of Bloomberg's company was that he was usually in much worse shape than Harry was. When he and Gladys first wandered into a marital lull a few years ago, Bloomberg and his wife, Brenda, were already in the throes of an operatic divorce that produced public threats and a legal Armageddon. As Harry's money situation worsened, Bloomberg was dealing with the punitive Third-World economics of divorce, and had moved into a crummy cinderblock apartment that catered to students. Bloomberg was a philosophy professor who taught an ethics course in the business faculty, because basically no one was interested in philosophy anymore and everyone wanted to know what they could get away with in business.

It took almost an hour to walk to the restaurant. Harry had saved on gas, on parking—the walk represented a net gain.

Bloomberg was waiting for him, swirling wine in a glass then bringing it to his nose and inhaling, as Harry walked into the restaurant. He had dark, greying hair he wore swept back, was overweight, his bulk covered by an expensive jacket. He looked vital and messy, with the thick hands of a tradesman, though Leon Bloomberg had never held a hammer. The circles under his eyes, bluish rings, gave him a look of melancholia. Bloomberg had a face that announced its suffering. And who could suffer like the Jews?

"Harry," he said, getting up to embrace him.

"Leon."

Their waitress arrived, an Italian woman in her thirties, a light sway to her walk, a dusting of moustache. Harry briefly imagined the two of them in Tuscany, their dark-haired children playing with wooden toys on the terrazzo tile of their converted farmhouse. Harry a successful something. She filled their water glasses and poured wine for Harry. Bloomberg and he quickly ordered.

"Do you ever regret your divorce?" Harry asked after the waitress had gathered their menus.

Bloomberg shrugged. "I lived in a loveless world. Twenty years. Though I don't trust my memory on this. Divorce is a hotbed of revisionist history. Brenda is a woman whose sustenance for twenty years was her dissatisfaction with every aspect of me, of us. Now she needs to find new meat to chew. Not an easy thing. I saw her at the supermarket, pushing her cart with its meagre vegetables, and I waved. It's remarkable: you live with someone for decades, share a bed, every flaw on parade in those rooms you share, and then you see one another and you wave like it's a neighbour whose name you can't remember. I went to a therapist. She told me not to think of Brenda as part of myself but as part of my life. These distinctions. I don't know that the therapist was worth the trouble. We fell in together, Brenda and I, because we were always the last two to leave a party. We were the most argumentative, and we left together, arguing politics even as we undressed in that miserable apartment she had above the grill. We smelled like hamburgers and fried onions. No wonder she became a vegetarian."

Harry sipped a little of the excellent Barolo that Bloomberg had ordered. Which was worse: to be trapped in a loveless marriage or be trapped by divorce-induced poverty? Both had the power to diminish. Bloomberg should have divorced years earlier. Now he was of a certain age, his vitality seeping away. It was that vitality—that restless intellectual energy, his indulgent appetite for food and wine, the naturally uninhibited force within him that greeted the world—that made him attractive. Women were attracted to vitality and shunned its opposite. Would he find another partner? Romance was like the stock market, a tenuous conceit propped up by misplaced faith. Gold was worth $700 an ounce because we collectively suspected it might be. Then we wondered why other people would think that, and we worried that they'd stop thinking it, and the only solution was to stop thinking it first, and so Harry sold his gold stock. And gold went to $1,800. What woman will invest in Bloomberg?

"And you and Gladys?" Bloomberg asked.

"One of those lulls," Harry said. "Did you ever have an affair, Leon?"

"Only after we'd sailed into the abyss. That was ten years ago, mind you. Brenda and I hadn't had sex for more than a year. That was my watermark. I was like one of those prisoners who are counting the days. If there was no sex within a year, I would break out of my cell and seek it."

"And . . ."

"It was life-affirming. A student, which presented challenges."

"A student. Leon, you're an ethics professor."

"The beauty of modern ethics is its elasticity, Harry. Every discipline has it now. Even physics, I'm told. The universe is a curved path of endless errors aligned to support life. Or it's something else. Anyway, she was a mature student—thirty-two years old. It's the age of relativism. Democracies use torture to ensure freedom."

"People steal to preserve wealth."

"Exactly. It's a glorious time for ethics."

Harry ate a little of his orecchiette and goat cheese and roasted kale. They drank the Barolo and ordered more. They commiserated about prostates, money and the dull-witted administrative mire of the university. Bloomberg was childless, so Harry didn't bring up Ben. But he told Leon about his mother's stroke.

"She's fine now," Harry said, "but it's one more thing. How is your mother?"

Bloomberg shrugged. "When she turned fifty, my mother sat me down at the dining room table. She said she had something important to tell me. 'Leon, I'm dying,' she said. I was eight years old. 'It could be cancer,' she said, 'it might be something else. What do these doctors know? The whole world is sick.' She sat on our porch for a year. Then the next year. She was on that porch, publicly dying for fifteen years. She loved dying. She was very good at it. The neighbours would drop by, less so after the first few years. But she had an audience. Then my father actually died, upstaging her. She moved to a condominium, and those years, they weren't so good. A decade of dying in private. What's the point? In the retirement home, though, she's thriving. It's a competition there. Who is best?

Who is the queen? Those who actually die are disqualified, of course. But Ada, she is the champ. She's a small woman, and she's getting smaller. I could carry her in my pocket now. She's ninety-three. Still dying with flare. I go every Sunday. I pray for both of us that it's my last visit."

After dinner, Bloomberg drove Harry home in his battered, wheezy Civic, filled with paperbacks and smelling of spilled coffee. In front of Harry's house, Bloomberg took a joint out of his pocket and lit it. Harry hadn't smoked dope in more than twenty-five years and had never embraced it, even back then. It made him lethargic and worried; it made him feel middle-aged—the irony of a drug that could make a nineteen-year-old feel like he had a crushing mortgage. When Bloomberg went to hand him the joint, Harry waved it away.

"It's not like it was thirty years ago, Harry. Try it—it will lift your spirit."

Harry took an experimental toke and handed it back. Bloomberg took a deep drag and shuffled through the CDs that were lying on the floor. He picked up a Keith Jarrett disc and put it in the slot. "Shenandoah" came on.

As they passed the joint back and forth, Harry told him about his father's money, his missing inheritance.

"What does that money mean to you, Harry?" Bloomberg asked, his face ballooning with held breath.

"It's what my father left." Dale hadn't taught him to box or tie a Windsor knot. His contribution as a father was distilled to money, and now that was an illusion. "It's the only thing he left."

"Money carries a burden. Just lay it down, Harry."

Lay your burden down; financial advice reduced to Negro spiritual.

They finished the joint and Harry felt an unfamiliar tingling and a gentle paralysis. He looked at the dashboard of the Civic, which suddenly seemed intricate enough to launch them into space. The dials were alarmingly complicated, indicating, he noted dully, speed, trajectory, compression, latitude and ennui. It would take weeks to master them. Keith Jarrett's piano was heartbreaking. Bloomberg held one monstrous hand up, a finger pointing upward. The hairs on his hand were long enough to groom.

"Here's a case history I give my students," Bloomberg said. "True story. A crooked fund manager steals a widow's life savings. He can't resist the cliché. She's wiped out. She has to sell her house and move in with her son, a plumber of limited means. This loss, it eats her. She's a child of the Depression. She withers, she dies. Was her death caused by the fund manager's theft? Who knows? Who can be sure? But the son thinks so, and he's filled with rage. He broods for a month, but he can't live with this injustice. He goes to the man's office and confronts him. The man tells him to take a hike. The plumber picks up a minor golf trophy and beats the fund manager to death with it. Of course he goes to jail. Three lives are ruined. Did any of them deserve their fate? Did they deserve to die? In the West, we're told that life is sacrosanct. Some lives more than others, perhaps, but still.

"Ethics is the study of possibility," Bloomberg continued. "You see each choice as a tree branch that diverges, and each of those branches goes off in another direction and produces new branches. Your father's money vanishes, you get obsessed, lose your job, hold up a convenience store, get shot by a rookie cop. What becomes of your son? Your wife? A new tree, with fewer branches."

Bloomberg talked on. Harry tried talking but found he'd lost the knack. The car engine wasn't on, and the windows fogged. Perhaps they were trapped. It happened in northern countries all the time. People stuck in their snowbound cars for days, living on trail mix and gum.

When Harry finally opened the door, after fifteen minutes or nine hours, it was a release; a new universe opened up. Bloomberg slowly drove off and Harry let himself into his house, examining the key with newfound curiosity. He walked with exaggerated quiet and peeked into his bedroom. Gladys was asleep. He got up to his third-floor study with difficulty. The room moved in lazy undulation. Harry lay on the sofa, his coat still on. His hand was in his pocket, though he didn't remember putting it there. When he pulled it out, it held a penny. He brought it up to his face, looking at the year—1978—then turned it over to examine the profile of the young queen.

I've been there, it said.

Where?

Buckingham Palace. 1991. In the pocket of a man named Terkel. He went to see the changing of the guard. When he pulled out money to pay for the taxi, I fell on the floor. Picked up by the cabbie who went to Omaha to visit his brother a year later. They fought like badgers. He bought a Hershey bar at the Piggly Wiggly, and I moved around that town for a dreary decade. I've seen a lot.

You're almost worthless.

Glass houses, Harry.

You're endangered. Black rhino.

But I'm still here.

Isn't your whole life spent in the dark? In pockets, in cash registers.

That's what makes the light so glorious.

And now you're mine.

That's what you're supposed to think.

TWENTY

HARRY DROVE WEST PAST THE ROW HOUSES that had been erected for railway workers more than a century ago, now mostly renovated and filled with hopeful young families who lived alongside the original working class, a dwindling crowd of urban hillbillies who sat on their porches and smoked resentfully.

He was on his way to meet his students and observe the Occupy movement first-hand. The windshield was briefly bleached in the sun's glare, then the streets were suddenly eclipsed by a dark cloud. He got stuck behind a streetcar. In the back window, a small boy waved and smiled, but when Harry waved back, the kid gave him the finger. Harry turned south, parked and walked toward St. James Park. The Occupy campers had received eviction notices but were standing fast. His class was waiting for him near the gazebo, as specified. Harry did a head count. One short. "Who's not here?"

"Davis," Verma said.

"He'll find us," Harry said. "So, as we discussed in class, we split up, move around. Talk to people. Record your impressions. I want a sense of not just what the people here are saying, but how the media is working it. How will this history be written? What is this moment? Is this the beginning of a revolution? And if not, what is it?"

They nodded and moved along, a few staying in pairs, nervous about integrating and approaching strangers, even these open-armed Woodstockians. There was a chant in the background that involved Afghanistan. The clouds were low and flinty. Stained blue and orange tents were staked around the park. Sleeping bags lay in heaps. A radio journalist that Harry recognized moved through the crowd like a predator. Harry guessed he was looking to interview the mentally ill to use as clips for the drive-home show.

Money had congregated around privilege, hard work and luck, but it would never embrace this collection of kaftans, down jackets, Sherpa hats, hand-knit sweaters and CRUSH THE BANKS placards written unevenly on cardboard. The scene was medieval, the layers of clothing and makeshift tents, the hygiene and beards and feudal demands: a Breugel fair. Harry passed a circle of people playing guitars and singing raggedly about justice for the earth. A woman held a sign that read, WHAT DOES MONEY MEAN?

A form of kinship, Harry thought. Money established hierarchies and punished the unlucky. He thought of those lottery winners who ended badly. They gave Corvettes to everyone at their high school reunion and were back repairing dishwashers before the year was out. Money conferred a sense of power to those who had it and a sense of possibility to those who didn't. At least, it used to. As long as everyone believed life would get better, the plutocracy was celebrated.

But when that necessary fiction crumbled, you were back in the fifteenth century.

Most of the protesters were too young to have experienced capitalism's golden moment. Harry had grown up in lockstep with the first suburbs; both he and the suburb had been so perfect in their conception. The city's first real shopping mall had appeared in an optimistic suburb. And here was the miracle: in those stores, in that mall, they sold washing machines and refrigerators and candies and cosmetics that were manufactured ten blocks away. The workers drove to the factories in cars bought from the local Chrysler dealership and then assembled the Frigidaires and made the chocolate-coated raisins and Pink Lady eyeshadow and had coffee breaks and flirted with co-workers and went bowling together, and on Saturday they drove to the mall and bought the very things they had manufactured themselves and then had them delivered to their modest, perfectly kept-up homes, and on weekends they barbecued burgers and drank beer, and theirs was the best system in the world, and if the Russians could just take a break from that depressive drinking contest they called an economy and drop by for a barbecue, they'd give communism the heave-ho. But economies aren't static. Another mall was built. A bigger mall. The old one withered, though it didn't die. It gravitated toward bargains (discount clothes), then junk (Chinese toys, appliances that didn't work). The original mall anticipated the poverty that would come.

Now the city, like other financial centres, no longer manufactured much. It moved paper around in complex swirls, it shovelled money from building to building. The economy was fragile and opaque. The world of his youth had been gone for decades. All those gleaming Bel Airs being washed in driveways, outdoor hockey, two brands of jeans, Presbyterian cooking—all of it breathing its last. The factories quietly leaving, moving offshore, the workers losing their jobs to Malaysians. The suburb losing its way.

Who was next? Would the sons of Rosedale find themselves scalding pigs in ill-lit abattoirs, standing in puddles of blood? Would they seek solace in beer and large families? Every empire collapses eventually, Harry thought. They lose energy and die of heartbreak.

He saw Verma interviewing a woman in her forties, recording it on her phone camera. Briscow was passing a joint to a woman with dreadlocks wearing an ironic ill-fitting pinstriped suit. Harry approached an earnest-looking man in his twenties with a Hutterite beard and introduced himself. The man was a Christian, representing the faith community, he said, committed to non-violence. His name was David, and he said he came from a small town no one had heard of.

Harry asked one of the questions they'd decided on in class.

"What do you hope to accomplish, David?"

"To raise awareness of a dangerous and growing economic inequality."

"Do you think you've done that?"

"Definitely. The key is sustaining it. I mean, this isn't my first rodeo. I've been arrested four times. Everything peters out. The media moves on. It has its own agenda."

Are you hoping to get laid? Harry didn't ask this. This man was pure of heart. But even God's soldiers had needs.

"We believe another world is possible. This is what the Reign of God looks like," David said, sweeping his hand. "People talking, dialogue, sharing."

Harry moved on to a man who wanted to talk about the evils of the Tokyo Electric Power Company, the need to put baking soda in the drinking water to soak up the radioactive dust that had blown over from Fukushima. Harry thanked him for his views and walked on past other snatches of conversation that drifted toward him.

"The global rising of the human spirit . . ."

"The mainstream media doesn't want to tell you about Argentina."

"Make money real."

"Two words: Arab Spring."

"Banking used to be a crime—read your Bible."

Capitalism has become a carnival, Harry thought. Every week a new scam was revealed, some of them so complex that armies of accountants were needed to sort them out. But others were remarkably crude. The simple dream of a greedy child, boldly acted upon; a company made of make-believe.

And still we line up to be hustled. Harry remembered the amusement park he went to as a child, an itinerant midway set up in a small town near their cottage. There were rides and rigged games run by northern Ontario hillbillies, their lean rural faces and natural suspicion, bad teeth hidden by tight, thin-lipped smiles. One summer, a ride malfunctioned and a girl was crushed when the giant teacup she was sitting in spun off its moorings and flew twenty feet and landed on its side. Harry couldn't remember if she was killed or not. The next year, when the hillbillies set up their rides, almost no one came, and Harry remembered looking at the deserted fairground and those workers staring at him with a look of what he knew to be hatred.

The sun broke through in optimistic bursts, but winter lurked. Whatever solidarity existed here would leak away as the cold set in. There were some who would stay, and that would create hierarchies—the hardy and faithful sharing their disdain around oil lamps at night in the tents. Those who had left bringing them food and flannel shirts with a feeling of guilt.

He walked up to a yurt that housed a library, but it was barricaded against the eviction order. A Native tent with a sacred fire was also barricaded. The eviction notices had been handed out politely, and the police were on record as saying they would enforce them, the first hint of steel from the city. Harry noticed police cruisers lining the street. A few cops in yellow jackets walked through the scene.

Harry stopped to talk to a group who were roughly the age of his students, and asked them about leadership: Did they have a spokesperson?

"We're not into hierarchy," one of them said.

"We're all free to speak our minds."

"Does that make for a fractured message?" Harry asked.

"Leadership makes for a fractured message, because it doesn't represent the people—it represents the leader and his interpretation of what the people want."

"What do the people want?" Harry was genuinely curious.

"What they've always wanted," one of them said cryptically.

"And what is that?"

"Justice," said one of the girls. She was very pretty, pale in a black wool hat, the kind of girl Harry would have fallen for as an undergrad.

Are you enjoying yourselves? Harry wanted to ask. Instead, he said, "Could you burn Rosedale down? Burn it to the ground?"

They looked at him like he was a police plant, then shuffled away from him suspiciously.

His cellphone rang and Harry picked up.

"Harry." It was Dixie, calling to threaten exposure or offer sex or inquire about money.

"Dixie."

"Harry, I don't want to give you the wrong impression. I mean, I know you aren't trying to cheat me out of anything."

Harry nodded. Why was she changing her tack? Perhaps her lawyer had given up. If she'd actually had a lawyer.

"We should work together, Harry. I mean, it makes sense. Pool our resources."

Harry wondered what resources Dixie had. If they were useful, she wouldn't have called him. She had her unnamed source, she had a rumour. But maybe she now grasped the hermeticism of old money. Trying to gain entry to it was like re-entering the earth's atmosphere; you had to approach at precisely the right angle. If you didn't, you'd either bounce back into space or burn up. Dixie, with her harsh tan and suburban highlights, didn't know what that angle was. So she'd come back to Harry.

"I mean, it had to be someone he worked with, don't you think, Harry?"

"That would be my guess."

Dixie mentioned a few names. Harry imagined she had a list of suspects that she was crossing off, the way a television detective might. Her voice had dropped slightly, a forced huskiness, a phone sex voice.

If it did turn out that there was $3 million in Dale's estate, and it was all recovered, this relative stranger would be receiving more than half of it while Harry settled for roughly a million. This bothered him, he realized. It hadn't bothered him when there was only a few thousand at stake, but a few million was another story. It also bothered him that one of the reasons Erin hadn't been much help in all this was that she, as the wife of a quasi-investment banker (and with a successful design business of her own, she would add), would rather that nothing was found. Because it would kill her to see Dixie receive a fortune, even if it meant Harry would receive one as well. Erin didn't need the money and would probably contest the will in court and spend the next three years tying it up and severely reducing the total through ongoing outrageous legal fees. There might even be legitimate grounds: Harry had thought it was odd that Dale had chosen such arbitrary, non-rounded percentages, and perhaps it could be argued that this in itself was evidence of an unsound mind.

After working through some uninformed conspiracy theories, Dixie finally said, "We need to hire someone, Harry."

"Didn't you already hire someone? What about your lawyer?"

"Oh, him," Dixie said. "I mean someone who knows about these things. A detective or something."

Harry didn't want to let her know he had already hired Tommy Bladdock, even if it meant Dixie might offer to split the cost. She would start calling for daily progress reports. She might even sleep with Bladdock in an effort to gain the advantage. He wanted to keep contact with her to a minimum and resented that he was bound to her by that arbitrary fuck.

"Do you know of anyone?" Dixie asked. "Some kind of . . . money detective who specializes in this stuff. Harry?"

"I'll look into it, Dixie."

"You must know someone who would know—"

"I'll look into it."

Having established in her mind that the two of them were now partners, and that Harry was losing patience, Dixie began to chat aimlessly about how a new cloud had been invented. Something she'd seen on the news. Harry looked past the eat the rich signs, past the woman with a clown nose wearing a pup tent for a dress who was doing a soft shoe dance, and thought he saw Ben. It looked like him, slightly hunched, that furtive air he'd developed.

"Not invented, I guess." Dixie rambled on. "Discovered. It has something to do with pollution. It looks like a thundercloud, except it isn't. Where the hell are you, Harry? It sounds like a circus or something."

"It is. I'm downtown, doing research in the park."

Harry walked toward the young man who looked like Ben. When Gladys was pregnant, she suggested that Harry read to the fetus. He'd lain awkwardly across the bed and read hesitantly from Pliny the Elder's *Natural History*, Book VII—"Indeed, what is there that does not appear marvellous when it comes to our knowledge for the first time?"—as Gladys ran her hands through his hair, a sensual moment of familial connection. But he never repeated it; Ben only got the one excerpt.

As his son grew into adolescence, Harry wouldn't admit to being afraid of him. In Ben, he began to see his own impatience and natural unease distorted as in a funhouse mirror, looming large and curved. As an adolescent, Ben grew taller than Harry, a fact Gladys pointed out to every visitor. When called upon, Ben obediently shuffled over to prove his mother's point, standing mutely beside Harry, the awkward prince waiting to kill the king.

Now Dixie was asking him just what kind of research happened in a park, but Harry cut her off. "I have to let you go, Dixie. I'm right in the middle of things here."

"Oh. Well, then, okay. I'm glad we've cleared things up, Harry."

"Mmm."

"Okay, then, so you'll call when you've had a chance—"

Harry was close enough to see that it was Ben. "Gotta go, Dixie." He pressed End and put his cell away.

He moved quickly through the crowd, aware that he looked like someone's desperate father searching for a child who had joined a cult.

"Ben," he called, when he was twelve feet away.

Ben was talking to a girl who was wearing mime makeup. He said something to her and she gave him a Marcel Marceau wave and walked away.

"Ben, hi, what brings you here?"

"Dad. You know, it's the place to be. Sarah was here, but she had a class. Why are you here?"

"I'm teaching. I brought all the students down to see a revolution first-hand."

There was a brief silence. Harry was grateful for the ambient noise, the swirl of slogans and Native drumming. Dale had looked at Harry and seen little of himself, which would have been dismaying; Harry looked at Ben and saw too much of himself, even more dismaying. The debts passed down through the blood, condemning offspring to the same struggle.

"Any thoughts about when you two are going to get married?" he asked Ben.

"We don't know. It might be one of those things where it just . . . I mean, we aren't, like, 'making plans' people." His hands were in the air, articulating quotation marks, a habit that had become a tic.

"If there's anything I can do," Harry said.

"Well, it isn't going to be a 'ceremony' ceremony or anything, Dad. You don't have to book the ballroom at the Holiday Inn."

"You're going to write your own vows?"

"The other ones are totally sexist."

Ben would procrastinate, then eventually abandon the task. The job would be left to Sarah, who would produce a manifesto. Harry stared at Ben's unruly head and wondered if he had failed to be a "parent" parent.

"There's so much bullshit in the world, we don't want to add to it," Ben said.

"No."

A young man in jeans and a puffy parka came up and shook Ben's hand in a complicated way, and Harry moved off a little so the two of them could catch up.

All families were geometry, Harry thought. His was a triangle, one that formed and reformed over the years, mostly as a scalene, with no equal sides, one line sloping away obtusely; sometimes as an isosceles, with two equal sides, the last side stranded between them; and occasionally, gloriously, as an equilateral triangle, all sides the same length. At first, mothering had been paramount, and Harry hovered over the mother and infant, a useless appendage. Several years later, there was a period of masculine bonding, and Gladys found herself an outsider, a tourist who didn't know the language. On holidays, they sometimes found symmetry and balance, equilateral at last! Now Ben was poised for flight. He hadn't been anyone's ally for a while. They were inescapably scalene. What would remain when one side of the triangle was suddenly gone? What geometry lurked?

Harry looked at Ben chatting with his friend, both of them lit by the joy of being part of something that incorporated rebellion and partying. They lived on a blissful socialist plane. The concept of money wouldn't make an impression on Ben until Harry and Gladys were dead and both Ben's bank account and refrigerator were empty.

Harry remembered a Christmas when Ben was a baby. He and Gladys had gone to Florida, partly to escape a brutal winter and partly as a corny idea they were going to embrace. They'd rented a house that belonged to a friend of a friend, a modest bungalow with a pool. Harry went to the Liquor Barn and found a promising Sancerre for a fraction of what he'd have to pay at home and bought six bottles. They exchanged gifts on Christmas morning, and in the afternoon they picked up takeout and drove to the beach and drank two bottles of the

Sancerre, pouring it into plastic cups. Ben sat in his car seat under a beach umbrella, and they stared at him like he was the baby Jesus.

He had brought Ben to see Dale when he lay dying in the hospital. Ben had little curiosity about his grandfather, had spent little time with him. And Dale's dementia made conversation either impossible or strange. Talk of the markets (a safe starting point) could abruptly veer into talk of hemlines, an abrupt sentence on building materials, insights into the Nixon administration, golf tips. Ben didn't seem to make the connection that someday it would be him lying on the bed, wrinkled and addled. When you're fifty, you can see sixty, sense seventy. But twenty only sees itself, an everlasting present tense.

Ben said goodbye to his friend and turned to his father. "So, I should be heading back, Dad. You going to hang?"

"For a bit. Until the shooting starts."

A crowd gathered by the yurt, where the grounds had been flattened into mud. Police approached from King Street, a wall of yellow jackets. A man in black, wearing a balaclava, jumped onto a picnic table and began leading a litany.

"Our demands . . ." he began.

"Our demands," the crowd repeated.

"Were not met . . ."

"Were not met."

"But we are not over . . ."

"BUT WE ARE NOT OVER."

The police approached in a line, intending to dismantle the yurt. A woman sang, "Everyone here is a hero of the people."

This was democracy at its messiest, Harry thought. At this level it looked like anarchy, an unwieldy affiliation aligned against the robber barons: elderly hippies, students, Natives, economists, the homeless, the generic partiers, seekers of crowds in any form. They had megaphones and endless negotiations among themselves. They posted non-hierarchical political guidelines on the Internet, and their message was fractured and diluted, and now all that inchoate emotion and sense of injustice was being channelled into a final stand. It was the last week of November, and they were past their eviction date. Winter was approaching. The public was losing interest. And now the police were here, organized and single-minded, veterans of sensitivity seminars and violence.

The cameramen moved in, sensing, finally, the clash that the camera loves. Forty days of peaceful protest had been trying. Forty days of John Lennon songs and earnest interviews.

Harry saw Verma shooting the scene with her phone. A Native man approached the line of police and invited them, through his megaphone, to "Come and join the circle." The cops remained impassive. Harry spied Briscow and the dreadlocked woman swaying on the edge of the crowd.

Several different chants went up, competing for space, none of them able to gain traction. Harry felt the moment build, that instant when the air was charged and something could happen, when pent-up anger was finally released, when rocks were thrown, shots fired. But this only lasted a moment. Harry felt it subside.

He lingered for another twenty minutes. People were still waiting for something to happen, but it was over. Within a week, the park would be deserted, the garbage collected; perhaps there would be a dusting of snow that would cover any physical trace. The collectivity and energy and anger and hope that had been here for forty days would disappear into the historical fabric of the city, with its gift for progress and amnesia.

TWENTY-ONE

On the evening news that night, Harry glimpsed August Sampson's corpse in a grainy cellphone photograph. The trunk of the 1993 Honda had been popped by a helpful city worker who was readying impounded cars for auction. And there was August, his skin yellow with disease and purple with cold, the colours of Easter preserved by winter in a dead fetal curl. Citing an unnamed source, the newscaster speculated that a deal between Sampson and some organized crime element had gone sour and he had been murdered. He had stage four cancer of the liver and was dehydrated. An autopsy was pending.

The car was registered to Andrew Wortham, who had a nondescript, small-time criminal record, and whose license had been suspended for drunk driving, and who appeared to be long gone. There wasn't anything resembling a coherent narrative. August would have turned eighty-one in July, the newscaster said. There was nothing that connected Wortham to August Sampson.

—

Harry called Bladdock. "You saw about August Sampson?"

"Poor bastard."

"This must be connected somehow."

"It's getting a bit ugly." Tommy paused. "Look, I wouldn't read too much into it at this point, but there may have been something else going on with BRG."

"Like what."

"Like another scam."

"Two Ponzis?"

"I don't think Señor Ponzi is involved. I'm guessing the fund was dirty."

"What fund?"

"BRG got into a hedge fund—Spectre Island. Claimed gains of five hundred percent, which by itself should have maybe rung a few alarms. Securities is taking it apart. Most of Spectre was in a company that was towing icebergs to shore to melt for bottled water. Allegedly."

Harry had put $10,000 of his own retirement fund into Spectre Island. That money, he recognized instantly, and with an awful familiarity, was gone.

"So BRG has some kind of scam going on inside, but they're also involved in Spectre Island?"

"At this point it looks like they were a victim of Spectre Island."

"You think they got taken by this fund, and they started stealing from their clients to make payments?"

"Possible. Or the other way around. They looked to the fund as a way to make up a shortfall. An odd investment for BRG, but the modified Ponzi didn't make sense either. The thing with a Ponzi is, once it starts, it's usually just a matter of time. The scammer lives with that. It can end two ways: you leave your entire life behind and find an island. Or you go to jail."

"So wouldn't it be odd for a guy in his eighties who is already dying to start something like this? They can't be looking at August."

"Maybe it's the dying part we should be looking at. I mean, that's the third way out."

"But August—what, he goes to an island and lives out the last two months of his life on the beach? He doesn't need twenty million for that."

"He wasn't the only person dying."

Harry took a moment to register. "You think my father . . ."

"I don't think anything. But I have seen everything. And I just want to prepare you for the possibility, no matter how remote . . ."

"That he took the money."

Bladdock was silent for a few seconds. Harry visualized him taking off his glasses and cleaning them on a polo shirt that advertised a corporate golf tournament. Harry calculated the cost of this gesture to be roughly two dollars.

"Look—for me, personalities don't enter in," Bladdock said. "I'm numbers. I go where they lead me. I'm a scientist. If the numbers say Gandhi stole the cash, then . . . I don't have any evidence it was your father. But if I was a cop, I would say that at this point Dale is a person of interest."

If his father had taken the money, where was it? What if he had taken it, then was too addled by dementia to remember where he put it? Harry tried to imagine his father arriving at this decision. What was it Ebbetts had said? That you stay too long in this business and one day you wake up in a foreign country. Did Dale suddenly feel he was no longer moored to that world, that he no longer owed fealty to his colleagues and investors? It would have been a repudiation of everything he had lived by. But if Dale was a criminal, then surely any money that was legitimately his would go toward fines or reparations.

"Either this is a train wreck," Bladdock said, "or it's genius. Could their CEO have put this together?"

"Press is essentially a fraud," Harry said. "Maybe too much of a fraud to execute this kind of fraud. August, who knows? Where's the motive? He doesn't have kids. He dies in the trunk of a Honda."

"Who does that leave?"

"In the company? Dick Ebbetts is a candidate. He's leaving the company. Maybe this is his severance package."

"We'll find it," Bladdock said.

"The money?"

"We die alone, but we leave paper."

The sound of Harry's debt was an annoying buzz, a fly moving quickly through a windowed room, crashing repeatedly into the glass. He called Ebbetts. A voice other than Ebbetts's instructed him to leave a message. "Dick, it's Harry. Call me back. I miss our little chats."

Gladys came in the front door, carrying groceries in a canvas bag with the name of a defunct magazine on it.

"August Sampson is dead," Harry said. "He was found in the trunk of a car. Murdered."

"That poor man. Murdered? Wasn't he already dying of cancer? What could be the point?"

"Maybe he was going to confess."

"To what? You think August took that money?"

"He must have been involved somehow."

Gladys put the bag on the counter and began placing groceries in the refrigerator and on the pantry shelves.

"I have to go and check on my mother," Harry said.

"Fine. I'll make some dinner."

•

Harry drove north in his dependable car. Felicia was back in her apartment, though there were residual effects from her episode. Fear was one of them. When Harry visited her the day she got back from the hospital, he noticed a subtle hitch in her movements, a wavering motor control. It was something she worked to conceal. That was why they drank their tea from mugs instead of the delicate cups and saucers she preferred. They would have rattled tellingly. She had to recalibrate specific movements, finding compromises with her physical self. Messages that had been instantly relayed now arrived through more complicated channels. Her hands didn't do exactly as they were told, and her memory sought names and words, some part of her brain opening cupboards to find them empty.

Today, she greeted Harry at the door, smiling. She offered him a glass of wine and he accepted. They sat and talked for a time about the cottage. It had been a happy place for her, and she liked to retreat to that memory. It was part of the mnemonic spectrum that was vivid and accessible; her short-term memory was now suspect. But she recalled sitting on the dock at sunset with precision—the taste of the air, the sound of Harry and Erin in the water, a final swim before dinner, the call of loons.

They hadn't had a television at the cottage. Instead, there were board games stained with the faint red circles of wineglasses. The days began slowly. Felicia swam every morning, a curative after a night of cocktails and stale stories with the neighbours.

Harry had measured his growth on the kitchen door frame there, several lines bunched together each summer with satisfying gaps over the winters. The simple worry Will I grow tall enough? soon gave way to the more complicated Will I have sex? Will I know what to do?

It was at the cottage that all the mysteries unfolded. The adults reeled through the evenings, while the teenagers stole liquor from the cabinets and mixed it with Coke or orange juice and experimented with one another in the boathouse.

Harry told Felicia about August.

"A good man. Lonely. An odd life and an odder death. I wonder how he got mixed up in all that."

"He must have been working with someone. Ebbetts? Press?"

"Press is certainly a candidate," Felicia said. "He was all appetite. He took lovers because he needed a witness for all that he admired in himself. He purposely slept with the wives of men he knew. A form of score-keeping, I suppose. Press felt inadequate among some of those men. So he fucked their wives. Not an original idea."

"Do you think he and August did this together?"

"If August was involved, then someone like Press or Ebbetts would have to be. Someone who is evil enough to take the initiative. I can't imagine all of them working together, though."

They chatted for a while longer, then Harry got up to leave.

"You're fine, though, aren't you?" he asked his mother at the door.

"Of course, dear." Though she put a hand on his arm to detain him a moment, something she would never have done in the past.

Harry drove home thinking that he would need to hire someone to spend some time with his mother, a nurse who came by and played cribbage with her and monitored her health and alcohol intake. Felicia's money would likely last exactly as long Felicia did; she would leave a net worth of zero, a perfect balancing of the books.

Harry was inching toward the idea that they would need to sell the house. It was the only real option. Gladys would be mortified to let it go, the most sustaining emblem of the middle class, their anchor.

Two days later, Harry read in the newspaper that Devonn Isis, twenty-three, and Wayne Jewkes, twenty-six, had been charged with the murder of August Sampson. Jewkes had confessed that the two of them had driven a brown 1993 Honda Accord that had belonged to Jewkes's mother's long-departed ex-boyfriend, Andrew Wortham, to Lombard Street at 5:30 a.m. on December 9, and in that darkness, shared a joint.

The reason they found themselves sitting in a borrowed shit brown Honda at 5:30 a.m., discussing the merits of August Sampson's Mercedes 5.5 E-Class, was that they had been approached by a guy who said an elderly man would be arriving there at 6:00 a.m., and that the man was dying and so it wasn't even murder really, and when they were done, they could have the man's $87,000 Mercedes.

Wayne and Devonn had a fledgling drug business, and they saw the Mercedes as a fundamental building block, Wayne told the reporter.

Wayne had seventeen prior charges. It was discovered by the reporter that the last four movies he'd rented from Action Video were *The Terminator*, *Dirty Harry* and two Charles Bronson movies. Wayne was the randomness of modern life, his past a muddied line of failure that stretched to small northern towns and seasonal work and the reliable alcoholism of his mother's boyfriends.

August Sampson arrived, as predicted, at 6:00 a.m. and got out of his Mercedes. Wayne grabbed him and attempted to stuff him into the trunk of the Honda. Sampson resisted and Wayne hit him on the head with a handgun and, with difficulty, managed to get him into the trunk.

He looked up to find that his partner had chosen that moment to leave Wayne with a body in the trunk of a car that didn't have any keys in the ignition. Devonn had driven away in the Mercedes.

What the two constables—Jane Hudek and Wilson Claimant—saw through the window of their patrol car at 6:10 a.m. was Wayne Jewkes standing in the middle of the road, holding a gun and screaming. When he saw the patrol car, he yelled, "You do not know who you are fucking with," and walked toward them, firing at the windshield. Hudek threw herself below the dash, took her weapon out, opened the passenger door, leaned into the small V defined there, steadied herself and fired two shots at Wayne, one of them hitting him in the shoulder and stopping him. Wayne slumped onto the asphalt, and Hudek and Claimant approached slowly. They kicked his weapon away and Hudek called it in.

The Honda, which was sitting two streets over, was towed away, and seventeen hours later, August Sampson emerged from that trunk on a bitter, cloudy afternoon.

The question was, why did a very low-level drug dealer kill a very successful money manager who was dying of cancer?

Over the next three days, the picture failed to get any clearer. There was an interview with Devonn's grandmother, who said Devonn had a good head for numbers, for business, but that patience wasn't his strong suit. An interview with one of the women he'd had a child with was merely a transcription of her negotiation to sell her interview to the reporter:

"I want 5,000 or f*** you."

"My newspaper doesn't pay for access."

"You gonna f***ing start or you don't get s***. This is a one-time, limited, do-not-f***-with-me offer."

A reporter traced Devonn's background, followed the trail to the feral red hills outside Kingston, the secret Jamaica that could be found at the end of a steep goat path among the lignum vitae trees. There were small wood-framed homes that ringed a gorge, and Devonn's mother lived in one of them. The sound of Marley moved nostalgically through the valley, and on a porch Devonn's mother sat and described the trajectory of her son's life for the reporter, the arc that had taken him from perfect child to a young man she didn't know.

Over the next two days, Dixie called six times, but Harry didn't pick up. He called Ebbetts six times but didn't leave a message. Bladdock called to tell him that August had given $7 million to charity before he died. Gladys told him that they had to consider their options, and Harry wholeheartedly agreed. Christmas was approaching, with its expectations and woe.

TWENTY-TWO

IN THE GREY, PESSIMISTIC, PRE-DAWN LIGHT, Harry told Gladys he was going to the BRG offices to talk to Press.

"What are you going to say?"

"I don't know. Maybe I should just slap him around until he spills the beans."

"You think he has beans to spill?"

"Either he does or Ebbetts does. Or both. I think Ebbetts is gone. I've left a dozen messages for that little bastard."

"Think about what you're going to say. Try to draw him out. Don't just go in there and vent."

Before he got into the Camry, Harry stood outside for a time in the brittle cold. He noticed his overcoat was fraying at the cuffs. The sun looked like a melted pat of butter behind the cloud. Harry drove to BRG and strode quickly past the receptionist.

"You can't go in there," she said as he went by. "Mr. Lunden isn't—"

Harry entered Press's office to find him at his desk, wearing a rumpled navy suit and a striped shirt with a few buttons undone. He was unshaven. It was possible that he'd been here all night. His face had once looked craggy and adventurous, but it sagged now, a mudslide. His eyes were red. Harry sat in one of the chairs facing Press.

"Harry," Press said dully. He didn't get up to shake Harry's hand.

"What happened to August, Press?"

"August." Press repeated.

Harry wondered if he was drunk. There was an empty highball glass on his desk. It was ten a.m.

"My father's money is gone, August is dead, I can't reach Ebbetts. What the fuck happened, Press?"

Press stared at his pristine desktop for a few moments. He was either drunk or medicated—or both. "August Sampson was my friend. We worked together for almost fifty years. In the trenches. Through Black October, through dotcom, 9/11, through peak oil and subprime. August was dying."

"And BRG was dying," Harry said.

"People got nervous out there."

"And no one gets more nervous than old money, do they, Press?" Harry said. "Because it isn't just money with them; it's the essential architecture of existence. It's Darwin and Adam and Eve and compound interest all rolled into one."

"When did it become 'them,' Harry?" Press said softly, looking up.

"When the money disappeared."

"You know we were never in the business of making money. We were in the business of protecting our friends. For years, for decades, we protected them from downdrafts, from Japanese meltdowns, from bubbles and shit decisions by the Fed, from currency manipulators, hedge funds, derivatives and every kind of godless paper that came down the pike." Press's voice gained force and volume. "We protected them from emerging markets and junior oils. What you don't understand is that this is a war. Men doing battle every day in six languages. There is no Geneva Convention. There is horror and brutality, and every day some poor bastard lies bleeding in the gutter and there isn't a damn thing we can do for him. He's gone, he's spilled milk. You move on. Our clients, our friends, we protected them from this. You spend your whole day wrestling with Satan, you're going to get dirty. Just ask God."

"You didn't protect my father. You didn't protect August. Tell me, Press, why would anyone kill a man who had a month to live?"

Press looked at the ceiling.

"How many of your clients packed up, Press? How many defectors?"

Harry had heard from Bladdock that several families had quietly decamped, taking their millions. But nothing was quiet in that world. Or, more accurately, everything was quiet, but everything was also known. Maybe others got spooked and took their money out too. BRG was getting old. It looked old. Press no longer had the breezy air of the guy who nailed the winning basket.

"What happened, Press? Give me the simple version."

"There is no simple version." Press's voice was a rasp.

"The company's falling apart, so August gives $7 million to charity," Harry said.

"August was in pain," Press said, as if this was an explanation.

"And you put him out of his misery."

The receptionist looked in nervously, then darted away.

"You put money into Spectre Island," Harry said.

"Water water everywhere." Press wavered slightly in his chair.

"Icebergs," Harry said.

"Titanic."

"I'd say so." Harry looked at Press's red-rimmed eyes, the spectral loss in them. He could feel anger welling up. "That money's gone," he yelled. "You empty fucking suit. Do you even know what happened here?"

"I built this company, Harry," Press said with sudden force. "What have you ever built? Felicia was right about you. You haven't amounted to anything."

It didn't surprise Harry that he hadn't escaped his mother's acid judgment, though it surprised him that she'd said this to Press.

"She was right about you, too, Press. She said you were a ruthless son of a bitch who would be eating out of a Dumpster if it wasn't for family money and August telling you where to put it."

Press stared at the empty glass on his desk. He picked it up and examined it like it was an ancient artifact.

"You took my father's money," Harry said. "You took other people's money. Did someone take your money, Press?"

Press put the glass down heavily. Harry doubted that he grasped the details of the scam. August was the brains. But how did he get involved with a hedge fund with no assets other than unclaimed icebergs floating stupidly in non-territorial waters? How did they make the same mistake as Harry?

"Your problem, Press, is that you can no longer maintain the facade of being Prescott Lunden."

Press offered a damaged smile. "Least of my worries."

Harry looked around the man's office, null in its decor, the subtle beiges and ancient carpet. There weren't any photographs, and the only painting had probably been supplied by the decorator.

"Our job was to preserve," Press whispered. "The barbarians were at the gate."

"You're the fucking barbarian at the gate," Harry said, standing and leaning toward Press, his hands on the desk. "Why was August downtown at six a.m., Press? The only reason would be to meet someone, someone he knew. But that person didn't show. Instead, two thugs were waiting. You set him up, didn't you, you heartless son of a bitch." Harry grabbed Press's shirt and shook him. It was like holding a rag doll. He pushed Press back into his chair. "Do the right thing, Press."

Press slumped, his mouth open slightly, and stared to the back of the room. He seemed to Harry to be on the verge of unconsciousness.

Press's secretary came in, looking afraid. It wasn't clear if Press was aware of her presence. His eyes were open. "Mr. Lunden, do you want me to call the police?" She looked nervously at Harry.

"Helen, why don't you do that?" Harry said. "Tell them that Mr. Lunden stole several million dollars from my father. Tell them he's a fraud. That he's been a fraud for thirty years. Tell them he has some information about the murder of August Sampson."

She stood there, unsure of what to do. Press's mouth was open, his eyes glazed.

Harry turned and left. He walked out to his car and sat there as it warmed. It still wasn't clear what Dale's role was in this. You could sleep with your wife's best friend, but you couldn't steal money from the neighbours. One was merely recreation, the other a commandment. But then you got to a point, didn't you? You found yourself sitting in your Jaguar with the garage door closed and a bottle of bourbon between your legs and the engine running, and a pop song was playing on the radio and you couldn't remember the title; it was on the tip of your tongue.

Dale had seemed so utterly in control when Harry was a child, the illusion of every son. Though in Dale's case, it was likely true. But his second wife left him and his brain unravelled, and he was left unmoored. The calm of the financial world, the dignified lunches with men who looked like him, had given way to a new paradigm of risk and complexity. The city was changing, the markets were changing. It was like a stage set that had been struck at the end of act one, the act two curtain opening to reveal a new configuration that conjured a completely different world.

Harry drove to the campus in the sharp light. He parked his car and walked to the classroom, where he was greeted by the spectacle of Briscow playing a game on his phone, his body tilting as he tried to evade the aliens or jump from the exploding planets in time. *Briscow, you vacant stump, will you find love? Will a woman reveal depths you never discovered on your own? Will you wander like a cloud and find that youth has flown and wisdom has failed to alight? Then return to that small town and measure out finishing nails in paper bags at the hardware store and retell your stories of the big city? "It warn't all it's cracked up to be."*

"Who would like a revolution?" Harry asked. "A show of hands."

Verma's hand edged upward. Briscow turned and saw it and put his own up. A few others followed suit.

"Verma the revolutionary. Could you burn Rosedale?"

"Metaphorically," she said.

"Maybe metaphor isn't enough. Look at William Lyon Mackenzie. He couldn't burn it. Maybe he should have. He was a folk hero. He ran for mayor and won. But he realized that politics wasn't where the power was, or at least he couldn't get hold of enough of it. So he looked to revolution. The revolutionaries met at Montgomery's Tavern to decide how to liberate the city, then went out looking to destroy the property of the one percent."

Harry's own ancestors were part of the ruling Tories that Mackenzie wanted to oust. Daguerreotypes of them had hung in his parents' house, mouths like zippers, etched straight across, closed and unyielding, people who may have felt communication was a sin. As a boy, Harry imagined those mouths unzipping to admit a piece of charred roast, like coal into a furnace.

"Mackenzie's ragged army was routed. The soldiers burned Montgomery's Tavern to the ground, and the revolutionaries were hanged or went to Buffalo or Australia. Mackenzie lived in the U.S. for a decade. But when he returned, some of the reforms he fought for had been implemented. Question: Will this be the case with the Occupy movement?"

"Maybe," Verma said.

"What went wrong with the movement, in your view?"

"Lack of focus. That's what you're going to say, isn't it, Professor Salter?"

"One of the problems with revolution," Harry said, "is that at the beginning, it's fun. It's invigorating. Walking on King Street, the Occupy movement felt empowered; they felt like Mackenzie's revolutionaries on Yonge Street. They stopped traffic. The police chatted with them instead of shooting them. The media took notice. They were the centre of attention. They were powerful. They had the power of numbers. They had the power of an idea whose time had come. Standard issue with most revolutions."

"But . . ." Verma said, leading Harry along.

"But they only had the power the state ceded to them. And at this stage of the revolution, you have to move fast, because your worst enemy is going to come from within."

"If you mean the handful of nutbars—" Verma said.

"The cranks, the anti-Semites, the conspiracists, the hangers-on. It wasn't just them. The focus dissipated rather than concentrated. The longer you leave a crowd, the less focused it becomes. The most effective people drift away, drift back to work. The indigent, the restless, the unemployed, the squatters and the opportunists keep arriving, waiting for something. When you are demanding action, is it a good strategy to publicly do nothing for two months? Or were they all just waiting for the violent to show up and work their magic?"

"Those people were really dedicated," Briscow ventured. Harry recalled Briscow sharing a joint with the woman in the pinstriped suit.

"Dedication is admirable. But the question here may be: Can you have a revolution without a leader? In the age of social media, can Twitter and Facebook replace Che Guevara or Mackenzie or Gandhi? Was the Arab Spring a new trend or a blip? In a way it comes down to physics—how to create and sustain revolutionary energy. Usually, there is a charismatic, galvanizing leader. But can we do it through sheer connectivity? When those people dispersed, what did they leave?"

"It's a first step," Verma volunteered. "This was Mackenzie marching. The problem has been identified. Support has been rallied. The next stage will be implementation, but this time as a political party, or a plank in someone's platform."

Harry looked out the window. A new building was going up, workers climbing around it like ants. Perhaps Verma was right; it was a first step. What was the next step? Do an audit of Prescott Lunden's reptile brain, of August Sampson's computer; find a trail that led to Dale's money and explained how BRG managed to bring themselves and others to ruin. Old money's greatest strength was to realize how ephemeral money is, how vulnerable. You could spend two generations amassing it through hard work and thrift, and it could be gone in a heartbeat. This they recognized. So they were cautious. And that's why the current market, with its short-term gains and inexplicable new tools was so offensive to them. These were the tools of destruction, not what you built with. One brick at a time. In the end, a solid building. The essence of shelter in a world where the very climate was in doubt.

August Sampson had been entrusted with the money of hundreds of people. Some of them, Harry knew, were unpleasant. More than a few were dishonest. The majority were probably decent people. As his cancer dug in, did August begin to see the world in its reductionist despair? At parties where people approached him in small groups to proffer their sympathies on his impending death, then scurried off in search of a drink, did he calculate the cost of the Scotch being poured, of the shoes and cars and waterfront property, the addictions, gardeners and implants? August had a facility for numbers, found joy in simple math and its enduring logic—and perhaps he translated those numbers into AIDS vaccines and African water wells.

Harry remembered seeing him at one of the parties where he had bartended as a teenager, lingering at the edge of conversations, nursing a Scotch and jingling the change in his pocket. The unsung mole who laboured below ground, a private, fussy man who lived through the numbers that crashed across his desk. August's life was one of fraternity, Harry guessed, but effectively loveless. There was no family or sparkling mistress. He was all work.

Maybe August welcomed his death, though he could have arranged a more peaceful end. He was tired of his own suffering, of the suffering on this earth, hadn't made peace with his loveless life. The aesthetic charm of the world was lost on him: glorious sunsets, autumn colours, the damp, sexual smell of spring, nature's unreliable majesty. He was unable to see anything uplifting in the human spirit, especially his own. He gave up on God and wanted out. But August wasn't here to support any of Harry's theories.

Perhaps August was the only one who knew where the money had gone. Press had looked defeated and bewildered. What had he been thinking? Harry wondered. Trying to trace the money? Or perhaps Press had moved beyond that and was recalling a long-lost love, a woman he met in the afternoons, admiring her Modigliani form as she lay in the tangled sheets. A tall, neglected woman with a fabulous laugh who came emphatically and captured his heart. And as Press drove home through the ravine in his Alfa Romeo, he tasted her on his fingers and knew that this was love.

Harry was part of the Occupy Dale movement, doing a little but not enough, hoping that wealth would somehow arrive. He wanted his students to feel anger for the oppressed of the nineteenth century: the Catholics and Methodists and Scots. Forget about the blacks, the women, the immigrants; their turn would come in the next century. But his students lived in the zippy declinations of the present.

Perhaps he had been no better at their age. Revolution had been in the air then (though only in the air). The smell of joints smouldering. Neil Young's tremulous voice. Sitting in small circles on the warm grass of the quad, pondering the pretty girls in all their imagined complexity. A yearning that usually reached a keening pitch sometime in early October. By then he was in love with an unapproachable girl, and the initial promise of the classes chosen in August had been betrayed. He'd taken the class Revolutionary Toronto, 1826–1841, a course that had not attracted the delicate Klimt beauties, tall and slim and disturbingly self-possessed. Instead, it was filled with the crowd that was raising money for Mexican fruit pickers, those who wore army fatigues, the unwashed, the zealous. They turned to one another for sex instinctively, politically, and Harry stood stranded on the sidelines. And now he was teaching the course.

Harry looked at the class. Had he been talking? Or had he been standing in front of them, lost in thought. Which was worse? Looking at Briscow, his lasting vacancy, it was impossible to tell. What will you taste on your fingers, Briscow?

Harry glanced at the clock and then at his students, their confused, expectant faces. His debt sounded like the keening at a Serbian funeral. "That's it," he said over that private din. The students filed out and resumed their ahistorical lives. Harry gathered his papers and followed.

TWENTY-THREE

It was after eleven, and Harry sat in the December gloom of his third-floor study. The phone rang, and he looked at the display and saw Bladdock's number and tried to divine whether it was good or bad news. He picked up. Bladdock's voice had the tenor of a child who can't wait to tell on someone.

"Sorry to call so late, but you should hear this. My guy at Securities says they actually started to take Spectre Island apart six months ago. Thing of beauty. Truly. Hedge was put together by a guy named Grimes. Richard Grimes. He had two partners, Bill Hubbard and Sylvia Dench. Short version: three years ago, they sell units by way of successive offering memoranda by a capital management firm and other firms pursuant to prospectus exemptions in the Securities Act, blah, blah. This nets $31 million. Basically local investors. So they go international by way of successive confidential private placement memoranda. Pick up another, I don't know, looks like maybe $40 million. They're giving themselves advisory and performance fees up the yingyang. Three percent of net asset value. And Grimes is the guy setting the NAV, which is based on four-fifths of fuck all. Basically, the strategy is taking long positions in equity-related securities, hedged by short positions in commodities. At least, that's how they sell it."

"Who's Grimes?" Harry asked.

"So far, he's a ghost. But he appears to be local."

"They're looking for him?"

"They're looking for the money."

"And how did this get to BRG?"

"That I can't tell you. Securities is looking into it at the moment. And I have to say, it's kind of a masterpiece. Grimes sets up two funds in the Caymans—Spectre Island and Ethical Ice—and then he puts the money into a company he controls—Glacial Pace—which is incorporated in Luxembourg and is supposed to be towing icebergs to Maine, where he got the state government to kick in the money to retool a former root beer factory. He's got at least two other shells set up in town, probably more, and he's basically playing chess with himself. But this pitch—I tell you, Michel-fucking-angelo. World's running out of fresh water, pollution, global warming, panic in the streets, yadda, yadda."

This all sounded sickeningly familiar. "So what happens if they catch him?"

"Well, the thing is, probably not much."

"Stealing $71 million is no longer a crime?"

"It depends on who's doing the stealing and who's getting robbed. Securities isn't exactly Eliot Ness. They nail Grimes, and what they'll likely charge him with is non-criminal fraud."

"What the hell is 'non-criminal fraud?' We have fraud that isn't a crime?"

"Yeah, I know. The optics aren't brilliant. But what it means, basically, is they can't prove *mens rea*."

Harry recalled his private-school Latin, long gone from the curriculum, he guessed. "Guilty mind? We all have guilty minds, Tommy. Difficult to prove, but universal, no?"

"It's the difficult-to-prove part that's key. What they're saying is Grimes didn't set out to screw everyone; he's a fuck-up, not a thief. The reason they say this is, apparently there is a deal memo with some sheik in Dubai and that bottling factory in Maine."

"And that's enough."

"Pretty much. It's weak, I know."

"What about the institutions involved. Are they culpable?"

"Well, the Cayman Islands Monetary Authority appointed controllers, but they're essentially covering their own asses."

"What about here—everything ultimately came out of Toronto, didn't it?"

"Yeah, but here's the thing, Harry. The reason no one ever really gets busted for this shit is that basically the Family Compact is still alive and well. I mean, the judges on this are playing tennis with the lawyers who are litigating—they came out of the same firm half the time—who are intermarried with the bankers, who have cottages on the same lake as the regulators, and there is one big happy inbred clusterfuck. So essentially, no one is going to take a fall. Not at BRG, anyway. Grimes, if they find him, will get banned; that might be it. If it wasn't for Sampson getting killed, this whole thing would never have gone public at all. I wouldn't be surprised to see Lunden walk on this. There'll be a few civil suits. They'll exclude him from the pack, but they won't bury him. His phone calls won't get returned. Maybe he gets a fine—hundred grand, something to put on the record."

"What if he's responsible for August's death—do we have 'non-criminal murder' now?"

"You get plutocrats killing each other, the peasants aren't out in the streets with torches. Who knows what'll happen with Lunden. My guess is those two kids will take the fall—eight years, out in five if they don't stab someone in the shower."

"If they find Grimes, how much do you think they'll recover?"

"Well, usually most of the money is gone with these things. It's like water—an ancient sea becomes a desert. Sometimes you get ten, twenty cents on the dollar. If they get him and there's some money left. They sell his assets—the Ferrari, the beach house, etc., but mostly it's Houdini time. We might get something from some of the enablers, but you're looking at six years of litigation."

Harry looked out the window. Branches from the huge maple swayed slightly. The maples had been planted during the 1930s as a government make-work project for the legions of unemployed. The park was filled with them; they lined the streets. Some of them were getting brittle with age, and after a wind storm, huge branches lay in the park like missing limbs. Fresh wounds in the trees.

"Tommy, ask your Securities guy who brought the hedge fund to BRG. Ask him if it was Dick Ebbetts."

Harry woke with a deep sense of loss. He plotted the financial arc of three generations. His grandfather amassing a fortune, partly through luck, then giving most of it away; his father building his own significant wealth and watching it get taken away, his brain firing in dull echoes. And now Harry looking for ghosts.

He felt a sudden need to do something measurable and

concrete. He decided to build a fence. They would sell the house, and this new fence would add value to it.

It was far too late in the season to be building a fence. But winter had failed to arrive with any force, and Harry stared at the grey, listing cedar fence they had lived with for more than twenty years and wondered how he'd been able to bear it. He wanted a sleek, stained cedar fence made of narrow horizontal boards, a clean Japanese look that would induce a Zen calm and ignite prospective buyers. It was too cold to stain, and the new cedar would grey slightly in the remaining winter months, but that might add a certain character, he thought. He got dressed and had a coffee and knocked on Mrs. Dackworth's door, hoping that it wasn't too early, though she lived alone and seemed to be up by six every morning, judging by the noises through the party wall. She opened the door and Harry examined her sweet, confused, retired face and gave her a pitch about replacing their mutual fence as she looked at him curiously. He was glad that he had helped carry things in for her and cleaned her eaves; for these reasons, she liked Harry and went along with his fence-building plan.

He had less luck with his other neighbours, a quarrelsome family of five. Phil, the father, was a gruff, unhappy man who fixed his car himself. Harry had had only a handful of cursory exchanges with him over the course of two years. A tired and likely hungover Phil came to the door in an unfortunate bathrobe and told Harry that it was the wrong time of year, that he wasn't going to have a goddamn fence shoved down his throat, that he had better things to do with his money and that the existing fence, which listed in two directions and buckled at every post, was just fine as far as he was concerned. He held a pugnacious expression after he delivered this speech, the kind that invited you to punch him.

Harry decided to build anyway. He'd leave the fence between his and Phil's yard as it was and build another one right against it, forfeiting six inches or so of his property (a forfeiture of roughly $15,000, he estimated, that thin strip of useless land).

He drove to the lumberyard, rented a post hole digger and ordered twelve ten-foot pressure-treated four-by-fours, twenty-two two-by-fours and four hundred one-by-two cedar boards that he spent an hour sorting through, discarding the ones that had too many knots or were too grey or were miscut. They'd arrive by two p.m., the man said. Harry also ordered eight bags of quick-drying cement, then left with a bag of galvanized nails, two bags of crushed limestone and the digger, and stood for a moment, trying to think of anything he'd forgotten. It had been decades since he'd built a fence.

When he got back, Gladys was sitting in the kitchen, drinking coffee and reading a novel.

"Where were you?" she asked.

"Lumber store. I'm building a fence."

"It's winter."

"The ground's not really frozen yet."

"Oh, Harry. What has possessed you?"

"I've already cleared it with Mrs. Dackworth. She'll pay for half the materials used on her side."

"Why didn't you clear it with me?" Gladys twisted the espresso lever out and hammered the old grounds into the steel compost container on the counter. "You don't think this is something I should have a say in?" She ground some beans and yelled over the sound of the grinder. "I'm guessing the Manson family isn't on board," she said, her head gesturing toward Phil's. "How much is this going to cost?"

"I'm doing the labour myself. It will add $15,000 to the value of our home."

"Only if we sell it," Gladys pointed out. "Is that your plan?"

"It's an option."

She gave him a bleak, angry look.

Harry went down to the basement to find his power saw, which he hadn't used in almost a decade. He looked in the furnace room, taking out plastic bins and opening them to find old photo albums, baby clothes, ski boots, ancient bills. And finally the orange power saw. After another ten minutes he emerged with a hammer, a crowbar, a plastic level and an extension cord. He dragged it all outside, then went inside to find an old sheet, which he draped over their outdoor table to use as a work surface.

"Harry, do you know how to build a fence?" Gladys asked.

"It's like riding a bike. It all comes back."

Harry examined the fence, its grey pickets like uneven teeth. He suspected he could pull half of it down by hand. He pulled a post toward him, and it moved more than a foot. It was warm for the season, though still cold, edging below zero. The sky was clear to the south but overcast with deep blue clouds above him. Once he got moving, he'd warm up. He began pulling the boards off, using the crowbar to pull the top of the board out, then using his weight to push down. The nails were rusted, some of them almost disintegrated, and most of the boards came away easily. An hour later, one side was exposed. He did the south side, then pulled the posts. Some of them weren't cemented. The ones that were had rotted above the cement and simply broke off. He stacked all the wood in the lane and went in and told Gladys that he was calling a junk guy to come and collect it, and if they had anything else that needed throwing out, now was the time.

Gladys looked out the back window to the newly naked yard. "We're so exposed," she said. "How long will it take you to build the new one?"

"The wood is supposed to be here at two."

"Isn't it an awfully big job?"

"Not really."

Harry hammered in stakes and tied a string and marked the post holes along the line, then began the hard work of digging the holes. He was quickly sweating with the effort. It was almost dark by the time he had them all done and realized that the wood hadn't arrived yet. He called the lumberyard to find that there were problems with the flatbed truck and they'd have to drop the wood off tomorrow.

"In the morning? I'm waiting on that wood."

"I'll make a note," the lumber guy said.

The next morning, Harry was up early, wandering the desolate backyard. Sparrows bickered in the forsythia bush. A black squirrel raced along the electrical wire. It was bitter, and the air had a metallic tang. Gladys came out with her coffee, a parka over her pyjamas.

"There is a point in every job," Harry said, "when it looks worse than it did at the beginning. It's like adolescence—those pimples and braces and gawkiness. But it will be a thing of beauty."

"You seem to be deliberately trying to make us more vulnerable."

"I should have consulted you. I just wanted to replace the squalor with beauty. You'll see."

"We can't afford it. You know we can't afford it. You just keep pushing. What is it you're after? This race to the bottom."

Harry observed the forsythia and imagined its bright yellow bloom in spring. "You'll be happy when it's up."

"Fuck you," Gladys said and went inside.

Harry couldn't recall Gladys ever uttering those two words, this most common of epithets, uttered a million times an hour globally—vehemently, ironically, from cars, in tavern parking lots, in bed. And now in their backyard. Harry looked at the house and then back at the barren mess and went back to work.

The truck with the wood arrived at noon, and Harry helped the man unload it. The flatbed was too big for the alley, so they unloaded at the front and Harry had to carry everything around to the back. By the time he was finished, his arms and legs were leaden. He needed to sit for a few minutes, remembering when he'd built fences one summer as a student, working for a contractor his father knew. He built fences, then painted them, shirtless in the summer air, dreaming of bored housewives who invited him in and revelled in his youth.

Now the yard no longer looked barren—it looked daunting. All that wood. The unbuilt form mocking him. A truck pulled up in the alley, a dilapidated blue one-ton Ford with a home-made box on the back, the sides built up with plywood. On the truck door, it read, mad jack's junk—you make it, i'll take it.

A man got out of the truck and walked toward Harry with his hand extended. "Mad Jack," he said, smiling and revealing surprisingly perfect teeth. His hair was long and grey. He was wearing a Jack Daniels sweatshirt in this cold. He looked at the old boards.

"This it?" he said.

Harry nodded.

"You wouldn't believe the stuff I've hauled away," Jack said.

Harry knew he was supposed to say, "Really, like what?" Then Jack would tell him about dead spouses, chopped-up pianos, epic Playboy collections, life-size statues of Elvis. But Harry wasn't in the mood. He only nodded and asked Jack if he needed a hand loading. Jack shook his head and started throwing the boards into his already pretty full truck. Harry placed a few of the posts in their holes experimentally.

"This one broad," Jack said over his shoulder, "calls me up, says she's got some junk, I say, 'I'm your man.' She says, 'You take anything, right?' 'Within reason,' I say. So I show up, this broad, built like a brick shithouse, got a set, you can tell she's a tough cookie. She's got a bunch of stuff, it's sitting out in the yard. Usual shit. I load it up. Then she says, 'Oh you know, I may as well get rid of this carpet, since you're here.' Says she needs a hand. It's in the basement. Go down, there it is, rolled up. She says she'll help me carry it out. We pick this thing up, weighs a ton. You don't have to be Agatha fucking Christie, I mean, there's something in there. I figure it's her husband. Guy's an asshole, one day she finally sticks a fork in his eye, you know? I put my end down. 'Lady,' I say, 'it's none of my business what you do in your spare time, but once it's in the back of my truck, it is my business.' She gives me this look. I open it up. There's a dog inside, Doberman. There's a lot of blood. This isn't natural causes. 'It's my ex-husband's,' she says. 'I got it in the divorce.'"

Jack put both his hands up. "Live and let live, that's my motto."

Harry ruefully shook his head, hoping this would be enough response for Mad Jack, but he started in on another story.

When Jack was finished loading and finished his gothic junk tales, Harry reluctantly gave him $240 in twenties, then went back to his posts. He staked them when he got them perfectly vertical, then put some crushed limestone in to anchor them and tamped it down gently. He put plastic around the post holes to form a small tent, then mixed and poured the quick-drying cement and put candles in and closed the plastic, hoping this small source of heat would be sufficient. He was worried that the cement might not cure properly and his masterpiece would come tumbling down. Its inception had already angered Gladys. It needed to be perfect. He went in and got more candles and arranged the small pots around the post, then resealed the plastic. It had the look of a demented vigil. All he needed was ten degrees Celsius.

It had taken longer than he anticipated and was getting dark. He went back inside and poured himself a glass of wine.

Gladys was hovering over a pot on the stove.

"It's cold," Harry volunteered. "But it's not bad when you're working. It warms you up." He sipped his wine.

Gladys lifted a lid and steam escaped. Harry thought of walking up behind her and embracing her. But her body would stiffen in response.

"I'm just going to get a start on those boards." He finished his wine and went outside.

The yard flooded with light when he moved past the door and triggered the motion lights. It felt colder. As he stood contemplating the stack of cedar boards, the lights went off. He did an exaggerated dance step and they came back on.

He cut two-by-fours and strung them along the top and a foot off the bottom. Harry remembered that the key to fencing was to have a solid, level beginning, because if you were off even slightly, that mistake was magnified over the course of the fence, each incremental error adding up until the finished product was a crooked mess. He took a strip of cedar, so light and easy to manoeuvre, and held it up against the first two posts. He took a few nails and almost put them in his mouth the way he had as a teenager, but it occurred to him that it might be getting cold enough to freeze them to his lips. As kids, they had put their tongues on metal posts on a dare on cold days. Jimmy Carson had his tongue freeze to the steel fence at school, and their teacher had to come out with a teacup filled with hot water to free him. Harry held the cedar and put a single nail in one end, then went to the second post and tacked it in, holding up the level with his left hand to get a reading, then marking it with a pencil. He retacked that end and rechecked the level, adjusting twice until it was dead-on.

He began the repetitive task of putting on the successive boards below it, using a shim as spacer. The boards were too long, but he would cut them on the post with the power saw. Gladys opened the door and uttered the word "Dinner."

"In a minute."

A light snow started to fall. Harry stopped to look at the boards that were up. The motion lights went off, and he did a sixties dance and they came back on. Carpentry was enviably linear; you cut and hammered and lo, it was built. It must be a satisfying profession: to build something palpable and useful. Harry suspected he was building the opposite in his classroom.

Harry watched his breath come out in small puffs that dissipated upward. He was breathing hard with the effort of his work. He stood in the chaotic yard and wondered how Press could have cheated his father, what combination of debt, desperation and moral blindness could have brought him to that moment. They were friends. Harry remembered a boxing match he had gone to with Dale and Press as a child, a rare outing and the single most vivid event from his childhood. He remembered the slap of leather on flesh, like beating a wet shirt against a rock. Muhammad Ali approaching slowly and letting go two long jabs that snaked out and seemed to snap at the point of impact. Then he danced sideways around the ring and stopped and reset and snaked two more jabs. Ali dazzled, hauling his celebrity behind him like a grudge. The rumour was the Muslims wouldn't let him drive his Cadillac.

The seven-year-old Harry was sitting in Maple Leaf Gardens with his father and Press and thirteen thousand people. This was the big time. A heavyweight fight between the former Cassius Marcellus Clay—the name the media had still held to—and the hometown boy, George Chuvalo. Chuvalo's face was a muscular spheroid that you could hit all day before you got his attention. He was a brawler: forty-seven fights, thirty-four wins, most of them knockouts. Harry still recalled the stats. Chuvalo had a chin like an anvil and a hard right hand. He loved the left hook. But he was a ham-and-egger. Clay was Zeus; he had beat Sonny Liston, the big, ugly bear. He had destroyed poor Floyd Patterson, toyed with him, bled him over twelve rounds. Clay had never been beaten.

"Clay's going to dismantle our boy," Press said.

"He's a gasbag," his father said. "Chuvalo lands a clean one, that boy's gone."

"He won't land a clean one. Clay's never been hit. Shiftier than a politician."

Harry sat between them, his head swivelling.

"Exactly. That's why if he catches one in the old snot locker, he's down. He's out."

Around certain men, his father's diction strayed. This was a prerogative of businessmen, to masculinize their grammar, to slap Aqua Velva onto their smooth cheeks every morning and then drop their g's over afternoon drinks. Press and Dale were what were once termed "men of the world," a breezy amorality suffusing every action. To a seven-year-old Harry, they were gods.

The arena held a soft haze of cigar smoke. Harry could barely see the ring. The crowd was enough, pulsing with blood. Men who leaned to one another and murmured certainties. When Chuvalo was introduced, they went wild. No one had ever knocked him down; this was his claim. He hung around. And you hang around to the fifteenth, anything can happen.

But Clay was snaking those jabs, each one snapping on Chuvalo's face like a wet towel. Chuvalo kept moving in, one half-step at a time, head lowered and weaving slowly, taking those shots like he was walking into a headwind. Clay taunted him, called him the Washer Woman. He held up his arms and invited Chuvalo to hit him. He pointed to his body—and stood there and let Chuvalo unload. Chuvalo took a few shots, then went low, below the belt. He went low again and the referee, a clothing salesman named Jackie Silvers, let it all go. Clay's trainer, Angelo Dundee, frothed in his corner, spittle flying into the ring.

A blond woman paraded the number fifteen, wearing heels and a bathing suit. Harry still remembered the way she walked, her feet pointed slightly outward, an exaggerated roll of her hips. Her outsized smile was genuine; she was happy to be at the centre of this.

The fifteenth round really brought out the bloodlust in the crowd. Three minutes left and Chuvalo was still hanging around. He was behind on points, but if he connected with that right it would be lights out. Chuvalo shuffled forward like a hospital patient, one foot then the other, moving slowly, dragging his feet along the canvas. Clay danced sideways and moved in, then magically appeared two steps back as Chuvalo let a tentative jab float into the smoke. Clay waltzed back in, and maybe he was tired, but Chuvalo landed a left to Clay's jaw, then three more in quick succession, then a right to the head. "Chuvalo may have hurt Clay! Chuvalo may have hurt Clay!" the announcer screamed. This was what was on the news the next day, that moment when the impossible was suddenly within reach. Clay reeled back, then collected himself. He shone with contempt. He snaked those jabs and watched them snap at Chuvalo's impassive Croatian head, a head genetically formed to receive the abuse of historic enemies, a face that could take a rifle butt. Clay jabbed and danced.

Chuvalo's face looked like it was growing golf balls, but Clay couldn't knock him down. No one could knock down George Chuvalo. He kept coming, walking into those punches like penance. When it ended, the crowd leapt to its feet, cheering the champion and the hometown boy, cheering their place in history. "They leadeth me into Toronto, Canada," Clay said afterward. "They leadeth me down the path of bad publicity. The sports fan shall follow me all the days of my life." His hands were sore, and he didn't feel like talking anymore.

After the fight, Press drifted off—perhaps to visit a mistress. Harry and his father walked down to Fran's and had grilled cheese sandwiches. In the diner glare, Harry examined his father, his unwavering hairline, the muscular forearms and capable hands. His nose was a subtle pattern of overworked capillaries. His shirt had his initials on the cuffs, and the cufflinks were small gold tennis racquets. One hand was draped over the seat of the leather banquette, as if it was around someone. He usually drove with his elbow resting out the open window, one hand lightly guiding the power steering. He had a physical jauntiness that was at odds with his naturally taciturn demeanour.

"You saw how Chuvalo kept coming," Dale said to his son. "He was outclassed, but he showed he had heart. That's what's important. Chuvalo's never going to be world champion, but he can live with himself. And that is worth a lot, believe me. Listen, this world isn't run by the smartest and the fastest. Sometimes it's the guy who hangs in there."

If he said anything else that night, Harry couldn't remember it. They sat and ate their grilled cheese sandwiches. Every table talked about the fight. George was a hero, but Clay was a god. Someone was going to shut that man's mouth, but Christ he was beautiful. It had rained while they were watching the fight, and the streets were black and slick and reflected the car tail lights in bleeding trails. The neon along Yonge Street beamed. The city was poised. You could feel it. The money was beginning to flow toward it, and this grey mass would bloom.

It had gotten much colder. His backyard project seemed suddenly quixotic. Stars were visible, and Harry searched for the Big Dipper and Orion's belt, the only two constellations he could identify. There was the sudden visceral shriek of raccoons fighting, perhaps with an unfortunate cat or dog, or with one another. The shrieking escalated, the pitch high and desperate and deathly, and for a moment Harry wondered if it was his debt he was hearing. The snow fell harder, small, bitter pellets coming from the northwest.

Gladys poked her head out the door, as if she was going to call him in for dinner again. "Do you want a divorce, Harry?" she asked.

Harry looked at her, searching for context. Snow pellets bounced off his face. She had asked in such a perfunctory tone. Do you want fries with that? But Gladys wasn't given to idle threats, nor was she ruled by emotion—this hadn't been delivered in a rage, to be regretted the next day. Perhaps this was what Harry's mother had asked his father that night on the lawn.

"No."

Gladys closed the door.

Harry ran a chalk line down the centre of a post and carefully ran the saw up, cutting the overhanging boards. He spent more than an hour putting up the next section. When he was done, he stood back and observed his fence, two panels covering eighteen feet. He looked at his watch and saw that it was almost eleven o'clock. The lights went off again and Harry started his dance, a series of steps taught to him in middle school as preparation for the first school dance. It was a pastiche of loony movement that involved hitchhiking and shooting imaginary pistols, physically misremembered by the flailing Harry, who now summoned the light, gyrating and twisting in the illuminated snow.

TWENTY-FOUR

HARRY SAT IN HIS CAR in the shade of the expressway with the burden of Christmas upon him. He could feel the commuters above, hundreds of thousands inching home to a new set of frustrations. Ahead was a pixilated mural of red tail lights. He nudged into the right-hand lane with difficulty, then exited without signalling, narrowly missing a cyclist who was weaving through the stalled traffic.

"Fucking idiot!" the man yelled.

"Bicycle path, moron!" Harry yelled back, pointing to the bicycle path fifteen feet away. The windows of his car were closed and tinted. The cyclist was long gone.

Harry hated cyclists, their self-righteousness, their courier invective, the raised middle finger as they went by. He hated this army of spandex shitheads. When he cycled to work, in good weather in the spring and fall, he hated the rage-filled drivers, hated their cramped, vengeful souls.

He drove north, parked, then walked briskly. There was no

snow on the ground. The temperature was above normal. The city was grey and naked, and the holiday decorations looked bereft, like they were for a dress rehearsal rather than the actual season. He wanted to get Gladys something thoughtful and unexpected for Christmas, something conciliatory. Christmas was an opportunity to soothe things between them with a gesture.

He went into a store and stood in the aura of its ethically derived scents. He pressed the plunger of a tester, and a small glop of viscous lotion spilled out, some of it onto his hand, some onto the floor. He rubbed it into his wrist and sniffed. Peach. The lights seemed very bright. A rock version of a Christmas carol played. A small boy yanked on his mother's hand, pulling her off-balance. An elderly woman took cream from a tester and spread it carefully over her deeply lined face, then left. Two teenagers giggled.

A very pretty girl was saying something to Harry, smiling. "Circus time is swell," she said again.

Harry stared at her flawless skin and dyed hair. She had a tattoo peeking out from her V-neck T-shirt, an Asian character of some kind.

"Circus time," Harry repeated.

"Citrus-lime. It also comes in citrus-lime. The body lotion. If you're, like, a citrus freak."

Circus freak. Uncommitted syllables rounded into marbles that rolled freely within her so-called sentences. He was uncomfortably hot and left the store and stood for a moment on the sidewalk, relieved by the cold air.

He was swept into Williams-Sonoma on a sea of people chattering into phones. This building used to be a cinema, the largest in the city. Harry remembered watching *Apocalypse Now* here as a student, sitting in the front row of the balcony, leaning against the rail and lighting a cigarette every time someone on screen did, back when you could smoke in the upper seats.

In front of him were espresso machines of exquisite beauty: Gaggias and De'Longhis and Ascasos in red enamel and brushed steel. He looked around the room, at the Zoku dicers, OXO colanders, Emile Henry Artisan Ruffled Pie Dishes. None of this would do.

Harry went outside and jostled once more. A dapper black man in a wool topcoat shoved a pamphlet toward him.

"I thought February was Black History Month," Harry said.

"Sick Kids," the man said wearily. "Sick Kids Hospital Foundation."

The pavement was pocked with dark spots where gum had stained, its half-life still mocking. Snow would have been welcome, a context that had gone missing.

Gladys was home, not feeling well. Every Christmas Harry got sick, a ritual that Gladys now thought was psychosomatic. This year Harry was fine and Gladys was in bed. Harry wondered if she would prolong it to avoid the faculty Christmas party and the unhappy weight of New Year's Eve. They had been invited to a dinner party that Harry didn't want to go to. But the alternative was daunting: to stay home with one another and have a silent dinner.

Harry walked along Bloor Street, examining the elaborate window displays. His cellphone rang, and Harry saw Dixie's number displayed. He would have to deal with her at some point.

"Dixie."

"Harry. Finally."

"It's been a busy time, Dixie. Christmas, etc. Sorry I didn't get back to you."

"My god, with everything that's happened."

"All of it bad."

———

"But they're going to find that money. They know who took it."

"The recovery rate for these things isn't brilliant." Harry was tired of Dixie, tired of her expectations.

"But they'll find some of it."

What irritated Harry most was that Dixie was a distorted version of himself. In her hunger for that money, he saw his own hunger.

"They might, Dixie. Then it's doled out to various stakeholders after a hierarchy is established." A hierarchy where neither of them would be near the top.

"But when will this all happen?"

"It won't happen, Dixie," Harry said, unable to keep the irritation out of his voice. "The money's gone. The chances of us seeing any of it are remote, and if we do see anything, it will be ten cents on the dollar and it will arrive seven years from now after acrimonious litigation eats up eighty percent of it. I'm letting it go, Dixie. Maybe you should do the same."

In the silence that followed, Harry imagined Dixie calculating desperately, wondering how much might be waiting, how much hope to invest. Harry wanted a clean break. He stood in front of the Holt Renfrew window, filled with mannequins that had slightly creepy penguin heads, dressed in Dolce & Gabbana suits. A stuffed life-sized reindeer wearing a cashmere sweater was lying down with an arrow sticking out of it. One of the D&G penguin people held a bow. Harry lingered for a moment and pondered this narrative. A few presents were littered around. One of the opened presents had a plastic heart in it. The dead reindeer glanced up at Harry. I died for love.

"But can't we—" Dixie began.

"If you want to go after the money, Dixie, you should talk to your lawyer. But I'm through. I have to run. Merry Christmas."

He pressed End.

Harry went inside Holt's and looked at scarves. The most expensive was $3,295. A saleswoman smiled at him, instantly assessing his clothes and shoes, reading his face. Nowhere was there written the word "money." There were people with money who dressed like bums, but it was a very particular uniform. Good clothes that should have been discarded: hardy tweeds from London, Ralph Lauren oxford cloth shirts with frayed collars, overcoats bought at this very store more than a decade earlier, brogues that had been made to order fifteen years ago. But that wasn't Harry.

The dull white noise that was his debt suddenly increased, building until it shut out all other sounds. The saleswoman said something; Harry watched her lips move and waited until they stopped, then said he was only browsing, hoping he wasn't yelling. He stood rooted for a few moments, hoping the noise would subside, but it didn't.

The saleswoman stared at him blankly. A handsome Latina. His head had once been crowded with women like this, all of them complex and passionate and tasting of earth and olives, constructed from cinema and cliché.

Harry got onto the escalator, gazing upward into the atrium, the crossing of escalators, the solemn lines of shoppers. Full lips bloomed on ancient faces. Tastefulness in all things except the flesh. He rose through the ranks, his debt getting louder, bringing in symphonic flourishes—the sudden sweep of a dozen violins, trumpets sounding, an oboe. Voices joined in, a choir of thousands celebrating the apex of the retail year, when credit was stretched and desire sated. This was the cathedral, the spire rising past Armani and Burberry, past Gucci and Prada. He could hear Gladys's voice among the multitudes, her soft, lovely soprano. And Ben's unsure tenor. All the debts and personal obligations of the holiday season forming a "Hallelujah Chorus" in his head.

On the top floor a bass drum joined in, a martial touch. Harry nodded at a saleswoman whose mouth formed a pleasant query. He wandered the top floor, past the messy tables of sale clothes, the symphony screaming inside. It wasn't just his own debt, but those around him, the city's, the nation's, all nations. The whole system was straining, Marx seeking vindication among the ruins.

He was jolted suddenly by a vision of a sickly future in which their house was gone, his marriage collapsed. Then he would quietly disappear from Ben's life, the way Dale had. Harry's job could end without warning. Polyps could flourish like mushrooms within him. A wasteland awaiting, burned stumps still smoking. Not a living thing for miles.

He circled quickly to get on the descending escalator, his debt getting even louder. Harry continued down, seeking escape. He looked for familiar faces. But Felicia wouldn't shop here now, and Erin was too organized to be shopping this close to Christmas. She would have wandered through here in late November, two days marked off on her phone calendar, a nice lunch booked nearby. Back on the main floor, cymbals arrived in a Teutonic clash. Horns blared, a bass thumped. Instruments and voices blended, heading toward an awful crescendo.

Harry walked into the men's department. He had come here with his mother to buy a suit for graduation. His father had wanted his tailor to make the suit, but his mother argued that Harry would look like a musty old stockbroker at his prom; he needed something fresher. So they came to Holt's and Harry dutifully tried on suits, wishing he were elsewhere. In the end, they bought a navy suit and he looked a bit like a stockbroker anyway.

Harry stood over shirts that were folded on a tray. They were regularly priced at $388, on sale for $254. The crescendo finally resolved in a single screaming note that exploded in Harry's head. He brought his hands to his ears and bent over, trying to stop the noise. A salesman came over and said something, leaning down to Harry's Quasimodo pose. The noise finally stopped, and Harry slowly straightened up, filled with relief. There was a ringing still. The salesman was saying something, but Harry couldn't hear. A few people stared. He wondered if he'd yelled anything.

Behind the salesman was his childhood friend Jimmy Carson, who looked at Harry with curiosity as much as recognition. Jimmy the drinker. He had done time for fraud, "a soft jolt," as they say. Or maybe only a fine. Insider trading, something like that. Harry couldn't recall any details. His thick, handsome face had begun its ruin, the veins streaky, the eyes bulging against the pressure of that flesh. Harry wondered if Jimmy was still married, if his wife had waited for him, like in a country and western song, or if she'd fled.

The salesman had a hand on Harry's arm. "Sir, are you all right?"

"Fine, fine. Thank you." He could hear again, though the voice seemed to be coming from a great distance.

"You're sure? Perhaps you should sit down."

"I'm fine."

Carson approached. "Harry," he said. "Jesus, man. You okay? You having an attack of some kind?"

"Tinnitus," Harry said. "Hearing. It can get a bit . . . adventurous at times."

"What's it been . . ."

"A while."

"Years. How are you?"

"Good, good. And you, Jimmy, are you still in . . . what was it? . . . arbitrage?" Harry asked.

"With Jennings Albrecht. God, that was a while ago."

"You're on to bigger things."

"There are no bigger things. Everything's small now."

"But money's still money. It's still moving around out there."

"A little. I'm with Mercer Beem. You remember they got carried away on that quant model. We've repositioned ourselves. Look, Harry, do you know anyone on the University Endowment Fund Committee? They took one in the nuts. Big time. I mean like a billion and a half. Poof. Their impulse is to hunker down. I'm not arguing with that. The thing is, we could make them well, but I need to get into the room. You know Althorp, Davis, any of those guys?"

Harry shook his head. If he did know them, he wouldn't be sending ex-con Jimmy Carson to sell them the latest version of derivatives. Jimmy, who watched from his window while Harry's father hit his mother. Jimmy, who sold naked pictures taken from a nudie magazine at school, who used the money from his sixteenth birthday to hire a prostitute.

"I was sorry to hear about Dale," Jimmy said.

"Thanks, Jimmy. You heard about BRG?"

"Hard to miss. A surprise." Jimmy's face had a sudden wariness.

"They took my father's money. Cleaned him out." Harry assessed Jimmy's face, blotchy under the light. "How hard is it, Jimmy?"

Jimmy assessed him coldly for a minute, then shrugged and smiled his ex-con half-smile. "It's all out there, all that paper—ABCs, CDOs, SIVs, subprime, NINJA loans. You sit in front of that screen and it's like you're in a snow globe and everything is fine, then you turn it upside down and suddenly all that paper is floating and you can hardly see there's so much of it, and you reach out and try and grab as much of it as you can."

"And then?"

"And then the problems start."

Outside, dark clouds moved in from the northwest. He called Felicia to check in. Marcie, the Barbadian nurse he'd hired to stop by twice a week, answered. Felicia was in the bathroom, she said, so he asked Marcie about his mother's health, her drinking. Marcie said she had a few gins in the afternoon when they played cards. Which meant another six or so in the evening. Felicia was intent on going to Italy, a trip that made Harry nervous.

"Do you think she should be travelling, Marcie?"

"If something's going to happen, it's going to happen."

"That's a great comfort."

Harry told Marcie that he'd be over tomorrow morning, then hung up. He continued along the street, past the armed guard in front of the jewellery store, the crush of shoppers, the pre–Boxing Day blowout sales. Harry breathed in deeply, yoga breaths that took it all in, the sense of communion as they thronged. He had read that the world's wealthy had $32 trillion stashed offshore, out of reach of the tax man. All those secrets. The unbought espresso machines and Canali suits.

Harry checked his phone for the number he'd entered this morning. He'd phoned the real estate office and gotten the cellphone number for Del, their agent from years ago. He'd left her a message this morning, saying he wanted to chat.

He entered the number. She picked up, and Harry could hear her talking to someone else. Ten seconds went by before she finally addressed her cellphone.

"Del, it's Harry Salter. I left you a message."

"Harry, great to hear from you. How is that adorable house?" Harry could hear her again talking to someone else, pointing out the features in a house they were in. *Did you notice the darling sconces?*

"I'm thinking of putting it on the market, Del. I need to get an idea of what it would go for."

"Off the top, Harry, sight unseen, which I never do, but since I was the agent, blah, blah. That neighbourhood—through the roof. I'd say eight ten on a bad day. Eight fifty if we get some cowboys blowing their brains out in a bidding war."

"A place on the block went for $900,000 in June. Bigger than ours, but in the ballpark."

"Well, June. Everyone loves June. December, not so much. Christmas is good for divorce and suicide. It's death for real estate. You don't want to show it until early spring if you can hang on. January, everyone feels poor after Christmas. Credit card bills coming in. Heating bills through the roof, not that we've actually had winter. February, everyone's depressed. March, they start to stir. Then April is the new beginning. Why not take on more debt? The world is green."

"I'll see, Del. May need to move a little earlier than that."

He wondered what she looked like now. Twenty years ago she had been an intense woman who didn't seem to have any life outside selling houses. Dark-haired, distracted, sexy. But he'd get two other agents to give an opinion before he chose who to go with. He could hear Del talking to whomever she was with. *You will die when you see the master bedroom.*

"Let's chat this week, Harry," Del said before turning again to her clients.

Harry pressed End.

If they sold the house for $850,000, there would be roughly

$420,000 left after paying off the mortgage, line of credit, real estate agent's fee, taxes, legal fees, credit cards. They could pay cash for a very modest, possibly cheery condo downtown, cycle everywhere, get out to more plays, go to cheap, hip restaurants. No more ants or mice, no more damp basements. No more debt. Harry still wouldn't have any money. His retirement was perilous, his employment tentative. He would be broke, but he'd have slain the dragon. A rebirth, then, not a retreat.

The wind came charging through the tunnel formed by the buildings, a chaotic gale that blew in more than one direction at once. A snowflake sped by erratically. The shoppers were in dark hues, grim and purposeful, hunched against the wind, moving in ragged single file like mine workers on a shift change. Harry darted in and out of a dozen stores, the Christmas music lively and annoying. His debt revived, and now sat in his head like the Memphis horn section that had played on those Stax soul records he'd loved as a kid. It had a jaunty, danceable rhythm. In the end, he bought his mother a literary mystery novel that was set in Florence. He got Ben a boxed CD set of The Band, and Gladys got a pashmina. In his heart, his house had a hundred bidders; it sold for a million. He was free.

TWENTY-FIVE

"Do you think we'd have been happier if your father had left us money? If he'd *had* money." Gladys asked. It was New Year's Eve, early in the evening. They carefully sipped wine. She was wearing the pashmina he'd bought her for Christmas, a modest hit.

Harry wondered if his father had been happy when he'd had money. When Harry visited him in the hospital for the last time, the day before his breathing mercifully stopped, he talked to Dale about the mercurial stock market, seeking common ground, though there was no sign that Dale understood anything. Harry had anticipated his father's death with impatience. He couldn't keep that thought away, even as he stared into that tightened face, into Dale's inscrutable eyes. What had made his father happy? Dick Ebbetts thought Dale had been in love with Tess. Harry had seen her in a restaurant a few months ago. Not a beautiful woman, though she carried herself with extraordinary grace and had a confidence that drew people toward her.

Perhaps that was her only interesting quality. But it was enough. And Dale still felt that loss even as his flesh was being eaten.

"Relieved, perhaps. I don't know about happy."

"What happened, Harry?"

It wasn't clear whether Gladys was asking about the money or about them—what had happened to their marriage.

"I think Press and August were running a scam to deal with all the defections," Harry said. "They'd made a few bad bets and lost some clients, and they needed a way to keep the company solvent. Maybe Dad was their first victim. They realized he was ailing and found a way to take his money. But it wasn't enough. They needed more."

"But murder. That's a leap, Harry. They were all such friends."

"I think Press was worried August would make some kind of deathbed confession. He had called me. I think he was getting ready to spill."

"And Press had him killed? My god."

"I don't know for sure. Press would have rationalized it—August is a few weeks from the end. Bladdock said that BRG then got taken themselves by a hedge fund—a scam that was based on hauling icebergs to shore, then melting them, bottling the water and selling it to Dubai. My father got taken by his friends, then they got taken themselves. I wish I could appreciate the poetic justice."

"Please don't tell me how much we owe Bladdock."

They sat in the quiet of early evening, sipping wine. Outside there was a light snowfall. Snows had come and gone, never cold enough to stay.

"Ben and Sarah have decided to split up," Gladys finally said.

It saddened Harry slightly that Ben would confide in Gladys rather than him. Though perhaps it was the decisive Sarah who had told Gladys.

"They're awfully young."

"She was good for him in a way. But perhaps it's best they split up before it becomes destructive, before her natural dominance begins to diminish him, to damage him."

"You have a clinical view of relationships, Gladys."

"I didn't used to."

"Are you sure?"

Gladys shrugged. She had probably thought there would be, if nothing else, security. That Harry's family would provide that.

"You heard about Dean?" she said.

"No."

"He has one of those awful undefined ailments. Epstein-Barr, maybe. Anyway, he's exhausted all the time. Has difficulty dressing, apparently. Can't work."

Harry recalled Dean's mating dance with Gladys.

"Satori is devoting herself to him. Paige told me. She's taken a leave from work."

"The art world has lost a great scrap dealer."

"Harry."

"What if I had Epstein-Barr? What if I sat in my stained pyjamas, staring at frost patterns on the window for eleven hours a day?"

Gladys poured more of the wine into both glasses.

"Would you devote your time to caring for me?"

"You feel Epstein-Barr coming on, Harry?" Gladys asked.

"A touch. In my throat."

Gladys laughed. "How did we get to palliative care so quickly? Didn't we skip a step?"

That glowing moment you saw in Ralph Lauren ads. All the handsome generations and their golden retrievers. Harry remembered the man who had assaulted him at the sausage stand. What would three generations of his family look like? A police lineup.

They were sitting in the living room. Harry looked at the fireplace and wished there was a roaring fire. He couldn't remember the last time they'd used the fireplace. When they bought the house, they hired a company to clean the chimney, and to Harry's surprise, a Dickensian urchin showed up. He might have been sixteen. He walked upstairs and went onto the roof through the bathroom window, leaving a trail of soot. His face was actually blackened, like Dick Van Dyke in *Mary Poppins*. They made fires that winter, but somehow the ritual died.

They'd almost finished a bottle of wine and it was only eight o'clock. They wouldn't last until midnight, and there was no point in going to a New Year's party and leaving at 10:30.

"I think we should sell the house, Gladys."

"For our sins," she said.

"I talked to Del, that real estate agent. She thinks we might get $850,000."

"You talked to an agent already?"

"I just wanted a ballpark figure. We could pay off debt and buy a condo downtown. Everyone's doing it."

"Admitting defeat?"

He could see Gladys calculating their life, houseless. The sudden loss of this symbol. No longer rooted to the land. He suspected she had been secretly edging toward this cliff as well.

"A new beginning," Harry said.

"Is that what we're calling it?"

TWENTY-SIX

THE ODD THING WAS, in the new year Harry got a call from Ebbetts.

"You know, Harry," Dick said, "you work with this stuff for thirty-one years, but you never actually see it. It exists in the fevered minds of a million peasants praying for a miracle. It sits in our hard drives. We watch it grow. Sometimes we watch it die.

"The world comes to us. A fourteen-year-old tapes six sticks of dynamite to a pipeline in Uzbekistan. A hurricane murders three million Florida oranges. A kid invents a cure for oil. Every crisis is an opportunity. There is a clinical trial, a drought, a war, an outbreak. We find comfort in misery. We short happiness, find solace in whatever. We survived the killing instincts of the herd; that was our accomplishment. That is nature's point. But every step of human progress brings us closer to the abyss. I leave you with this, Harry: our mothers gave us life, but it is money, and money alone, that preserves it."

The police asked Harry if those were Ebbetts's exact words—"money alone preserves it."

"To the best of my recollection," Harry said.

"Preserves life."

"Yes."

Bladdock's last gift, which came with his towering invoice, was that Richard Grimes, the architect of the water scheme, and Richard Ebbetts were the same person. Grimes was his real name. He'd changed his last name years ago.

When Ebbetts reflected on his work, Harry thought, he must have seen something immaculate. It was holy in its perfection. To create something out of nothing was more than a talent. Even God needed clay to create Adam. But Ebbetts had willed nothingness into existence, had given an absence life. Was this not the greater miracle?

The first step had been to identify the obvious: all life depends on water. And water had everything the market loved: it was elemental in its simplicity; it was necessary and transparent and familiar and increasingly politicized. He chose Dubai, that artificial playground, with its one-note economy as the canary in the mine. Creating a critical water shortage in the desert wasn't a leap. There would be one sooner or later anyway.

Ebbetts's initial prospectus stated that American aquifers were being depleted to alarming levels. In his quietly alarmist literature he demonstrated how this wouldn't be a slow transition but a sudden, horrifying drought. What would a single year of failed crops look like? The rainforest was going. More than 120 million litres of oil was reported as spilling into waterways annually on average (with some spectacular spikes upward). It was held by certain environmentalists that this figure represented roughly ten percent of actual leaks and spillage. There were gas pipelines still made of wood. The world was returning to desert, and its nations would revert to tribalism; dozens were already there. Ebbetts had compiled hundreds of stats, had downloaded the most dramatic images of drought from the Internet. He argued that it was water, not oil, that would trigger the apocalypse. All of this was either true or plausible, or at least not easily disproved.

He convinced the Maine government to subsidize the purchase and retrofit of an abandoned root beer factory and announced that a Dutch architect had been hired. When the crisis hit, the literature stated, certain countries would be left behind. There would be nominal humanitarian aid, but as desert claimed parts of Africa (where 250 million were already at risk), the resulting turmoil would be catastrophic.

A global crisis loomed; the only question was of degree. Ebbetts grounded his fund in humanitarian principles, stating that one percent of profits went to an NGO that dug water wells in Ghana and the Sudan. They had already brought water to forty-seven villages, the prospectus happily declared. His website was imaginative and apocalyptic. His company had a rich history of profit and humanitarian spirit.

No one guessed that, in fact, it had no assets and no employees and was not operational. Perhaps, Harry thought, there was a moment when Ebbetts considered actually starting a water bottling enterprise that took advantage of icebergs in non-territorial waters. It might be viable. But it would interfere with the purity of his empire, which was vast and complex and contained almost entirely in his head. An actual company would involve lawyers, employees and unions. There would be payroll and taxes and company picnics. He'd need boats, international agreements, accountants, sick days, office flings and engineers.

That was capitalism at its messiest. His own version was sleek and profitable; it was the beautiful physics that capitalism had been moving toward since Jesus threw the money changers out of the temple. In his first statement, Ebbetts claimed a 494 percent return on Ethical Ice.

The funds increased due to the inflated value of the two iceberg stocks. Ebbetts would have seen the shadow of something at BRG. He realized that August and Press had their hands full, and their minds were distracted by their own theft. *Mens rea.* He was winding down, plotting his escape. Almost all of his energy had gone to setting up the fraudulent funds. His two partners were in charge of selling the units; they were considerably more charming than Ebbetts and spent lavishly on entertainment. Ebbetts would have known about the redemptions at BRG, quiet family fortunes that had left in the night. There was a tension in the company that hadn't been there before. And Dale was losing his mind and August Sampson was dying.

Ebbetts waited until the desperation was at a keening pitch. On that front, he was like a dog, hearing noises that humans can't. He could hear the tension, and it was into that wonderful moment—a moment, if it was audible, that would have sounded like cats being murdered—that he pitched Spectre Island to Press and August. He gave them the water argument, the Dubai layout, and fed them documents that he'd spent weeks on. This wasn't anything BRG would get behind under normal circumstances, but these weren't normal circumstances. Sitting in Press's office, folded into his leather club chair, his feet on the thin, ancient carpet, Ebbetts would have treasured the slow, delicious moments that made up this seduction. He was selling two con men the Brooklyn Bridge, the identifiable apex of his professional life. And he only had a professional life. This was it.

All of what he'd said in the prospectus was true, more or less. At least, it would probably be true at some point. And that's what investments were, weren't they? You accurately predicted the needs of the future. You anticipated behaviour, you factored in stupidity and greed and human nature, and you were left with something. And then you bought it and waited for the world to catch up.

Ebbetts had worked at BRG for thirty-one years and had been treated well. He made between $225,000 and $300,000 most years. He hadn't made any friends. He was, as he was told every two years or so, a valued employee. Harry understood that this was what his people were best at: distance. They set up an invisible barrier, and somehow you knew where it was and that was as close as you dared approach. Ebbetts was the vulture who hopped toward the carcass after the lions had finished, after the lurking hyenas had had their fill.

Ebbetts had convinced Dale to put money into Ethical Ice. At that point, Dale's mind was itself like an iceberg, slowly drifting in non-territorial waters. What had he seen, Harry wondered, when faced with that proposal? Dale had spent his life being conservative in his work and non-conservative in his life. But he'd made money in the oil sands, one of his few forays into the unknown. Perhaps he saw another opportunity, one final score. The business had been changing around him. His knowledge was no longer valued. And what he did know was splintered like a mirror, shards picking up small, distorted images and flashes of light. There was no coherent picture, just the half-knowledge that he'd made money, that in his time he had been a player. Maybe he was hoping to leave something for Harry and Erin, a comforting thought.

There were civil suits against Grimes, Hubbard and Dench. Bladdock said they'd probably find him or one of the other partners. Money trails were hard to cover. Harry joined one of the suits, another lottery ticket.

One of the newspapers had found an escort agency that Ebbetts used—Gentlemen Only. His tastes, said the Hungarian proprietor, gravitated toward dark-haired women in their thirties, though a few were into their forties. In twenty-three years he had spent $1,879,660 on these women. Maybe, Harry thought, he felt that this contact would make him more comfortable with other women, that he would be more marketable. But it probably only made him more comfortable with other escorts. One of the girls—Tamara, age thirty-seven—said in an interview that Ebbetts tried to lure her out of the life, wanted to marry her, but she had turned him down. Most of the time they didn't have sex, she said; they simply went for dinner or to a function. It was like a marriage, the pleasant chat over an expensive dinner, the silent ride home, a chaste kiss.

Altogether, it looked to be roughly $70 million that was gone, taken from the original fund investors and BRG clients and Dale. This was on top of the $30 million August and Press had taken out of BRG. It was noted that Ebbetts's Yorkville condo had been sold to a French lawyer in November. That same week, Felicia's house was sold for $2.4 million to an Indian businessman who owned a chain of discount optical stores. Ebbetts's leased BMW had been returned without complication. There was no trace of him.

APRIL

HARRY DROVE EAST THROUGH THE CITY, to a street unlined with trees, rows of tiny bungalows framed by naked yellow grass. This would have been a working-class neighbourhood back when there was a working class, before they were edged out by the underclass. These yards, Harry guessed, would have once been impeccable. The backyards would have had gardens with tomatoes and zucchini in them, draped over trellises built by Italian workers who sat on their small front porches in singlets and were happy merely for the evening breeze.

Now the front yards were scrofulous and littered, the concrete walks buckled, the paint peeling. Walls had torn shingles in the pattern of bricks. Many of these people were renting, Harry guessed. He went to number thirty-two and knocked on the door. The porch had been crudely enclosed with chipboard and mismatched windows. Inside were piles of newspaper and lawnmower parts, cans of paint and oil, a reclining chair. A woman finally answered. She was just over five feet tall, in her late sixties perhaps, though she looked older, her face lined, her sour grey hair thinning and stretched tight over her scalp. The house smelled of cigarettes.

"Ms. Grimes?" Harry asked.

"I paid those taxes. You got no right."

"I'm not with the tax department. I'm here about Dick. He worked with my father."

"Dick."

"Dick Grimes. You're his sister?"

She smiled, revealing oversized dentures the colour of ear wax. "You're looking for Dick, you should have come by fifty years ago. That's when the little shit lit out."

Her name was Charlene, and she told Harry that Dick had left as a teenager. He'd never threatened to leave or thrown a tantrum, the usual teenage bullshit. Their father had left when Dick was one, and some of the boyfriends their mother had weren't what you'd call father figures, and the last one, well, he was a piece of work. Max. And Max laid a beating on Dick, and maybe that was what did it, but he was gone after that, and she figured he'd be back in a few days, a week at most. Their mother phoned the police after two weeks, but what were they going to do? Never heard a word from him, not in all this time.

"What's he doing now?" she asked. "He was always good with numbers. I told him he should work in a store."

"He worked in the stock market."

"That'd be about right. A shrimp, but I guess you can't hold that against him. He rich now?"

"Yes, he is."

"A regular millionaire."

"I'd put it at around twenty-five million."

"I'm his sister," Charlene said quickly. "I looked out for him." Her eyes glittered briefly with a sibling instinct the colour of coal. He played by himself as a child, she told Harry. Whole street filled with kids, and they'd go out in the morning and come back for dinner or not till dark, gone for twelve hours playing hockey or on their bicycles, lost in the ravines, doing whatever. But Dick stayed inside. Too rough and tumble out there. Too much life for him. She didn't know what he got up to.

Harry stood on the stoop and chatted with Charlene for a while. She offered him a cigarette and he took it, the first one he had smoked in twenty years. The air carried the first of spring. They smoked and chatted about Dick. Across the street, a man dragged his garbage to the curb. In the shade, there were still a few patches of dirty snow. A boy went by on a bicycle, wearing a T-shirt, anxious for summer.

The sun was weak in the afternoon sky. Harry drove north and crossed the ravine and parked near the gates of Mount Pleasant Cemetery. A few people milled. When he got to his grandfather's crypt, he saw that the stone angel was gone.

Harry looked out along a low swale dotted with stone spires and Celtic crosses. The city's builders contained beneath five feet of fertile soil. Tens of thousands who had dreamed in technicolour. Each one added singly to this heap, carted north after solemn prayer and laid down amid a crowd of distracted friends. The failure was palpable, an aroma that lifted out of the ground in spring, the rot of near-greatness, the essence of mortality.

His mother was recovering well. She might live another twenty years, though Harry guessed her liver would betray her. She was fragile and couldn't bear fragility. Her final years would be a fresh argument.

Ben had found a new girlfriend, an uncomplicated business major, and Harry was buoyed by the laughter he heard when they were together. Sarah had been a foreign country—Ben was intrigued but never at home.

Dale was perched on a modest swell. His money was gone, come to dust like a living thing. Harry didn't mourn his father's passing, or even the passing of his money. He mourned the absence of possibility, the procrastination of his life with Gladys, the failure of his own imagination. They had gotten $800,000 for the house, paid off all their debts, bought a modest condo in the heart of the city. They'd sold the reliable Camry, too. They cycled and walked, urban pioneers. They had almost convinced themselves it was a fresh start.

Harry stared out at the granite markers rising out of the ground like early wheat. A flatbed truck with a winch lowered a pebbled gold coffin into a hole. Harry had failed to inhabit his own life. His father, for all his many flaws, had inhabited his; this was one area where he was a success.

Eventually Harry would be in this cemetery, staring up from the gloom of his coffin through the tangled roots into the empty sky. His ragged suit, the dry skin drawn tight, his last thoughts still rattling in the yellowing skull, the words lost on prevailing winds, the quiet deceptions, the fears of a child standing in new clothes among strangers on the first day of school. The hours collected like dust, the channel changer limp in his hand. Money swirling in useless eddies. What is left in that memory, what caress lingers, what unspoken love? His essential stats on the headstone, the enduring cold. Who will stare down with love in their eyes? Who will lay daffodils gently on the stirred earth and linger under the April sun? Who will pay to have him carted to the boneyard?

The sun was low, a wink of light against the horizon, the last of it, beckoning.

ACKNOWLEDGEMENTS

I am very grateful to Nino Ricci, Ken Alexander, Gail Gallant and Ellen Vanstone for their early, astute reading of the manuscript. I'd like to thank my agent, Jackie Kaiser, for her support and insight, and my editor, Anne Collins, for her infinite patience and wisdom. And finally, my wife, Grazyna, for her ongoing support and editorial judgement, and my children, Justine and Cormac, my shining beacons.

DON GILLMOR is the author of the bestselling, award-winning, two-volume *Canada: A People's History*, and two other books of non-fiction, *The Desire of Every Living Thing*, a *Globe and Mail* Best Book, and *I Swear by Apollo*. His debut novel, *Kanata*, was published in 2010 to critical acclaim. He has also written nine books for children, two of which were nominated for a Governor General's Award. He is one of Canada's most accomplished journalists, and has been a senior editor at *Walrus* magazine and a contributing editor at both *Saturday Night* and *Toronto Life*. He has won ten National Magazine Awards. He lives in Toronto with his wife and two children.